THE ART DEPARTMENT
A FAMILY HISTORY MYSTERY

NICK CHURTON

First published in 2026 by Wrate's Publishing

ISBN 978-1-917970-11-2

Copyright © 2026 by Nick Churton

Typeset and Edited by Wrate's Editing Services

www.wrateseditingservices.co.uk

Cover illustration and design by Rachel Middleton

All rights reserved. No part of this publication may be reproduced, stored in a retrieval system, or transmitted, in any form or by any means (electronic, mechanical, photocopying, recording or otherwise), without the prior written permission of the publisher.

This book is a work of fiction. Names, characters, places and incidents are either a product of the author's imagination or are used fictitiously. Any resemblance to actual people living or dead, events or locales is entirely coincidental.

A CIP catalogue record for this book is available from the British Library.

To my sons Oliver and Alastair

CHAPTER
ONE

'This is nice,' said Dimity Arrow to her husband, Felix, as she added a scoop of berries and a dash of honey to her bowl of porridge. 'We never seem to have a quiet breakfast together. You've either been at Witch's Lawn or scrambling around some county pile looking for clues or curios.'

'Either that, or you are up at the crack of sparrows for services at St Margaret's,' Felix replied.

'We're like ships passing in the night.'

'At least we have the nights to pass,' replied Felix with a grin.

Since their wedding, Felix and Dimity had settled down to life in their upper-floor flat above Felix's office, studio and shop on the border of Belgravia and Pimlico.

'Talking of Witch's Lawn, have you heard from Eliza recently?'

Felix raised an eyebrow. 'Recently? My grandmother is never off the phone. I'm surprised she hasn't already called this morning.'

Dimity laughed. 'She's excited about Saturday.'

'I'm excited about Saturday; you have a day off. Do you think Bidian will be there?'

'I'm sure the whole gang will be present.'

'Now I'm the one getting excited. I love Witch's when it's busy. Oh, I haven't told you – I had a call yesterday from someone associated with Yuri Volkov.'

'The Russian billionaire?'

'The very same. Apparently, Volkov has just bought a huge house in the Cotswolds, and they want to talk to me about the restoration, if I'm interested.'

'And are you?'

'I'm meeting Volkov at the house on Wednesday.'

Dimity smiled. 'Ah, that interested.'

'Well, it's a money-no-object job on a jewel of a property. It would be silly not to.'

'And the surprises keep on coming,' Dimity observed dryly.

Felix smiled at his wife. The surprises *did* keep on coming. He'd started the year unmarried and ended it with a wife, and a grandmother he hadn't known existed.

'You never know where these things lead,' said Felix.

'Quite. Look what happened when you were asked to investigate Witch's Lawn.'

Felix laughed. His newly discovered grandmother, Eliza Arrow, owned the Tudor hunting lodge whose secrets he had been commissioned to unearth. It had changed his life. Witch's Lawn was no ordinary house, and Eliza Arrow was no ordinary grandmother. She was a spry ex-spy approaching a hundred and the latest in a long line of Arrows doing shadowy, dangerous, and sometimes dirty, undercover work for the Crown and state since Henry VIII was on the throne. To Felix's delight, Witch's Lawn was a treasure trove. The house had wonderful furniture, priceless art, a hidden room and a fascinating tower that had contained the biggest secret of all. Today, the house was in Eliza's care, but one day, Witch's Lawn would come under his stewardship. It still made him dizzy to think about it.

Fortunately, there was a team who helped to run the place, and they would also become Felix's responsibility. West, Cairo and Frankie were three retired Special Forces operatives ostensibly in place to protect Eliza from any bite back that might resurface from her past. Then there was the gardener, Julius, who made up for his lack of fighting skills with a formidable intellect. The four retainers had become Eliza's surrogate family.

Nothing was as it seemed at Witch's Lawn.

* * *

'Grandma, Grandma!'

Eliza Arrow turned away from her conversation with her lunch guest and looked towards the new voice in the room. Strictly speaking, she wasn't this child's grandmother, but it was flattering and endearing that the excitable Rosie considered her so. The little girl was Felix's goddaughter. Despite all the surprises Eliza had experienced throughout her long life, nothing had prepared her for the new family she'd recently discovered.

'Rosie, can't you see I am talking to Sir Bidian?'

'Yes, but, Grandma, this is very important.'

'What is so important that you wish to interrupt your grandma, child?'

'West says if he finds me, he will chase me around the garden.'

'Well, that *is* important. You had better hide well, or start running, my dear,' Eliza said, amused at Rosie's thrill at being chased, and her not being old enough to understand it was by a ruthless and deadly ex-Special Boat Service trooper.

'Where shall I hide, Grandma?'

'Only you should decide.'

'That is not very helpful,' Rosie said with a pout.

Eliza smiled. 'Often in life you have to help yourself, my dear; this is as good a time to start as any.'

'Humph. What about in that room through there?' Rosie said, pointing to a door.

'It's called a larder, a small room where food is stored.'

'Yes, there.'

'That's a good idea. Now you better get hiding – or running.'

The little girl bolted into the larder.

Eliza smiled broadly. It had been a wonderful year. Partly because of Sir Bidian's intervention, she had, for the first time in forty years, a real-life family in the form of her grandson Felix and her dear friend, Dimity, who was Felix's new wife. Plus, Felix and Dimity had adopted the roles of aunt and uncle to their friend Santa's daughter, Rosie, giving the single parent some time for herself.

Rosie might as well be my grandchild, Eliza thought, for all the time she now seems to spend at Witch's Lawn.

Yes, the past year had been a delight and one of the happiest times in her long life.

'I'm sorry, Bidian, where were we?' Eliza said to her one-time trainee.

Sir Bidian de Butts, the head of MI6, laughed. 'Please don't apologise, Eliza; Rosie is a lovely little girl, she has a lot of spirit. It is nice to see.'

'She reminds me of Athene,' Eliza said. 'A little too much

for my own good sometimes. I often think that Rosie has the spirit my daughter had when she was six. But I enjoy having Rosie running wild at Witch's: her shouting, laughing. Even her crying breathes more life into the place. There is no compensation for family loss, but, given time, life sometimes brings back some balance, doesn't it?'

Bidian nodded. 'I think life must, Eliza.' He knew all about how Eliza's daughter had died in the line of duty when only a young woman, and how Eliza had recently discovered Athene had left behind a son, Felix. 'I've also noticed that West, Cairo and Frankie make rather good childminders, even though they are here to mind you. The only times I have ever seen West smile is when he's with Rosie. It's very confusing – I still tend to think of him as a professional killer.'

'Even soldiers like West can have their soft sides, Bidian. Cairo mothers Rosie, and Frankie acts like a Norland nanny – in much the same way she acts towards me, I might add.'

Bidian laughed. 'It's always good to see you so well looked after, Eliza. And I must say, you are looking the picture of health.'

'You young flatterer! Just look at me, a stooped and wrinkled old woman several inches shorter than she used to be. I've been increasingly feeling my age for forty years at least.'

'Hardly that stooped or wrinkled, Eliza. I've always thought nobody radiates youth quite like you, even the young. And you are still the most elegant near centenarian I've ever met.'

'And how many near centenarians have you met?'

Sir Bidian laughed. 'To be fair, not many, but I don't think one loses elegance however old one becomes. Just look at elderly ballerinas.'

'Perhaps elegance has some memory.'

'Well, there is certainly nothing wrong with your memory, Eliza.'

'All in all, I have no complaints, Bidian. I have enjoyed several lifetimes, and this current one is more comfortable than most people experience at my age. But now I'm just an old lady, retired to the Chilterns.'

'An elderly woman with many secrets. Talking of which, we have had a strange communication from one of our people in Moscow.'

Any further discussion was curtailed as Felix and Dimity entered the room.

'Oh, sorry to interrupt, but have you seen Rosie?' Dimity asked Eliza.

'She's hiding from West.'

'I think we should be getting her back to Santa.'

'Is it that time already? These days fly by so quickly – too quickly. Have you had tea?'

'Yes, in the kitchen with Cairo.'

'Good. Before you go, tell me what you both have planned for the week ahead. I like to imagine you getting on with your lives.'

'Usual church things for me – all a bit routine, I'm afraid,' said Dimity, who had recently become an assistant priest at St Margaret's in Eaton Square, Belgravia.

'And I have a meeting on Wednesday in the Cotswolds with a prospective Russian client called Yuri Volkov,' Felix said.

'Yuri Volkov, the oligarch?' Bidian asked.

'Yes. He wants to restore a big mansion. I've been asked to assemble a historical report and pitch for the restoration job. It could be a massive cash injection for the firm, not to mention a high-profile project that would be good for PR.'

'I'd be interested in your opinion on Mr Volkov, Felix. You can tell me when we meet on Thursday. Now, I had better be getting along myself.' Bidian turned to his host. 'Thank you for a wonderful lunch, Eliza, I've had a most enjoyable day. I'll talk to you about the Moscow communication on another occasion; it'll keep for now.'

Sir Bidian bade goodbye to everyone except Rosie, who was still hiding in the larder.

'How do you feel about working with Bidian?' Eliza asked her grandson seriously. 'I can't say I'm entirely happy.'

'Well, I will know more once I've spoken to him later this week.'

Eliza turned to Dimity. 'And what do you feel about Felix joining the intelligence community, albeit on an arm's-length basis? It's not without risk, you know.'

'You're asking the wrong person, Eliza. My mountaineering came with considerable personal risk. Anyhow, I think recklessness runs in the Arrow family. It's in the genes; it seems inevitable somehow.'

'I know, but getting involved in espionage – even at arm's length – can have unpredictable, and often unforeseen, consequences.'

'Well, I will listen to Bidian and see what he wants me to do,' Felix said. 'I think he only wants me to observe and report when I have the chance. I'm sure he doesn't mean me to get into any clandestine spy stuff.'

'You will find that there is an invisible line between casual observance and spying; a line that sometimes you don't realise you have crossed. Also, the people you have under observation often use a different line. Anyway, I think you will find Bidian has a bit more than casual observation in mind.'

'Does the head of the Secret Service often talk to you about these things?'

Eliza ignored the question. 'Well, if you do decide to step into the shadows' – she raised her teacup in a mock toast before reciting the centuries-old Arrow family saying – 'I wish you peace and lesser sorrow.'

'Well, I'll find out what Bidian has in mind. I must say, he seemed quite interested in Yuri Volkov.'

'Bidian is interested in *every* powerful and wealthy Russian living here. It goes with the territory, Felix, and I also have a feeling such things might touch on the reason Bidian has for meeting you.'

'You already know about this meeting?'

'Some things. Now, I think you had better find Rosie if you need to get back.'

'Do you know where she is hiding?' Dimity asked.

Eliza smiled. 'I do, but I couldn't possibly tell you. After all, I am very good at keeping secrets.'

CHAPTER TWO

In Moscow, half a day earlier, it had been a typical January morning. The temperature was minus ten degrees, and the traffic was almost at a standstill. The chandelier-lit Metro, so grand when empty, was now a wave of slow-moving, heavily wrapped commuters.

Róisín Kelly had left behind the winter smell of ingested alcohol and boiled vegetables and now inched up the steps and out of the marble-covered interior, before making her way to a small café, where she stopped for breakfast.

For the fifteen million people who, like Róisín, lived in the Russian capital, the average day was like this: work, fast food and road congestion.

Róisín had arrived in Moscow from Ireland when she was in her late twenties, almost forty years ago. At that time, the city seemed alien and unfriendly. Like today, her breath had frozen in her nose, and the population seemed as frigid as the weather. Little did she know when she'd first arrived that this was just a mask. Behind the stony faces of the people lay a hidden humanity and warmth.

Moscow had become her adopted city; she loved and hated it in equal measure. It was a place where she felt completely at home but utterly foreign. To her, it was a city of ironies. The winters were harsh, but in summer, when the trees finally bloomed again, Moscow became warm, green and T-shirt comfortable.

The people intrigued her. She had never become used to how much Russians drank, but she had come to enjoy drinking with them. She liked the vodka-fuelled, late-night debates, where she found herself tumbling into a world where everything was confused. Increasingly bizarre pronouncements, peddled by rumour and social media, were argued as truths. One night, she was asked to prove how smoking causes lung cancer. On another occasion, she was told that overeating mayonnaise brought on migraines.

Despite the casual misogyny, rudeness and scant privacy, Róisín had slowly become used to Moscow and its people, and she felt, in turn, they had become used to her.

Under ordinary circumstances, she would have felt safe in the city. However, her situation was far from ordinary, and she had grown weary of the crushing pressure and constant peril of her double life. She felt this more now than at any time since she had left Belfast. Moscow would be hard to leave, but she had to try.

After breakfast, Róisín made her way to the Tretyakov Gallery. Since retiring from the Irish section of Russia's Federal Security Service, the FSB, she maintained several part-time jobs. She taught English, French and German at a private business school, and took on freelance translation work. Her other occupation was acting as a gallery guide to visitors from different countries. But this work was a labour of love, as she adored the art as much as the place itself.

Within the gallery, there were over a hundred thousand works of Russian national art. On its walls were the country's cultural identity and the story of how artistic creativity played an essential role in its history. Róisín could never tire of these works: she found something new to enjoy each time she went.

Her part-time jobs gave her a comfortable enough living. She could maintain a busy social life and afford one or two modest holidays every year. To get away, she chose the Black Sea for the beaches and the Caucuses for the mountains. She hadn't been out of Russia since the day she had arrived.

The five people she had travelled with to Russia were strangers from Londonderry. She had come from Belfast, where she had been living off the Falls Road. To avoid any unwanted attention from the British security services, the small IRA group had endured a rough journey on a stinking trawler to Iceland, where they were transferred onto a Russian tanker for its return journey to the Motherland. Once they reached Moscow, Róisín never saw her travelling companions again. They were young hardliners bent on terror and were in the Soviet Union to master that trade under experts at the KGB.

Róisín, on the other hand, had worked within the IRA command structure in Belfast and was seen by the KGB as a valuable political and intelligence asset, as she had specialised in infiltrating loyalist groups. During a period when Russia was supplying arms to the IRA, she became a KGB advisor on Northern Irish paramilitary affairs. Eventually, what had been a temporary secondment to Moscow became permanent. This suited both the Russians and the IRA, but staying in Moscow had also been Róisín's choice – an initial month-long debrief in Moscow had led to an affair with her inquisitor, a Russian army officer.

The romance had fizzled out within two years, but by then Róisín had new documents and a work permit. In the end, her lover, who had reached the rank of lieutenant general in the GRU, the Russian army's intelligence division, chose to stay with his wife and young family. Róisín bore no grudge, although she was upset at first and was left feeling extremely alone. But she understood and managed to maintain a detached friendship with the man. They met for a walk or dinner in an out-of-the-way restaurant every month or so, which was pleasant. Her ex-lover also told her things.

When Róisín first came to Russia, she felt under close surveillance, but over time, she sensed the eyes on her lose focus, until she eventually didn't feel them at all. Within five years, she was granted full Russian citizenship.

The affair and her work had brought Róisín into contact with men of senior rank from the army and security services. She had kept up several of these acquaintanceships – and the friendships she forged with some of their wives and girlfriends – so her social group now came from military, security and cultural circles. She never mixed the three, nor did she seek the company of the Irish, difficult as that was when there were fourteen Irish bars within Moscow's inner ring road and at least six within walking distance of her apartment. With the Irish, the six-degrees-of-separation rule was often reduced by half. Everyone seemed to know someone or was linked through family or friendships. For that reason, Róisín avoided the Irish and, for a different set of reasons, the British too.

Given her self-imposed rules, life in Moscow should have been simple. However, her instinct and training meant she was constantly trying to identify important information from everyday tittle-tattle. It was both exhausting and dangerous.

*　*　*

After a long day in the gallery, Róisín returned home to change. She applied a little make-up and replaced her skirt with warm trousers. Over a light blue shirt, she added a navy cardigan. Despite her almost seventy years, clothes still hung well on her tall, slender frame, and she was ever thankful for her family genes. Around her neck she tied a silk scarf, selected from the small stack of identical orange Hermès boxes in her wardrobe. She could never afford such luxuries; they had been occasional and welcome gifts from her former lover. Róisín put a comb through her short, salt-and-pepper hair, which she had cut every five or six weeks at a fashionable salon a few blocks from Red Square. Wrapping up against the freezing night air, she headed off to her rendezvous.

This evening, Róisín was seeing a younger girlfriend with a loose tongue and a taste for vodka. As always, there was a lot of entertainment on offer in Moscow, with many cultural activities to choose from. Róisín enjoyed watching sport and supported a local hockey team. She regularly attended matches, and although she loved watching the games, the club's association with the Russian military sometimes provided her with useful introductions and information. But this evening, having read some good reviews, Róisín and her friend had decided to see a one-person play about the life of Rachmaninov and had been lucky enough to get tickets.

After the performance, and despite the wide choice of cuisines on hand, the two women decided to stay with Russian food, and they discussed the play as they scrunched through fresh snow to their chosen restaurant. They ordered beef stroganoff with fried potatoes and drank beer. Róisín sipped from her glass but soon ordered another bottle for her friend.

After the meal, Róisín suggested they end the evening at a nearby bar. It was dark, noisy, and crowded, but she pounced on an emptying small corner table for two.

'Vodka?' Róisín asked her friend, already knowing the answer. She ordered Zyr from a passing waiter.

Róisín poured out a full glass for her friend but only a small amount for herself.

'Have things been any better at home?' she asked her friend, who had a disturbing history of marital problems.

'No. If anything, they are worse.'

The friend took another gulp of vodka.

Róisín knew the husband, who worked for a secret service branch, to be a cruel man.

The friend glanced about her and looked reassured by the noise and dim lighting that lent the two women privacy.

'Look at this.' She rolled up a sleeve to expose a bracelet of purple bruising around her wrist.

'He did this?' Róisín asked, prodding the emotional fire and pouring another glass of vodka for her companion, who nodded as tears began to trickle down her face.

'I'm frightened for the children.' She took another mouthful of vodka.

'Why don't you leave him? You could go to your parents in Nizhny Novgorod and never return to Moscow.'

'That would only make things worse.'

'How could they get any worse?'

'My husband is the devil – he and his cohorts.'

'His cohorts?'

'He is in a special unit. It's called Unit 29155, or something like that. I'm not supposed to know, but I do. They are working on a plot that will undoubtedly hurt someone, somewhere. I don't understand how he can live with himself.'

'How did you find this out?'

Róisín's friend suddenly looked worried.

'You can tell me,' Róisín said soothingly. 'No one recognises us here and we can't be heard.'

'I hear things,' the friend said in a hushed voice.

Róisín poured out another glass. 'What do you hear?'

'Well, not everything, but I kept hearing the word Nemezida. And then, when he was whispering to someone on his phone the other day, I also heard the name Bezrodny. When he saw me in the room, he screamed at me to get out. The last time my husband behaved like that was before a traitor was found dead in a foreign country. Russia was blamed, although the authorities denied it, of course. My husband was in a good mood for weeks after. I see things, Róisín, and I hear words.'

'I can see that you do. But please be careful whom you tell. It could be dangerous for you. It is OK between us, as I won't repeat what you say to anyone.'

'You are a good friend, Róisín.'

'I'm glad you think so. Now, I think we should get you home.'

By this time, the friend was in floods of tears, and, Róisín thought, with any luck wouldn't remember the conversation in the morning.

The following day, Róisín sat at her laptop and logged onto eBay. Years ago, to flag a dead drop, she used newspaper advertisements. Now she had developed eBay as her flag carrier. She put up specific items to sell on the auction site, finding cheap knick-knacks in local flea markets, which she paid for in cash. The items were unlikely to attract any interest from genuine collectors, as she set her reserve prices just high enough to ward off interest but not so high as to attract the attention of counter-intelligence officials. But her handler was aware that a new item for sale meant a new message at the dead drop.

Róisín's double life had started almost as soon as she arrived in Moscow. She had slipped a note into the coat pocket of an embassy translator. Contact was made, and over many years, trust was established through the passing on of reliable information.

Now she encrypted onto paper the names her friend had mentioned the evening before, signing off as Mara. Róisín didn't know the significance of the words Nemezida and Bezrodny, but her source was usually reliable; despite, or rather because of, her vodka-fuelled indiscretion and naivety. But Róisín felt the names were important somehow. She chose a cypher from Tommy O'Hara, one of the IRA's top code men. O'Hara had told Róisín he obtained it from "the best of the best" but hadn't given it a name.

With the message written faintly in pencil on the inside of a small, used envelope, Róisín screwed it up to look like a piece of everyday litter. She put on her boots, hat, coat and scarf, and set off on one of her usual habitual walks to Kolomenskoye Park. Once there, she walked through the Golosov Ravine, a famous beauty spot. The ravine's sides had been reinforced, and pedestrian paths and stairs built against its steep walls. In the summer, several springs bubbled up, creating pretty brooks along the bottom of the ravine. But today, these were frozen.

Róisín stopped at a sizeable, snow-covered boulder and sat on it for a moment to enjoy the stillness and quiet. She casually brushed some snow away and, making sure no one was watching, jammed the screwed-up envelope into a familiar crevice. Then, as if idly making designs, she brushed the snow back again.

Róisín liked this spot; she thought it had a melancholy feel, just like the Russians. Legend had it that the ravine was a time loop and when soldiers and peasants walked through its mist, they emerged on the other side a few decades later. Other folklore suggested the boulder brought happiness to women who craved a child. The boulder had never given Róisín happiness, but it did provide her with hope, which was almost as good. She hoped the boulder would save some lives – including hers.

As she began to walk back through the park, she thought of a time when she hadn't been called Róisín, Mara or the other names she used in different places. Sometimes, she felt she had forgotten who she really was and where she had come from. Now she wondered if anyone in her previous life remembered her, and if she could ever return to her real self.

CHAPTER
THREE

Yuri Volkov leant on a dusty windowsill, not caring about any potential harm to his expensive, bespoke, Savile Row suit. He had plenty of others. The whole house was filthy and damp. He had been told there was woodworm, dry rot, wet rot and lots of other structural problems he didn't care to know about or understand. But he would have all that put right. The building hadn't been lived in for several years – since the last owners ran out of money. Volkov had picked up the repossessed house for a song.

He turned and looked out of the window. The river, fringed by weeping willows, swept by in the distance. In the foreground was what once must have been a beautiful lawn. But now nature had reclaimed it as a field. He thought this room would be his office, and there would be a lawn again.

Volkov smiled to himself. So far, everything had worked out well. His life could not have changed more from his origins in a cramped communal apartment in Leningrad to a large English manor house in the heart of the Cotswolds. It was exciting.

Five families had shared the fourth floor Leningrad apartment. The Volkovs – mother, father and five children – lived in a sitting room, dining room and bedroom. All the families shared the hallway, kitchen and bathroom.

Now he could engage the services of Provenance Architecture & Law, a respected company specialising in the restoration of historic property. The firm would advise him on the renovation of this classic English country house and garden. Courtlands would be the most beautiful home in the Cotswolds. As the joint owner of Oliniya, Russia's second-largest energy company, and one of the world's wealthiest people, Volkov could afford almost anything his heart desired. And what he desired most was to become an English lord of the manor. This had proven more straightforward than he had imagined. The money helped. But people didn't quite know what to make of him. Some of this was down to his wealth, but some of it, Volkov suspected, also had to do with his looks. He was of average height but had a distinguished and memorable bearing, helped by Savile Row tailoring, which disguised a slight paunch. Volkov's thinning and receding hair was swept back on his head, exposing deep lines across his broad forehead. He knew people often compared him to the American actor Jack Nicholson. Like the actor, nobody seemed to know if at any moment Volkov would break into demonic anger or display a devilish smile. He liked putting others off balance, especially in business. But contrary to what most people might have thought, he liked to laugh, happily showing off two rows of perfect teeth thanks to the work of a costly Beverly Hills-based cosmetic dentist.

Volkov felt he was closer than ever to achieving his aim of assimilation. His elegant Belgravia townhouse and seats on the boards of several high-profile art charities, had put him within touching distance of his objective. His only child had recently been enrolled at Cheltenham Ladies' College – with the help of a large endowment for a new science facility. The final pieces were falling into place; he *would* become an English gentleman.

Volkov had been marked out as gifted by his teachers at a young age. He was sent to several schools for the brightest children and was encouraged to join the Young Communist League. Ultimately, he found a career in industry rather than joining several of his school friends in the military or security services. He finished his formal education at the Institute of Oil and Gas in Moscow.

'Mr Volkov?' called a voice from outside the room.

'I'm here,' Volkov shouted back to Felix Bohlin.

Upon meeting earlier, Volkov had soon taken to the owner of Provenance Architecture & Law. Bohlin appeared eager but also seemed to possess an older head than his age would suggest.

He left his windowsill perch and walked into the sizeable, wood-panelled hall, where he was met by a man dressed in a light tweed jacket over a plain, pale blue shirt with a knitted tie, beige chinos and stout brown brogues polished to a high shine. Volkov thought he had a bookish, set-in-his-ways look. This was emphasised by round, metal-rimmed glasses and an engaging smile.

'Have you seen everything?' Volkov asked.

'It would take me weeks to do that, and I must say, Mr Volkov, I should enjoy every moment. Courtlands is an extraordinary house. I'm afraid the fabric is in poor condition – that you already know – but it has all its original features and is not beyond saving... with the appropriate expenditure.

Following this meeting, my team will survey the house, and I'll be able to provide a rough-cost estimate.

'The house is fascinating,' Felix continued. 'I found some pitted masonry outside – possibly musket ball marks from the English Civil War. Otherwise, no one has messed around with the fabric. That makes it unusual. It's a blank canvas – there's nothing to undo before restoration. I was thinking you could follow Prince Charles's lead and provide young people with apprenticeships and on-the-job training in traditional crafts and conservation techniques, as he does on some of his restoration projects.'

At Prince Charles's name, Volkov suddenly became even more interested. To emulate the prince, to have the prince's name spoken in the same breath as his – that was what he wanted. Once it was completed, perhaps he could invite him to Courtlands. The restoration and his philanthropy could lead to an honour of some sort.

'How long will the restoration take, do you think?' Volkov asked with fresh urgency.

'Well, it's hard to say, but six months is enough for an in-depth survey so that we know exactly what we are dealing with. Then the roof and chimneys should take at least a year to be restored. While that happens, window replacements can be made and fitted, and any other damp ingress can be remedied. I imagine another year and a half on the interior basics with replacement plumbing and electrics, and then a year perhaps for decoration. So, I should think about five years altogether. Of course, garden design, landscaping and planting the formal gardens can fit in with this timetable. One shouldn't rush these things, but as always, it depends on the amount of money one spends and the number of good people one employs.'

For Volkov, five years was far too long. But, he thought, if he wanted to entertain royalty, this renovation must be done correctly. While the work was going on, his PR people could drip-feed stories to the press about his no-expense-spared and meticulous renovation. Perhaps a TV company could make a documentary programme or even a series on the restoration – he could sponsor the project. He would be the saviour of a national treasure. But Volkov still wanted to live in the house as soon as possible. Otherwise, his daughter's schooling would end before the renovations were finished.

'Try and halve the time. Make it less than that, if possible. I will pay the extra. You should start immediately. I haven't a day to lose.'

'With the right people, I'm sure we can save a great deal of time. But it will mean my devoting an awful lot of my days here too,' Felix said.

Volkov shrugged.

'Then, Mr Volkov, I will draw up a contract this week.'

Volkov brought the meeting to a close. Felix Bohlin had been vetted through several discreet channels, and Volkov felt he knew as much about the man as he needed to. Bohlin had come highly recommended. There were no skeletons in the cupboard personally, although his life was not straightforward. Bohlin was adopted and had recently married an Anglican priest called Dimity Fortuna: apparently a childhood sweetheart. And there was some business with an elderly woman who, unexpectedly it turned out, was Bohlin's natural grandmother, but these were just complicated modern family matters.

But he also knew he could never be too careful. Not with what was at stake.

Yes, Volkov thought, as he watched Felix Bohlin's car

disappear down the drive, he had come a long way from that cramped apartment in Leningrad and now inhabited a different world. But still, he could not forget Mother Russia; it was the heart of his being; it was the essence of him. He had come to enjoy the life he had made in England, but he belonged to Russia. His duty was to serve her. It was a price he was more than willing to pay – for the opened doors, the wealth, the life he led, and for Russia herself.

When asked, he would know what to do. When the day came, he wouldn't be called Volkov. He would be Nemezida, or Nemesis, as the English said.

The following evening, Volkov went to Covent Garden. Like many cultured Russians, he enjoyed the ballet and had been looking forward to seeing a programme that included a rare performance of L'après-midi d'un faune.

Volkov sat in his box next to his regular ballet-going companion, Maria Mirova. She was the widow of a Russian industrialist who had left her with enormous wealth. At an embassy function several days beforehand, she had mentioned to Volkov that she would like to talk to him about something personal when they were next alone.

Mirova had recently taken on a role as the unelected head of a small but highly influential and fabulously wealthy cabal of ex-patriot Russians who had made their homes in London. The purpose of the group was to provide the Kremlin with information independent of the Russian Embassy in London. She may have been unelected but everyone in the group knew that her authority was encouraged and approved by the Kremlin. Her allegiance to the Russian cause worldwide was in no doubt, especially by Yuri Volkov. So, unopposed, Maria Mirova became the de facto general secretary of this London group of powerful Russians.

In the event, when they were next alone, she had coyly proposed marriage. Although sweetly put, Volkov couldn't help but think it sounded more like a business merger.

Now, during the interval, Mirova leaned towards Volkov, and said, 'Yuri, I am a little surprised and hurt. I had expected to hear from you about my little suggestion by now. What is keeping you? We socialise in the same circles, enjoy the same cultural activities, and are keen collectors of important art. And we are still young enough. Think of the size of our combined wealth and art collection if we were married. Apart from a few Americans, we would be the wealthiest couple in the world. Just think about it.'

Yuri had thought about little else since Maria had first made her proposal. He could see the advantages. Wealth accumulation was one of Yuri Volkov's great passions, and there was no doubt that Maria had many important contacts, especially in the Kremlin, that would make them even wealthier. They would be an unstoppable power couple. Yet marriage was the last thing on his mind. It was only a few years since his wife had divorced him, and he was enjoying living the life of a single man once again. Plus, he wasn't sure how it would go down with his daughter, Lizabeta, who had been badly affected by her parents' separation.

Those weren't the only things that unsettled him, though. Somehow, he couldn't help sensing Moscow's powerful and controlling hand behind this proposal.

All this had weighed heavily on his mind. While Maria was helpful and even bearable company at social events and on private occasions such as this, he was happy enough on his own. He had freedom. Marriage to Maria Mirova, or any woman, would mean his life would never again be fully his own. Besides, this complicated and driven woman with her close ties to the Russian government was, he felt, an innocent-looking but dangerous individual. Perhaps it all would have been less worrying had he been in the least bit attracted to her. But he wasn't. She had a hard demeanour, and he had rarely seen her wearing anything other than ill-fitting trouser suits in unsuitable colours. She wore thick-framed glasses and leather shoes that her mother might have worn. No, if he were looking for a wife, she wouldn't be the answer.

Volkov had his own connections deep within the Kremlin, but he had recently been considering loosening those ties, despite how challenging that would prove. A great deal of help from Moscow had gone into the rise of his company – help for which he was genuinely grateful. Sometimes, when political influence was not enough to push through an advantageous deal, financial and other threats were brought to bear by the Kremlin. Remaining always at arm's length, Volkov reasoned that these were typical Russian business tactics and had turned a blind eye. But lately he had been feeling less comfortable. Now he viewed life from a different perspective – a Western one. Lizabeta, whom he had installed at Cheltenham to further her social advancement – and his own – was also helping him to see things in another light. So, this sudden and unexpected proposal from Maria Mirova couldn't have been more unwelcome.

Volkov was a careful man, and he had made some discreet enquiries about Mirova. What came back did nothing to reassure him. There were questions about her previous husband's death and malicious gossip that she may have had a hand in it. One night, Volkov dreamed he had become entwined with a black widow babushka.

The proposal gave him another complex problem. While marriage for him seemed out of the question, telling Maria so and not making an enemy of her and Moscow would not be easy.

So, Volkov had taken the only available option open to him and played for time, reasoning she would expect him to take the same care in considering the suggestion as she had undoubtedly taken before making it.

Maria had reluctantly agreed and flatteringly told Volkov she couldn't wait until they were married, before adding that he shouldn't take too much time as the union had Moscow's full support.

No, Moscow wants this, Volkov thought. Men in his position were in increasing mortal danger from an emboldened and vindictive Kremlin, for which oligarchs had become too much of a nuisance. The answer was usually assassination or life imprisonment, but forcing him into a marriage with a party fanatic would avoid the public outcry and inevitable diplomatic fallout that came with a political killing. Moscow would then have easy access to his wealth. Yes, he would need to tread very carefully indeed.

'Come, darling, we have such a wonderful life ahead working together to further our country's interests, and we don't want to let the Kremlin down, do we?' Maria said.

Suddenly, Debussy's music and Nijinsky's choreography lost their thrill. For the first time in many years, Volkov felt that his lifestyle in England was in serious jeopardy – as was his life.

CHAPTER
FOUR

Felix had expected his meeting with Sir Bidian de Butts to be held at the MI6 headquarters on the south bank of the River Thames in Vauxhall. He had been excited at the thought. Instead, they met at Somerset House, home of the famous Courtauld Institute, regarded by many as the world's leading centre for research into art history and conservation. Felix had visited the elegant and imposing Somerset House by the Thames several times before when researching a picture of a forebear, as well as in his student days. However, what the place had to do with Sir Bidian he hadn't a clue.

Felix sat in a beautiful wood-panelled office a mile downstream from the official security HQ. On the walls were some exceptional full-length portraits. He didn't recognise the subjects but did know the artists were Reynolds, Gainsborough and Romney. In front of him, on a large walnut desk, was a cup of freshly made coffee.

'You have some pretty spectacular pictures, Bidian.'

'Perks of the job, I have to say. They are just here while a gallery is being restored next door, but I'm not complaining.

'Now, tell me, how is the high priestess of St Margaret's?'

Felix laughed at this reference to Dimity. 'Mitten is fine' – he sometimes slipped into using Dimity's family pet name when talking to friends – 'she's busy as usual with all her parish goings-on.'

'Please send my best wishes.'

'I will.'

'Now, to business. How did you get on with Yuri Volkov? Did you get the job?'

'The contract is being drawn up as we speak.'

'Very good. I suspect you are curious as to why I want to know, and why I have dragged you here,' said Sir Bidian.

'I am curious to know what might be expected of me, and how government work might fit in with my business and new roles as husband and grandson.'

Not for the first time, Felix thought how Sir Bidian looked the epitome of a security chief – straight out of central casting, as the Americans would say. He wore a well-cut, navy suit with a faint chalk stripe, a starched white shirt with double cuffs, and a striped tie that signified something that Felix couldn't identify. On other occasions when they met, Bidian had worn an Old Etonian tie. But the striking feature of his appearance was the absence of a left hand, which was lost, Eliza had told Felix, during the Cold War. A worn-to-shiny brown leather glove covered a prosthetic replacement.

Sir Bidian settled back in his oversized leather chair. 'Of course, you want to know how this work might affect you, Felix. But first, let me put some things into context.

'At the heart of any state's international activities lies influence. The influence the state has on the rest of the world is vital for trade and security. The power a state can exert on other countries and individuals in support of its interests is all part of essential statecraft. It always has been. Diplomacy plays a significant and preferable role in this. But in the shadows lies espionage.

'As you know, despite ever-changing circumstances, we have been rather good at espionage over the years. Sadly, time and events have eroded our nation's global influence. It comes to every empire in the end. We no longer have the economic and military power we had to influence world events, so we must once again use our guile instead.

'Of course, it won't be the first time we've employed subterfuge. Before the Industrial Revolution and the Empire, we had to be subtler in using these tactics. For instance, we used people of culture or those talented in the arts – the celebrities of their ages – to gain access to the powerful, the wealthy and the influential in other countries. Those people carried messages, learned secrets, planted false intelligence, maintained backchannels, paid bribes, seduced, blackmailed and even, dare I say, tortured and assassinated from time to time. Above all, they kept the Crown, or our government of the day, informed and warned. As you have come to understand, Felix, your family members were involved in many of those activities over the centuries – although I'm not so sure about the torture and assassination part.

'Now that we don't have the global power we once had, developing new ways to influence our friends and foes is a topic that has occupied and tested us for some years. But you will have no trouble guessing that your remarkable grandmother gave me part of the answer. Eliza talked to me one day about our cultural and artistic influence over the centuries – our soft power. After all, her – your – family practically wrote the book. Before long, I realised that she wasn't reminiscing or giving me a family history lesson but suggesting to me in that very clever way of hers exactly what we should do. The extraordinary woman is a ghost. She plants a seed and watches it take root. She waters it some more and lets it grow. Then she backs off as if she had never been there – leaving one to imagine it was one's own idea all along. She was the best of us, Felix – she still is. I can tell you that even John le Carre's George Smiley character could have learned a thing or two from her. In fact, the other day I spoke to a retired spook who referred to Eliza as Georgina Smiley. I must remember to tell her that.' Sir Bidian laughed before continuing. 'Anyway, Eliza reminded me that the Soviets used art against us in the thirties and forties when they recruited Anthony Blunt as a spy – one of the infamous Cambridge Five. Imagine, Blunt was in MI5, was Surveyor of the Queen's Pictures and a director of the Courtauld Institute. And all that time he worked for the KGB. Doesn't bear thinking about, does it? It wasn't one of our finest hours. Eliza suggested to me that it's time for retribution. Poetic justice, or rather "artistic justice", as she put it.'

'So, what did you do after you received this ghostly brainwave?' Felix asked.

Sir Bidian smiled. 'Well, I did what I always do with these things: I put a lot of extraordinarily clever people together to tear the idea to shreds – except they couldn't. Ultimately, we agreed that sometimes, the old ways are the best for the soundest reasons. So, we hatched a plan. In certain circumstances, we see no reason why today we can't curry favour and disarm certain enemies and competitors, just as we did hundreds of years ago. We have called this social and cultural assimilation, or SCA, as we are keen on our acronyms. SCA is designed to get us deep into our targets' personal lives.

'So, we have set up a specialist group called The Art

Department. Where better to base this than side by side with the best art research establishment in the world?'

'Hiding in plain sight?' Felix suggested.

'Quite so: this place is groaning in artists, researchers and scientists. There's also lots of room; we can borrow useful facilities and tap into the finest expertise when we need to. If we follow the correct protocols, our small team should be able to go about their business quite unnoticed.'

'And is the first item of business my client, Mr Volkov?' Felix asked.

'Most conveniently, yes. This could be a proper dry run to get our systems working correctly and the team functioning well while going through our checks. But now it seems there are one or two background ambiguities about Volkov that suggest this could be more of a damp run than a dry one.

'Volkov has a weakness for art and culture, which suits us perfectly. The man might be all he would have us believe. But you never know, he might not be. So, this scrutiny could come in handy in helping us to get to know more about him. If he is hiding anything, he will be expecting our scrutiny. So, we will scrutinise from a direction he is probably not anticipating.'

'And if there is nothing?'

'Then he has nothing to worry about.'

'You mentioned "our small team",' Felix said.

'Yes, people with specialist knowledge and creative talent, like yours. But we will also need artists, copyists, technicians, historians and even musicians. I also have a jeweller in mind, a singular craftsman. Then we will add a layer of analysts, planners, computer geeks and possibly one or two shadier characters, as required.

'We mean to recruit a small group with particular skills – to hoodwink, cheat, forge, charm and intimidate their way into the homes, workplaces and playgrounds of some of the most dangerous, potent and influential people in the world – terrorists included. Fortunately for us, some of our enemies have in common a fascination and even a lust for works of art, either for money laundering, genuine investment, culture washing, fame, or fanatical collecting. It is these motives that make them vulnerable. And in my business, where vulnerability exists so does opportunity.'

'So, how far have you got in putting this team together?' asked Felix.

'We have five specialist recruits so far. You are one of them, if you agree to join us. Your business practice is a perfect front, and you travel worldwide visiting clients, so have a ready-made and scrutiny-proof cover.

'But first, I want you to meet the other team members.'

CHAPTER
FIVE

Sir Bidian led the way down a long corridor.

'The first person we'll meet, Felix, is Petro. He's a master in Eastern European art and is, or was, a monk in the Eastern Orthodox Church.'

'A monk!' Felix repeated in surprise.

'Yes, a man of hidden depths. I must say we had a stroke of luck with Petro. We get a good break occasionally, and he was one of them.

'One day, we heard from the Foreign Office that a Ukrainian, without any papers or passport, was seeking political asylum through our embassy in Paris. They told us that he was, or had been, a monk, and we knew from our own sources that a man called Vasyl Chorney, Russian by birth, had been visited by a monk just before he died – apparently from an obscure cancer that later turned out to be brought on from poisoning.'

'Petro murdered Chorney?'

'Most creatively, as it turns out.'

'Who was Vasyl Chorney?' Felix asked.

'As a delinquent in his early twenties, Chorney murdered Petro's parents and brother, and after that he became a mobster. He was a thorn in our side for many years. The tentacles of his organisation reached London and other major British cities. He had built up an extensive network of pimps, drug dealers and heavies. They were also becoming a real nuisance in trafficking illegal immigrants. But after Chorney's death, the syndicate fell into disarray through infighting. Although ruthless enough, Chorney's brother, who had thought he would take over the criminal empire, didn't have the brains or political skills to deal with the Russians. Now he's on the run, and the organisation is a free-for-all, with different factions within the Russian Mafia trying to take over. Happily, while it's in disarray there is less of a threat to us.

'After his family was murdered, Petro turned to the church for sanctuary. The monastery hid him from Chorney but also discovered and nurtured his creative talent, turning him into a world-class artist and leading authority on Eastern European religious art. He was just what we were looking for.

'After an intensive debrief, we gave Petro a new identity. Now he has the run of our studio, and until we have this latest project fully up and running, he will be doing some helpful conservation work for the National Gallery through the institute.'

'How did you persuade Petro to work for you?' asked Felix.

'It wasn't difficult. We accepted his asylum claim. Then we added a livelihood and an opportunity to continue doing what he loves in this remarkable place and work with us against the Vasyl Chorneys of this world. He's not keen on the Russian government or its expansionist intentions either. So, our stars are pretty much aligned. Oh, and he had a large amount of unattributable cash with him. Chorney had intended it to go to the new abbot at the monastery, but Petro felt it was the least he deserved and took it. Between the Treasury and us, we invest the money wisely. It should give Petro a nice little pension.'

'Invest as in launder?'

'The British government doesn't launder money, Felix,' said Sir Bidian, looking affronted. Then he smiled. 'Although it might give it a light rinse now and again when required.'

'And how is Petro getting on with the change of culture?' Felix asked.

'I think it fascinates him. But remember, we have taken him from one institution and put him in another, so the change is not as great as it could have been. We have had to warn him not to visit Orthodox churches in London on the outside chance some Ukrainian cleric visiting London recognises him. But what he seems to like most is central heating.'

Sir Bidian opened the door to a large room looking north over the magnificent classical courtyard of Somerset House. Tall sash windows allowed light to flood the vast space. Much of the room was empty, but there were areas with easels, giant blank canvasses and all the materials associated with artists' work.

Felix was hit by a smell that took him back to school and university art rooms. He picked out the mildly nauseating essence of egg tempera, the refreshing scent of mint and lanolin artists' soap, and the unmistakable aromas of oil paint, turpentine and linseed oil.

At a large worktable lit by a bright lamp sat a man deep in concentration.

Sir Bidian approached the table, and said, 'Petro, sorry to

interrupt, but I should like to introduce you to Felix Bohlin.' The man stood up from his stool. He was taller than both the others. The first thing Felix noticed was how long and lean he seemed. All his features were elongated: his face, nose, body, limbs and fingers. An unkempt and slightly greying beard covered his lower face. He wore a long, loosely fitting, brown warehouse coat that was gathered at the waist by a length of cord, which, Felix thought, was similar to a monk's habit.

The three exchanged pleasantries, and Sir Bidian asked what piece Petro was working on.

'I help restore religious paintings for National Gallery,' he explained. 'This from Crete – fifteenth century. It is beautiful, yes?'

Sir Bidian and Felix agreed.

'Well, I don't think we should interrupt you further. Thank you, Petro,' said Sir Bidian.

Felix shook Petro's hand.

Walking away, Sir Bidian turned to Felix, and said, 'Next is our super art sleuth. Her name is Ellie. More correctly, her name is Louise-Emmanuelle Lydden. Apparently, when little, Ms Lydden thought her forenames were a bit of a mouthful, so she called herself L.E., and Ellie she became. Her double-barrelled forename has been handed down the female line of her family for over two hundred years. Ellie gained a degree in fine art from St Andrew's University, and after her master's worked for Sotheby's and several private galleries, one in Mayfair and the other in Manhattan, before branching out independently as a freelance art researcher. A bit like you with buildings, but her speciality is discovering and producing the evidence on which clients depend for their art to reach the sort of value only positive attribution will bring. She has a particular talent for this. I'm convinced that she can smell an original from twenty paces. In the antiques trade, I understand they're called divvies – people with seemingly unnatural power to recognise exceptional items and tell genuine antiques from forgeries.'

'Where do you find these people, Bidian?' Felix asked.

Sir Bidian laughed. 'Well, it seems I'm a divvy in the spy world. But I mustn't take all the credit. I have a small team keeping their ears to the ground. They discovered, through delving through her bank records, that Miss Lydden's income was not very regular. The paydays, when they came, were OK. But unfortunately, at that time she had not had one of those for a while. So, I invited her in for a little chat. She passed with flying colours. Not that she knew she was being interviewed for a job.'

'What makes her so ideal?'

'She fits our departmental profile perfectly. She is a brilliant finder of things; she speaks Russian and French, and her family history is fascinating – and should be to you also.'

'Why's that?'

'One of Ellie's forebears was Louise-Emmanuelle de Châtillon, Princesse de Tarente. She had been a favourite lady-in-waiting to Marie Antoinette. The princess was fortunate to keep her head during the Revolution. The Queen arranged for her to escape to England, where an uncle of hers lived.'

'It's a nice story, but why is that particularly interesting?'

Sir Bidian smiled. 'Because the man who escorted Louise-Emmanuelle through the street barricades of Paris and across the Channel to our safe shores was one Robert Arrow. Your grandmother has a letter that says so.'

'So, my family was involved in the French Revolution?'

'Up to their un-severed necks, it would seem.

'Ellie has already proved successful, as she found two sisters we were looking for. The pair were in very great danger. Their names are Rani and Tiya De. I'm going to introduce you to them later. Now, I think Ellie will be in our little refreshment room.'

Sir Bidian opened the door and ushered Felix into a small room with a pine table, four yellow plastic chairs, and a worktop running along one wall with a kettle, coffee machine, hot plate and microwave. The woman sitting at the table looked up from a file she was reading, turned to Sir Bidian with a radiant smile, and said, 'Sir Bidian, how lovely. To what do we owe this visit?'

'Ellie, I want to introduce you to Felix Bohlin.'

Ellie had wavy blonde hair cut just above the shoulders, a clear complexion, and strikingly blue eyes. She wore jeans and a camel-coloured polo neck. A brightly patterned silk scarf added zest to her look.

'I was just explaining to Felix what a marvellous job you did in finding Tiya and Rani.' Ellie looked slightly embarrassed. Turning to Felix, Sir Bidian added, 'Ellie posed as an art buyer, and with our help managed to prize the sisters from their lair. They were living as illegal immigrants about thirty miles south of Miami. The RAF spirited them away to avoid creating a commercial aviation trail for their pursuers.'

'Why was anyone trying to find them?' Felix asked.

'Ah, well, I'm afraid the young ladies' interesting pasts caught up with them. A collector of the wrong sort discovered that his Picasso was not all it should have been.'

'They were dealing in forgeries?'

'Not just dealing,' said Ellie. 'Tiya was the forger, and an excellent one at that. She was a child prodigy. Her extraordinary artistic talent was discovered by chance in the Calcutta orphanage where the sisters went to live.'

'Rani, it turned out, was no less talented,' said Sir Bidian, 'but in numeracy – an extraordinary mind and an extraordinary young life. Before the orphanage took them in, the two girls had been living on the streets following the death of their parents from TB.

'Managed by Rani, Tiya started forging art to order, and the two became very successful on the online black market. Sadly, for them, the truth caught up with them. Word spread, and some sinister people were out for blood. Fortunately, Ellie was as good as we had hoped and tracked them down before anyone else did. With the noose tightening, Rani and Tiya were only too happy to accept our hospitality and protection in return for lending us their talents.

'Tiya continues to use and develop her considerable artistic skills here – especially under Petro's eagle eye. We have also arranged to make up gaps in their formal training with study at the Royal Academy of Art. We have sent Rani to GCHQ as a finishing school. They say she is quite brilliant in computing and almost unbeatable at chess. So, I have to say, both girls seem to be thriving.'

On the way back through the studio, Felix met Tiya and Rani. The two small-framed women in their mid-twenties, and only a year apart in age, had a striking facial resemblance and shared delicate features. Tiya was the more bohemian of the two; she wore a long flowing print dress over which she had added a well-smudged apron. A headscarf protected her hair from flicks of paint. Rani looked elegant in a fitted jacket and trousers. Without a scarf, her hair flowed long, straight, black and lustrous below her shoulders. Both women looked happy and relaxed.

Sir Bidian introduced Felix, who said how much he was looking forward to working with the sisters.

'Will there be any more in the team?' Felix asked Sir Bidian as they returned to the spy chief's office.

'I have one or two in mind,' replied Sir Bidian with a smile.

CHAPTER
SIX

Róisín sat alone in her flat feeling worthless and vulnerable. There had been no response to the message she had left at the dead drop, which added to her feeling of isolation.

Forty years ago, she had considered hers to be a loyal cause, one full of crusading zeal and the indestructability of youth. She was convinced she could make a difference and had stumbled on an ideal way to do so, but now she questioned her motives.

She thought again about the value of her leaked information. Surely the receivers of this bounty must have tried to discover her true identity. Did they ever wonder who their supplier was? Or did they take the information for granted, as they would do until the day it stopped – through their informant's death, senility or capture? Róisín understood that analysts would treat Mara as a double agent – they had to. But initially, at least, they would be confused over whose double agent she was. Still, if the intelligence received turned out to be genuine then why not take what was on offer? Who would care about the source if the information had real value.

Still grief-stricken by the death of her husband in Ireland, Róisín had initially let herself be swept along by events over which she had no control.

The turning point had been Mara. At a time when Róisín felt she had burned all her boats and could no longer return home, she created an alter ego that was focused and idealistic. Mara let Róisín slip into a character who was in control and made her feel valuable. In many ways, being Mara had helped Róisín become herself again.

The name Mara was connected to many countries, regions, religions and cultures. Róisín had adopted the codename knowing it would be impossible for intelligence analysts on whichever side to predict with any certainty the gender, leanings or origin of its creator. It amused Róisín that her cover name was actually the shortened form of O'Mara, inspired by the name of a corner shop in Belfast – something so arbitrary it was beyond the imagination of even the most brilliant and gifted analysts.

Róisín had let her coffee go cold. As she reheated the kettle, she wondered how many spies had let themselves fall into the situation she had found herself in. Quite a few, she imagined. Losing one's sense of self was a great risk when operating long-term under deep cover.

Now, four decades after she had arrived in Moscow, Róisín wondered if there was anyone left alive who remembered her or, if so, cared. As far as she was concerned, anyone important to her was dead.

As she sipped her fresh coffee, she wondered how useful the latest information she had passed on would be. She couldn't put her finger on anything, it was a gut feeling, but she felt something was about to happen, and it had to do with someone, or something named Bezrodny. Not for the first time, she wondered if this information could be her return ticket.

* * *

Sir Bidian and Felix completed their tour of the studio and returned to Sir Bidian's office.

'I'm delighted those pieces of our jigsaw are in place,' he said to Felix.

'They seem remarkable people, and you seem very confident in them.'

'I am. But one must be ever wary. However, I think Petro, Rani and Tiya can see our motivations are in line with theirs, and they know they may find themselves out in a very cold world if they stray.'

'You would do that?' asked Felix.

Sir Bidian looked him in the eye with a steely glare and let the question hang.

'Now, Felix, I have had some good news. I think the department is ready for business. If you agree, I should like to invite you to an evening of music in Cheltenham.'

'Cheltenham?'

'Yes, preliminary investigations show that Mr Volkov is not quite the common or garden oligarch billionaire he makes himself out to be. Whilst carrying out some research, our analysts have come up with more questions than answers. So, now we need to get closer to this gentleman, and I think we have created just the opportunity for us to do that.'

'Is this by any chance anything to do with Volkov's daughter being at school in Cheltenham?' Felix asked.

'It has everything to do with her being there. Our Russian friend is immersing himself in all things British, including having his beloved daughter educated at Cheltenham Ladies' College. I'm told she is learning to play the violin – enthusiastically, but not that well by all accounts,' he added with a chuckle. 'I remember my niece going through the same stage. It wasn't easy on the ear. But I digress. Fortunately, we have had a relationship with the college for over a hundred and fifty years. The school has provided us with some extraordinary analysts and operatives over that time, including your grandmother.

'We have arranged with the college for a programme of English music to be put on in their concert hall. The star performer will be the virtuoso violinist, Linqin.'

'Linqin? How on earth did you manage to get her? Isn't she booked up years ahead?'

'She is. But we have some pull in that direction. I won't say any more on that for the time being.' Sir Bidian gave a smile accompanied by, Felix thought, a twinkle in his eye.

'So, what has this to do with Volkov?' Felix asked.

'This is where we will make multiple contacts with the man and begin to infiltrate his life. Plus, the college governors can use the occasion to tap him for another substantial donation. Everyone is happy, even Mr Volkov, who buys more kudos.'

'But why the greater interest in him?'

'Because it transpires that in his younger years, Mr Volkov attended School 281 in Leningrad.'

'I suppose he had to go to school somewhere. Why is that one so special?'

'It was a school for high-flyers. But what makes it extra special is that one of his classmates was a certain Vladimir Putin.

'After the 1991 Soviet coup d'etat attempt against Mikhail

Gorbachev, Putin went into the security services and Volkov entered the energy business. We don't know if there is a link between them now, but it seems unlikely there isn't. Either way, we need to know.'

'And I am going to this concert to find out more?'

'You and Dimity, if she will go.'

'I am sure she will; she loves listening to Linqin. But won't our being there seem too much of a coincidence? After all, we have no other link with Cheltenham or the college.'

'It certainly would look too much of a coincidence. So, you will have to get Mr Volkov to invite you.'

'How on earth do I do that, Bidian?'

'I am in no doubt, Felix, that you will find a way.'

'Is this you testing me?'

Sir Bidian raised his right eyebrow. 'You could think that.'

CHAPTER SEVEN

'Bezrodny? Kazimer Bezrodny?' Eliza was astonished.

'We can't think of another Bezrodny,' said Sir Bidian. 'He was one of yours.'

Eliza nodded slowly. Good Lord. She'd not thought about him for years. Kazimer Bezrodny had been one of her best assets during the Cold War, providing priceless details of the Russian nuclear programme. That was before she'd had to extract him through Finland – a terrifying experience for them both. But the Russians had been getting suspicious – not about Bezrodny per se but that there was a leak somewhere. Eliza had always thought it had been the traitor, Kim Philby's doing. She had known Philby at MI5 reasonably well and still felt stung by his defection.

Sir Bidian and Eliza sat in the drawing room of Witch's Lawn surrounded by mementoes, trophies and treasures gathered by members of the Arrow family over five hundred years of shadowy duty to the state.

Eliza was familiar with every piece and its history. But she didn't live in the past, and, conversely, the older she became, the less inclined she was to look forward. The future was not a subject upon which Eliza wished to dwell. At her age, it was a dimension with limited possibilities, and with each passing day, those possibilities became palpably fewer. Now she lived for the day. And the days when Bidian visited were some of the best. Eliza and her protégé met every month or so. The visits helped to keep her mind sharp and engaged. Eliza understood Sir Bidian was doing this, somewhat against the rules, to entertain her, but also for another point of view on some sensitive or tricky matters. Eliza knew he shouldn't. But, she thought, she was still bound by the Official Secrets Act, as she had been, thanks to her father, since she was eighteen years old. She had never given away any state secrets and was unlikely to do so now. Besides, there was no one left to tell.

'Yes, Bezrodny was one of mine,' Eliza said. 'He worked for us for about eight years.'

'So, why the mention of him now after so many years?' asked Sir Bidian, looking perplexed.

There was a knock on the drawing room door. Eliza sighed in irritation and turned to see West enter the room.

'Tea's up, be with you soon,' said West in his usual flat, East London, matter-of-fact way, before promptly departing.

'West doesn't change, does he?' Sir Bidian remarked.

Eliza smiled. 'No, his is an acquired charm.'

'One I've never managed to find. But then West isn't here for his charm, is he?'

'No, he's not, but Cairo makes up for it.' Eliza didn't say any more, as at that moment Cairo came into the room carrying a tea tray.

'Good afternoon, Cairo, you are well, I hope?' Sir Bidian said.

'Never better, thank you, Sir Bidian. How could I not be,

THE ART DEPARTMENT

living in this house with Eliza?' Cairo smiled at them both, set the tray down on the coffee table and left.

'Bezrodny,' Eliza prompted as she poured the tea.

'Yes, when I was here for lunch the other week, I was going to tell you about a communication we had received from Moscow.'

'We were interrupted as usual.'

'There's nothing wrong with your memory.'

'Nor my lack of patience,' replied Eliza snappily.

Sir Bidian laughed but then looked serious. 'I seem to have a mole.'

'On your lawn or in your department?'

'Neither.'

'Then whose department?'

'The Russians.'

'My word, how high up?'

'I don't know, but quite a height judging by the quality of information we are getting.'

'Who is it?'

'That's the problem. I don't know that either.'

'You don't know the identity of your mole?'

'No.'

'Isn't that rather unusual?'

'Unprecedented, I should think.'

'How long have you had this mole?'

'Thirty years or more.'

'Over thirty years, and you don't know who it is?'

'No.'

'How on earth did it start?'

'The asset contacted Nigel Broadway at the Moscow station just before he retired and has been coughing up high-grade, but random, intelligence ever since.'

'A male or female mole?'

'I have no idea.'

'Has this mole ever asked for anything in return?'

'No.'

'A purely altruistic asset? That's rare, and hard to believe.'

'Nevertheless, that's how it seems to be.'

'So, how secure do you think this unknown asset is?'

'Seems very secure, and the information has become more valuable as the years have passed.'

'Suggesting career or at least influence progression.'

'That's what we think.'

'What sort of information?'

'It's mainly official government and security stuff.'

'So, a double?'

'It seems like it.'

'That we didn't recruit?'

'Not that I'm aware.'

'What do you call this mole?'

'He or she signs off as Mara. Could be anyone.'

'You've never mentioned Mara to me before.'

'I've never had the need.'

'But you're telling me now because Mara has mentioned Bezrodny?'

'Yes.'

'How does Mara communicate?'

'A dead drop.'

'Old school. Where?'

'Moscow. Kolomenskoye Park.'

Eliza nodded. 'Picturesque. How often?'

'Seven or eight times a year. We never ask for more. We take what we can get and don't look a gift horse in the mouth.'

'Sensible. But now you think you will have to ask for more?'

'We need to, as it's hard to imagine why Bezrodny's name has come up. Is there any reason you can think of, Eliza?'

'I don't think so. After all, any secrets he might have possessed were given to us years ago when we got him back to London. If he did have any other intelligence, it would be long past its sell-by date and of little or no value.'

'So, what on earth could it be?'

Eliza thought for a moment. 'The only thing that makes any sense to me is retribution. I'm afraid Mr Putin has no statute of limitations on traitors. We know that from Markov and Litvinenko. Then we had the attempt on the lives of Sergei Skripal and his daughter in Salisbury.'

'That's what we wondered,' Sir Bidian said.

'So, what have you done?'

'We've doubled our watch on Russians coming into the UK, from whatever direction. The last two assassins – intelligence officers – came in on false passports. And we have upped our scrutiny on all Russian embassy staff – although there could be a cell we don't know about that is independent of the embassy. It's all we can do for now. We want to look after Bezrodny as best we can. But we can't have Russian agents wandering around the UK with weapons-grade poison again. Just think what happened last time with that damned scent bottle.'

'Well, I have to say that if this is retribution on the FSB's part, then Mara must be in a highly placed position or have access to someone who is. So, what are you going to do?'

'Ask questions at the dead drop.'

'That's putting Mara at much greater risk.'

'I know, but what else can we do?'

'Have you ever had the dead drop under surveillance? Ever tried to find out Mara's identity?'

Sir Bidian shook his head. 'With so few random contacts every year, we don't have the manpower to cover it, and the park is too open and is often crowded. Besides, we think Mara always flags the drop after, not before, he or she leaves any material. It would be very sloppy field-craft otherwise. And after so many years undetected, Mara is clearly anything but sloppy. As for electronic surveillance, we didn't want to take the risk of discovery. If the Russians ever found the equipment or sourced a signal, they would use it and find out the identity of their mole for themselves.

'What would *you* do, Eliza?'

'I think I'd wait for the next dead drop. See if anything further is mentioned. I should imagine that if Mara is well placed and has specific information, he or she will make contact again sooner rather than later. What flag do you get to signal a dead drop?'

'A message hidden in Russian eBay.'

'Well, I'm afraid I don't know much about that. But it sounds like a modern twist on old school. And you can't identify the sender?'

'No, GCHQ tells me that our mole uses TOR.'

'Which is?'

'The Onion Router. Basically, it's a dark web system that gives users anonymity. Plus, our mole is probably using internet cafes rather than a home computer or mobile device for further security. We can't risk trying to hack the system as it might alert someone.'

'Well, I'm none the wiser about any of that, but I wonder how old this mole is?'

'Judging from the time he or she has been operating and

the age they must have been when they started this contact, then perhaps in their late sixties or even seventies.'

'So, probably coming to the end of any usefulness.'

'Oh, I don't know, Eliza, look at you.'

Eliza laughed. 'I'm not running around Moscow using dead drops for passing on state secrets. What about putting something on eBay, Bidian? Reach out that way. Do you think that would work?'

'We have considered that, and it might be successful. But we can't guarantee that only Mara will see it. I'm sure the FSB or GRU will have eBay and social media under the microscope. Lord alone knows what algorithm they have devised to catch patterns and hidden messages. I'm not sure it's worth the risk.'

'I understand your dilemma. On the one hand you want to protect a retired agent, but on the other you want to protect an active one.'

'Exactly.'

'Then you know the answer to that, or I didn't train you sufficiently well.'

Sir Bidian smiled at Eliza's steel. 'Oh, I do know the answer, have no fear, Eliza. You trained me very well. I just want to try and protect both.'

'Bidian, you're a romantic. You should know that all too often you can't do that. But if you still want to try, then I think you will have to wait for the next drop and hope it comes in time for you to do something about it.

'More tea?'

Sir Bidian declined.

'So, bring me up to date with Bezrodny.'

Eliza knew the service had found Bezrodny a small flat off the Cromwell Road in West London and a job in the Science

Museum's library, but little more, other than he had married an English woman he met at the library.

'There's not much I can tell you. Only that he and his wife retired to the south coast some years ago.'

'I take it his wife doesn't know anything about his past?'

'Not as far as I know. And Bezrodny has never put a foot out of place all these years.'

'It's odd that his name should come up now.'

'That's what we think.'

'Well, somehow you are going to have to find out why.'

* * *

News of the Cheltenham concert spread quickly. The programme consisted of Elgar's Violin Concerto in B minor and Thomas Linley the younger's Violin Concerto in F major. Tickets had sold out almost immediately.

When Felix next met Volkov to discuss progress at the Cotswold mansion, the subject of the concert presented itself easily. Volkov was clearly excited by the event and was keen to let Felix know about it, as well as how well his daughter was doing at school.

'Dimity, my wife, adores Linqin,' said Felix honestly. 'I was too late to book tickets when she last performed in London. I really must do something next time. Perhaps for her birthday.'

'But you must both come as my guests,' said Volkov. 'As the main sponsor, I have several spare tickets.'

Felix was beginning to feign protest, but Volkov raised his hand. 'Please do not say another word. It will be my pleasure. I will arrange for one of my assistants to send you over the tickets. I am pleased that I can make a wish come true for your wife.'

'It was as easy as that,' Felix told Sir Bidian over the phone later.

'I knew you would find a way,' Sir Bidian replied.

* * *

On the evening of the concert, the hall was full to overflowing and was made even more beautiful by some magnificent flower displays. Scent and excitement mingled and hung in the air. The sound of the orchestra tuning up in the auditorium added to the feeling of anticipation.

Felix said to Dimity, 'Look, there's Volkov, and I take it that's his daughter. But who's that woman with them, do you think?'

Standing next to the oligarch was a short woman who was a little on the heavy side for her height. She wore a midnight blue trouser suit, and her brown hair was severely cut in a straight line just below the top of her neck.

'Do you think she's Volkov's lady friend?' Dimity said. 'If she is, that can't be easy. Her body language with the daughter doesn't look comfortable.'

'You always notice these things. But next to Volkov, she does seem a bit mismatched. He is dressed so elegantly. They don't share a tailor, that's for sure. Yuri is very aristocratic looking, don't you think? Put a well-trimmed, full beard on him and he could be a Romanov. The woman looks very different with her large forehead and narrow eyes. They're Slavic features, wouldn't you say? Anyway, we'd better make ourselves known and offer our thanks.'

Felix and Dimity squeezed through the scrum of people in the foyer.

Volkov soon spotted them. 'Felix, I am so pleased that you

could come this evening. And this, I presume, is your beautiful wife, Dimity.'

Dimity held out a hand. 'Mr Volkov, I am delighted to meet you. Felix has told me so much about your house in the Cotswolds.'

'And it is a pleasure to meet you, Dimity. I think, with your husband, I can do something special with the house. Now, I must introduce my daughter, Lizabeta, and my good friend and compatriot, Maria Mirova.'

'Who are these people to you, Yuri?' Maria said in an offhand way, as though Felix and Dimity weren't there, and she wasn't much interested in the answer anyway. Her English was stilted.

Yuri looked embarrassed for a moment before replying, 'Felix is my property adviser, Maria. He is looking after the restoration of Courtlands.'

'A house I am still looking forward to visiting,' Maria said pointedly, while scrutinising Felix and then Dimity.

Yuri smiled weakly.

Dimity turned to Volkov's daughter, and asked, 'How are you enjoying Cheltenham, Lizabeta? I understand you are at school here.'

Lizabeta responded with a bright smile and said in well-polished English with barely a trace of a Russian accent, 'Oh I love it here. I have made so many new friends. It is wonderful to be in England.'

Volkov's daughter looked similar to most of the other privileged and confident teenagers around her. She wore the standard college uniform of a white shirt, tartan kilt and a moss-coloured sweater, the sleeves of which were pulled down to almost cover her hands.

A loud noise interrupted their chatter.

'That will be the ten-minute bell,' said Felix. 'We had better find our seats, Mr Volkov.'

'Please, Felix, you must call me Yuri. I insist.'

'Thank you, Yuri.'

'And we must also thank you again for inviting us this evening. We are both thrilled to be here,' Dimity said honestly.

Yuri and Lizabeta smiled warmly, while Maria Mirova turned her back. The parties separated to go off and find their seats. Naturally, Volkov and his party were in the front row.

Felix and Dimity found their seats halfway back in the stalls. 'Why do you think teenage girls tug the sleeves of their jumpers down to cover their hands?' Felix asked. 'I've often wondered.'

Dimity laughed. 'It's one of the little mysteries of life. But perhaps it's a comfort thing. I used to do it. I wore holes in my cuffs with my thumbs.'

'I remember.'

'I shouldn't say this, but I'm afraid I didn't take to Maria Mirova,' Dimity said.

'Whatever happened to goodwill to all men? You're supposed to see the good in people.'

'To do that, I find it helpful to know the bad in them. There is something about that woman. She certainly doesn't seem comfortable with the daughter. Did you see the look on her face when Lizabeta said how she liked being in England? Perhaps Maria would like her at school in Russia and out of the way.'

'Maria didn't seem keen to meet us, either,' said Felix.

'No. She could be the jealous type.'

'What? Do you think she wants Yuri all to herself?'

'Who knows?'

'If she does, I wonder how Yuri feels about that?'

'Well, he looked a bit uncomfortable I thought. But we might be doing the woman an injustice, and we don't know the real story,' Dimity said.

'Ah, there's the goodwill.'

As Dimity dug Felix sharply in the ribs with her elbow, the house lights dimmed. The hall immediately became hushed, and the conductor welcomed Linqin to the stage. There was a burst of loud applause. The beautiful and slender young Singaporean woman with signature black hair the length of her back was dressed in a scarlet full-length evening gown with a mandarin collar. She shook the conductor's hand and made a bow to the audience.

The conductor raised his baton, and the orchestra began the stirring opening sonata of the Elgar concerto. Linqin then elegantly tucked her violin under her delicate chin, set her bow and made her haunting entrance. What ensued was spellbinding, and it was followed by an equally affecting performance of the Linley piece.

At the end of the recital, the audience, which included a large number of the college's students, rose to their feet and chanted, 'More, more, more', as if they were at a rock concert or the Last Night of the Proms. When the small orchestra left the stage, the chanting continued.

After some minutes, the conductor returned to further great applause. When he had finally managed to quieten the crowd, he said, 'Ladies and gentlemen, Linqin has generously agreed to play another piece.' The hall erupted in applause. More time went by as the conductor struggled to regain control. 'Linqin has suggested that given the English theme of tonight's programme, she plays *The Lark Ascending* by Ralph Vaughan Williams. This will be the first time she has played this work publicly on English soil.'

There was pandemonium as everyone in the hall realised this would be an 'I was there' occasion.

'But before we start, I should like to say an enormous thank you to Mr Yuri Volkov. His recent most generous endowment will underwrite the musical work of the college, not just with its own students but with those from schools throughout the local area for many years to come.'

More applause followed. Felix couldn't see Volkov's face, but he imagined a wide grin. Linqin returned to the platform, and the sweeping and emotional piece that followed brought the house down.

After the concert, Felix and Dimity met Volkov and his party again. Volkov was looking extremely pleased with himself, and Lizabeta was bubbling with excitement. Maria seemed to be urging Volkov to leave.

The conductor, accompanied by Linqin, entered the foyer and headed straight over to them.

'May I introduce you to Linqin, Mr Volkov?' he said.

Felix saw that the Russian was a little awed. Volkov then blurted out his admiration and thanks to the violinist before lapsing into star-struck silence. Volkov's daughter seemed similarly afflicted.

Dimity filled the void in conversation by saying, 'I thought I knew *The Lark Ascending* so well, but somehow, Linqin, you gave it something more, which I can't put into words.'

Linqin gave a little bow. 'Thank you; it is a challenging piece but so beautiful.'

'But somehow it was different – besides the way you played, of course,' Dimity said.

'Well, the hall's acoustics are good,' replied Linqin, 'but then there is my violin.' She held up the violin case she was holding. 'It is as though it was made for the piece.'

'I remember reading somewhere that it is an exceptional instrument,' said Felix.

'Oh, it is,' Linqin replied. 'My violin was made by Bartolomeo Giuseppe Guarneri. Some say his instruments produce a finer sound than those made by Stradivari, and they are equally – if not more – valuable. Of course, I think this one sounds infinitely better than any other violin, but then I am biased, and I know its little ways. But I do think it has a more vibrant tone than a Strad. There are only a few Bartolomeo Guarneri instruments in existence.'

'I certainly thought the sound was a heavenly one,' Dimity said.

'And you should know,' Felix responded.

Everyone except Maria laughed.

'It is heavenly to me also,' said Linqin with a smile. 'Thanks to La Strega.'

'What is La Strega?' asked Dimity.

'Some of Guarneri's instruments have unique names. Mine is La Strega. I don't know why it was given that name originally, but in Italian, La Strega means The Witch.'

Felix suddenly felt the hairs rise on the back of his neck at the mention of Eliza's code name in the Spanish Civil War. He suddenly suspected why Bidian was so tight-lipped about being able to make the arrangements for the concert.

'Perhaps it's called La Strega because it will put a spell on you. It certainly did on us,' said Felix, recovering a little from the initial surprise. 'I should love to know how you found such a wonderful instrument. Violins like yours must be in huge demand by virtuosos.'

'Oh, they are. But mostly these instruments are in collections or bank vaults. The fact is the owner anonymously donated this beautiful violin to me to use during my lifetime, or at least until I stop my virtuoso work. Then I hope it will go to another soloist.'

'How amazing,' said Dimity. 'I wonder who would make such a wonderful gesture.'

'I don't know, it was extraordinary,' replied Linqin. 'But there were some stipulations connected with the loan. The first was that I did as much justice to the instrument as my talent and hard work could achieve; the second was that I never try to discover the identity of my donor.'

'How intriguing,' Dimity said.

'And it was amazing that the college could engage you,' Felix said, fishing for more clues. 'Didn't I hear you are booked up years in advance?'

Linqin smiled. 'That is correct. But there was a third stipulation – or rather request – connected to my having this instrument.'

'What was that?' Dimity asked.

'That when asked by my donor, I play – if I am at all able. All expenses are paid. This time, it happened that I was heading from Berlin to LA. So, I was only too happy to break my journey at Heathrow. But, as usual, I have no idea who made the request. It was arranged anonymously through my agent. But Mrs Mirova, Mr Volkov and Lizabeta, you might especially be interested to know that my violin was once owned by the great Russian composer and violinist, Vasily Pashkevich.'

'Pashkevich?' Volkov said, sounding surprised. Maria Mirova's demeanour changed, and she looked mildly impressed.

'Yes, he had the violin until he died in 1797. Some say Catherine the Great gave it to him. After his death, we know the instrument found its way to Vienna, but then it disappeared for almost a hundred years.'

'And you don't want to know who owns it now?' Maria asked, her tone making the question sound like a rebuke.

Linqin smoothly replied, 'In some ways, I should love to know, so that I can express my appreciation. But in other ways, not knowing makes it more thrilling. I often wonder if my sponsor is in the audience. It makes me strive to always play the best I can.'

'Your sponsor could be here tonight,' suggested Felix.

'Yes.'

'So, that is how you express your appreciation?' Dimity asked.

Linqin nodded and smiled.

'Well, you certainly honoured your sponsor tonight,' Volkov said.

'I'm sorry to break up the party,' the conductor interrupted, 'but I must introduce Linqin to the college governors. I also think there are many young people wanting autographs and selfies.'

The conductor proceeded to steer Linqin off through the throng.

'We should go, it's late,' Maria urged Volkov.

'I suppose we must. This has been a wonderful evening—'

Volkov was cut off by a man shouting, 'Yoo-hoo, Felix, Dimity.'

Felix turned, although he already knew the owner of the voice. 'Roger, what on earth are you doing here?'

'My dear, can't you tell?'

'Oh, I suppose you must have done the flowers,' Felix said.

'Of course I have "done the flowers", as you so prosaically

put it. I must say, it was nice to be asked. I just adore Linqin, don't you? Doesn't everyone? But I only agreed on condition that I was given a backstage pass so I could watch from the wings.'

Roger turned to Dimity. 'Hello, my darling, how is married life with this heathen?'

'All is fine, thank you, Roger. This is such a lovely surprise. I haven't seen you since you last took the members of our flower guild out for the evening. I don't think many of them knew what a hangover was until the morning after. The arrangements in church that week looked as drunk as the guild members must have been.'

'Ah, yes, petal, that was quite an evening. Now, are you going to tell Roger off all night, or are you going to introduce me to your interesting-looking friends?'

Roger turned to Volkov, who appeared slightly startled. Maria had the look of someone who had just trodden in something she regretted.

'Of course,' Felix said. 'Yuri, I should like you to meet Roger Strand. Roger is one of London's most leading and sought-after florists.'

Roger frowned. 'Not "one of", petal. London's *leading* florist.' Turning to Volkov, he added, 'I do everyone who is anyone.'

'Roger, meet Yuri Volkov, his daughter, Lizabeta, and his friend, Maria Mirova,' Felix continued. 'Yuri, as I'm sure you know, is the main sponsor of this evening, and as of a few weeks ago, my most important client. Yuri has bought Courtlands. You might have seen it in the news. My firm is managing the refurbishment and the interior and garden design. I'm acting as general project manager. It's an enormous undertaking.'

'But I have heard of you,' Volkov said to Roger. 'Many of my friends are your clients I think.'

'I'm sure they are, but I'm always looking for more business,' Roger said fearlessly. 'Cotswold mansions are a speciality. Let me give you my card. I only present it to people I take a personal interest in.' Roger gave Volkov a stage wink.

As outrageous as ever, Felix thought. But by the look on Volkov's face, he seemed pleased with the introduction. The same couldn't be said for Maria, while Lizabeta looked on open-mouthed. It'll be good for her education, Felix decided. He doubted whether highly camp florists made it onto the curriculum at Cheltenham.

'Now, I can't stand and gossip, darlings,' Roger said. 'There are some wilting violets and wallflowers to sweep up. Sadly, in this establishment, most seem to be female.' He let out another enormous laugh and was gone.

'Roger's shop is a few doors from my office and showroom in Pimlico,' explained Felix to Volkov. 'I'm surprised to see him here but once met never forgotten.'

'I certainly do see,' said Volkov. 'I think I will be using this card and his services very soon.'

'I am surprised people like that are allowed in a place like this,' said Maria with a snort.

Felix could see Volkov was embarrassed for a second time. Fortunately, it was then that the chair of the college governors came up and whisked Volkov and his party away.

'I can't believe Roger is here,' said Felix to Dimity.

'Can't you?'

'You mean...?'

'Do I mean that Bidian arranged it? I most certainly do,' Dimity said.

'Do you think Roger knows that? Perhaps he's lining him up for The Art Department.'

'Stranger things have happened.'

'Bidian did say there would be surprises. And talking of surprises, what about the violin? Do you think that has anything to do with Eliza – all that witch business is a bit of a coincidence, don't you think?'

'I think it might have everything to do with Eliza. So, we must ask her how that violin ended up in the Arrow family. Or perhaps Bidian already knows.'

'More of the family fiddling about with secrets, I suppose,' Felix said.

'Ha-ha, but Bidian is clever, isn't he? He now has in place Volkov's architect, and possibly his florist too. I wonder who will be next. Perhaps he thinks I can become his confessor. But that would be a conflict of interest. After all, God trumps MI6. But let me tell you about my conversation with Maria when I bumped into her in the loo earlier.'

'What did she say?'

'She asked me where we lived, how we met, and how long we have known each other. She was quite brazen about it.'

'What did you say?'

'I told her the truth. We have nothing to hide.'

'Except all the stuff we *do* have to hide. I think I should tell Bidian about her.'

'You'd better mention that she also said she would like to find out about the owner of Linqin's violin. She sounded quite serious. So, Bidian should be warned, and he should also know that Maria appears to have her claws in Yuri. I'm not at all sure about that woman, Felix. I think those claws could be very sharp indeed.'

* * *

The second mobile phone on Eliza's pretty Venetian chairside table rang and she collected herself. The phone, given to her by Sir Bidian and supposedly a special one with a high level of security, didn't ring that often, and when it did, it was not for gossip or chitchat.

'Hello, Bidian.'

'Eliza, I'm glad I've caught you.'

Eliza gave a silent snort. As if she would be doing anything else these days than sitting by her phones. But still, it was a kind sentiment.

'I've called to say that using Linqin to lure Volkov was an inspired idea. You haven't lost your touch. The evening was a complete success. The music was wonderful by all accounts, your alma mater made a packet, and, best of all for us, Volkov let Felix and Dimity a little further into his world. They're now on first-name terms. Plus, we may be bringing Roger Strand more into the fold. I'm told that Volkov seemed most impressed with him.'

'Roger was all down to you, Bidian, and I have to say it was rather inspired. I do like Roger. He makes me laugh. Dimity told me about his evening out with the women – and man – of the flower guild. He took them all to an Old Compton Street gay bar. It was hysterical by all accounts.'

'I can imagine – or rather, I can't imagine,' Sir Bidian said.

Eliza chuckled. 'Roger is simultaneously totally disrespectful and charming. He gets away with murder, don't you agree?'

'Don't give me ideas.'

Eliza laughed, and said, 'What? Getting Roger to do

someone in with a tulip, or assassination by posy? I hardly think so.

'But you didn't call me to talk about Roger, Bidian. What's on your mind?'

'I can't hide anything from you, can I? Yes, there are two major things on my mind. The first is the woman Volkov was with at the concert. She has come as a bit of a surprise. We must do some more investigating, but it seems she is the extremely wealthy widow of another oligarch and is often seen with Volkov. It turns out she's part of a very exclusive Russian set in London, but as far as we can tell, she has few, if any, contacts with the Russian Embassy, despite practically living next door to it.'

'A feeling in your water, Bidian?'

'Yes. Her name is Maria Mirova. Volkov's association with her and this group gives us more questions to answer.'

'You're wondering if this is an ex-pat social group or something more sinister like a cabal?'

'Precisely.'

'And the other thing on your mind?'

'I thought I would tell you that after Cheltenham, Felix has formally agreed to join the programme.'

Eliza closed her eyes for a moment. She had resisted asking Felix what he was going to do, not wanting him to think she was meddling.

'Do you think he will be all right, Bidian?'

'What do *you* think, Eliza?'

'I hope he will be. I couldn't bear to lose him,' replied Eliza with a slight catch in her voice. Having lost her husband at Dunkirk, and her daughter, Athene, on active service, and having given a lifetime of service to her country, Eliza felt she had sacrificed quite enough.

'I'm sorry, I didn't mean to upset you.'

'It's OK, but I still do get upset, even after all these years. Father and daughter never came home, and Arrows always come home – look at Felix. I know he's keen to do his bit, and in a way, I want him to. That is what we Arrows do. But promise me, Bidian, that you will do everything in your power to make sure Felix does come home – always comes home. I couldn't bear to lose another. Felix is all I have of my husband and daughter. It would finish me off. Promise me, Bidian.'

'I promise, Eliza,' Sir Bidian said solemnly.

Eliza composed herself, knowing Bidian could guarantee nothing of the sort but still comforted by his words. 'I don't think I have ever mentioned this to you, but I see so much of my daughter in Felix. Sometimes, I even get confused. It is not just that they look so similar, but their mannerisms are the same. I also want you to make sure Dimity comes home.'

'I'll make sure she always returns too. Dimity seems to come as a job lot with Felix.'

'You were never going to keep her out, once Felix was in.'

'No, I see that now. But having a woman of the cloth on the team gives us some interesting options.'

'So, how is the art team shaping up?' asked Eliza, moving the conversation along. Since she had floated the idea of The Art Department to Bidian, she had taken a particular interest in the project.

'Oh, rather well, I think. Our other players are all in place, although I might add to their number as we go along. We will have to see what we need in the weeks ahead.'

CHAPTER
EIGHT

'Do I get to hear how we secured the services of Linqin?' Felix asked Sir Bidian during a meeting several days after the concert.

He laughed. 'I've been waiting for you to ask. Eliza said I could tell you. I do love all this stuff connected to your family. Apparently, it was one of your forebears who made it possible. Linqin's violin belonged to Richard Arrow. It seems that during the War of the Spanish Succession, he acted as attaché between our Queen Anne, the Duke of Marlborough and Leopold I. Richard would be about your ten-times great-grandfather, and he was a very talented musician by all accounts. The emperor gave him the violin as a thank you in the early 1700s. But I think such a gift suggests he might have played a larger role than that of a simple attaché.'

Felix shook his head. Being part of the Arrow family was to be in a constant state of wonder. 'Well, I hope the whole thing doesn't backfire, Bidian. This Maria Mirova told Dimity she would like to find out the name of the violin's owner. Dimity felt she was quite serious. We don't want her snooping into family things too deeply.'

'I'll talk to Eliza and ensure the firewall is extra secure, even to the most inquisitive.'

Felix nodded. 'So, when did you learn about Linqin and the violin?'

'Not until I was discussing options with Eliza a month or two ago.'

'Is my grandmother still on the MI6 payroll? Because if she isn't, she should be.'

'Indeed, she should.'

'Where do we go from here?'

'Well, we have our Trojan horse; that's you by the way, Felix, and now we bait several other hooks.'

'You enjoy this, don't you?'

'The scheming, the planning and the execution, yes – when it goes right – but when the execution or the outcome goes wrong, there is nothing worse.' Sir Bidian looked at his gloved prosthetic hand for emphasis. 'Now, let me have your thoughts on Volkov.'

'There's not much to say, really. He played the sponsor very well and clearly enjoyed the celebrity he achieved in being so generous. His daughter seemed sweet enough, but a little uncomfortable around Maria Mirova. I had the impression the girl couldn't wait to get back to her friends. But that's normal at her age, I suppose.'

'I'm sure you're right. But you're not keen on Mrs Mirova, are you?'

'On first meeting, no; she was very offhand. Plus, when she met Roger Strand, she made it perfectly clear to his face that she was homophobic. She didn't try to hide it and was openly

THE ART DEPARTMENT

offensive. I could see that Volkov was embarrassed. But more alarming was Maria's conversation with Dimity in the loos.'

'Do tell.'

'She was all questions. She asked about my business and my dealings with Volkov, and she wanted to know where Dimity and I live.

'Dimity reckoned Maria wasn't just making small talk; she was asking less-than-casual questions about our lives.'

'Well, at this stage, that is both interesting and mildly concerning. While we are finding out about Volkov, Maria is digging for information about you. That sets off alarm bells. Why would she want to do that? I wonder if we have touched a nerve.'

'Dimity and I couldn't figure out what Maria was to Volkov. First, we thought she was a girlfriend. But there was no show of any affection between the two of them, and there is certainly no love lost between Lizabeta and Maria. A happily blended family it isn't. It seems a strange arrangement. Maria didn't even try to be friendly. Dimity said she thought her a controlling type.'

'That's just the sort of important insight I need,' said Sir Bidian.

'So, what's your next move?'

'Well, this is where The Art Department comes in. We need to get closer still to Volkov. You told me that he wants to fill his new house with important pieces of art. We know that he has the means to purchase them. So, I think we need to introduce him to several people who can help – our people. At the same time, perhaps we can tempt him with an item that, even with his great wealth, he might not otherwise be able to obtain.'

'How do we do that?'

'I want you to work up a plan with the group. Use Ellie, she will have ideas. Find or create something that will lure Volkov. Perhaps the man has nothing to hide. But along the way, we can build up a picture and see if he has any extra-curricular activities going on with the Russians. We will have to see what develops.'

'Does that include Roger Strand?'

'Ah, Roger.'

'I know you know Roger, Bidian. He did the flowers at our wedding.'

Sir Bidian smiled. 'An interesting character with a wide social circle and client base.'

'Do I take it that it was you who got him involved in the Cheltenham concert?'

'You never know when a gregarious florist will come in useful.'

'Does Roger know?'

'Not yet. I'll see how things go and then, if necessary, sound him out later. But a man with such a huge personality and vast network can hear a great many things from a great many people. Let's say he has passed the first test and, it seems to me, he could fit in perfectly at The Art Department.'

'So, as Dimity pointed out, you now have Volkov's architect and possibly his florist in place.'

'Dimity's very astute.'

'An understatement. So, what's next?'

'We introduce Volkov to his art consultant.'

'And how do we do that?'

'It's more a question of how *you* do that.'

'I feared that might be the case. Who is Volkov's art consultant?'

THE ART DEPARTMENT

'Ms Louise-Emmanuelle Lydden, of course. You will have to find a way of introducing her into the conversation.'

'I sow the seed, water it a bit, let it grow and then step away, leaving Volkov to think it was his idea?'

'You are learning fast – helped by hundreds of years of inbred skulduggery, I might add.' Sir Bidian laughed.

'What will Ellie do?'

'If everything goes to plan, Ellie will set up a snare. That is something our field people can't do. They would never be able to come across as the genuine article. It takes years of gaining specialist knowledge, especially in the art world.'

'What sort of snare did you have in mind?'

'Well, more than one snare really. If anyone in our line of country is fearful of discovery, they tend to be on the lookout for one principal threat, not several at the same time. We will create multiple dangers.'

'Hence Ellie, Roger and me; anyone else?'

'At some stage, I expect Rani will become involved. Petro and Tiya will stay in the background – Petro because of his Ukrainian history and Tiya, well, she is an artist, not a spy. Then there's your wife.'

'Dimity?'

'If she is agreeable, she has the perfect cover. Her church is even close to Volkov's townhouse. I was thinking of a music recital or an art exhibition at St Margaret's. That would draw him ever closer. Remember, Felix, if our suspicions are correct, he must keep up a cover one hundred per cent of the time. We only have to catch him out once. The nearer we are to him, the greater the chance we have to do that.'

'Yes, I see. Do you think the church would agree to an event?'

'Well, they won't know the real reason, and Dimity can see

if Volkov will sponsor the thing – the extra money for the church will be a great incentive. And I have a couple of other ideas.'

Sir Bidian fell silent.

'But it looks as if you're not going to tell me those.'

'Not yet.'

CHAPTER
NINE

Felix was meeting Yuri Volkov at the Russian's London home in Belgravia. The cream-coloured stucco house, typical in appearance to most other Georgian buildings in the affluent London district, was beautifully appointed; sumptuous even, Felix decided. In the ground floor reception room, he thought he recognised the hand of a celebrated London-based Persian interior designer – so well known in creative circles that he was simply referred to by his forename. Layers of antique textiles in exciting but harmonious colour combinations, embossed leather walls, warm and discreet lighting, groupings of pictures and well-placed *objets d'art* and furniture were the designer's statement and signature. But there was another hand at work here. And because all the elements of the interior blended together with such expertise, it took Felix a moment to notice. It was the smell of roses.

'Do I detect the skills of Roger Strand here, Yuri?'

Volkov smiled. 'Yes, you do. Thank you for the introduction. Since meeting him, he has been regularly supplying and arranging the flowers here.'

'They look and smell wonderful.'

'It makes a big difference to the house, and when she is at home, my daughter loves them.'

'I must say your house looks fabulous.'

'Thank you, I had Tamerlan decorate.'

'I thought I recognised his hand. But is this the sort of look you want at Courtlands?'

'No, otherwise I would certainly have engaged Tamerlan again. For me, he suits town best, using a blend of international styles. Or I'd hire him for a traditional riad in somewhere like Marrakech. At Courtlands, I want an English country-house style to reflect the architecture and the setting. It might be romanticism, but I believe I will only get that level of authenticity from an English designer. So, a John Fowler look, but updated. I want it to appear as if it has always been the same, but at the same time not look out of date.'

Felix was impressed. Volkov had done his homework and seemed to have a genuine interest in the decorative arts. 'You set quite a challenge, Yuri.'

'One I am sure you will rise to, judging by the other work I have seen your company do.'

'That's kind of you.'

'Credit where credit is due, isn't that what you British say?'

Felix smiled and nodded his head. The conversation had opened up nicely, and now he took advantage. 'I was going to ask you, Yuri, have you thought about furniture and pictures for Courtlands?'

'Not in any great detail. I know that I want to collect some outstanding English furniture for the house, and in that, I hope you will guide me. Perhaps you will keep me informed of pieces that come onto the market and of major sales at the auction houses. Perhaps we could go to some of these together?'

'That is an excellent idea. What about art?'

'Again, I think I want to concentrate on British painters. Will you be able to assist me there? Most of the experts I know are concerned with Russian artists.'

'If you want nice pictures to go on the walls, then yes, I can help you. But I suspect you want a grade or two higher than that.'

'I suspect I do.'

'Then you need a specialist, someone who doesn't just know what is coming up for public auction but also has an ear to the ground of what is in the market privately and quietly.'

Volkov nodded his agreement.

Bingo, thought Felix.

'Do you know such a person?' Volkov asked.

'I know one or two.'

'Who would you recommend?'

'Well, it is difficult to choose. But if discretion is important, then I should try Ellie Lydden.'

'Ellie Lydden? I have never heard of her.'

'I am not surprised. She keeps out of the limelight and is rather shy. But she is known in the trade as being super discreet. That's why she has such an impressive client list — if you could ever find out who is actually on her client list.' Felix chuckled to himself. He was beginning to get into the role.

'Tell me more.'

'She is English and from a very aristocratic lineage. One of her family members almost lost her head in the French Revolution. I think she had been a lady in waiting to Marie Antoinette and later may have travelled to Russia to carry out the same role for a tsarina.'

'To Russia, a tsarina?'

'Apparently so. Ellie went to St. Andrews University, where she read history of art. She followed it up with a master's and then worked for Sotheby's in New York before setting up on her own. She has no gallery or office – she just goes where the work takes her. But her forte is investigating provenance and unearthing hidden gems, especially for those collectors who prefer to have no fuss. That is perhaps why you have never heard of her.'

Volkov gave Felix a look that conveyed his complete understanding. 'I think I would like you to introduce me to Ellie Lydden.'

'I'm not sure I know how. I've only met her once myself,' replied Felix, with partial honesty. 'She could be anywhere at the moment.'

Sir Bidian had told him that a big lie should be built on a strong foundation of innocent truth. Then there was less on which to be caught out.

'Please find her,' Volkov said, his tone suggesting he was used to asking for things and then getting them quickly.

Felix thought this was as far as he should go on the subject and changed tack to give Volkov a report on the work at Courtlands.

A survey had been quickly but thoroughly carried out. Scaffolding and a tarpaulin cover were in place, and a considerable team of workmen, some of them living in caravans parked by the house, had begun stripping back the vast roof. Felix's head garden designer, already with two gold medals from the Chelsea Flower Show to her name, had started the design of the gardens, including the reinstatement of the sweeping lawn to the river.

Volkov nodded his appreciation. 'Are we ahead of schedule?'

'I should say we are.'

'Very good. Now I want you to start searching for furniture. I am happy to go anywhere to see the right pieces. And I want to meet this Ellie Lydden.'

Felix knew that Volkov wasn't the sort of man one said no to. 'I will begin tracking both down and let you know immediately when I have any news,' he said.

Volkov gave a curt nod. The meeting was coming to an end. Taking this cue, Felix said, 'Well, I had better let you get on. I am sure you must be very busy.'

'Not too busy to discuss Courtlands and art,' Volkov said in a gentler tone.

Seizing the opportunity, Felix added, 'Talking of art, my wife's church, St Margaret's in Eaton Square, is putting on an exhibition of religious paintings and icons. I think there will be a section displaying Russian pieces. I thought it worth mentioning to you.'

'I am glad you did. I have one or two excellent examples myself. My friend, Maria, shares my passion for art; she will also be interested. Why don't you suggest to Dimity that she call me to tell me about her plans? I may be able to help.'

'I certainly will. But I should warn you about something.'

'Warn me of what?'

'My wife is shameless in asking for money, donations and sponsorship.'

Volkov laughed. 'A man in my position quickly gets used to it; it is, how do you say, like water off a duck's feathers for me. But for the right causes, I am willing to give my generous support.'

'Then I will ask her to get in touch. She will enjoy seeing you again, I'm sure.'

'And I would very much like to meet her again. Tell her to call me soon.'

* * *

'You're a natural,' said Sir Bidian to Felix the next day at Somerset House.

'Oh, I don't know about that.'

'Think about it, Felix, you managed to introduce Ellie's name to Volkov and establish that you will be with him for buying trips – or at least some of them. Then, on top of that, you managed to interest him in an exhibition of religious paintings. We might even be getting a line into this Maria character.'

'I know, but there wasn't an exhibition of religious paintings until you created one.'

'A rather good idea, I thought.'

'That's not Dimity's view.'

'Really? Why's that?'

'When I told her, she said we had no right to mount an exhibition at her church without saying something about it to her first. She said the vicar hasn't the time to organise the next service, never mind an exhibition. According to Dimity, he's too busy turning himself into a celebrity priest.'

'Something she finds most frustrating, I imagine. But don't despair, I have had a quiet word with the bishop who, earlier in his career, was a high-ranking army chaplain in the Guards. My old regiment, as it happens.'

Felix raised his eyes to the ceiling. 'And they say the old boy network is dead.'

THE ART DEPARTMENT

'Maybe on its last legs but still breathing. Anyway, I'm sure Dimity will put on a good show. By the way, how is the team getting on with their plans to lure Volkov?'

'Very well, I'm told. Ellie has identified a Russian artist with just enough fame and mystery. While documented, not much is known about his life or work. Ellie assures me this provides the ideal background. From what Petro and Tiya have seen of his other work, they feel they can create a miniature that will deceive anyone.'

'And enough of a masterpiece to tempt Volkov?'

'That's the idea. But it seems an awful lot of work just to infiltrate Volkov's life. Is this really a dry-run exercise, Bidian?'

'Actually, I don't think it's a dry run any longer.'

'But isn't it enough to have Roger and me in the camp? No pun intended.'

Sir Bidian laughed. 'Roger doesn't yet know he is in our camp. But the more fishing lines one has off the back of the boat, the more chances one has of catching something. It's also that Volkov has been very good at keeping his nose clean since he arrived in the UK. It makes me wonder if he's too good to be true. If so, he really doesn't want to be under scrutiny from the press or government agencies. The wrong sort of scrutiny might be unwelcome. We need to have something up our sleeve to use against Volkov if required. It would be useful if we could tie him to the illegal art trade somehow.'

'But if what he buys – on the supposed black market – is a fake, is he guilty of anything?'

Sir Bidian smiled. 'Ah, but Volkov won't know it's a fake. And the threat of exposure could give us some means of leverage.'

'Is leverage another word for blackmail?'

Sir Bidian smiled again. 'It is.'

'So, what's the next step?'

'We must make arrangements to have Ellie meet Volkov.'

'How do you suggest we do that?'

'I propose we wait for four or five days, then you call Volkov and tell him you can arrange a meeting with Ellie. You are to effect the introduction.'

'Effect the introduction? Is that code for hold Ellie's hand?'

'What did I tell you, Felix? You're a natural.'

CHAPTER
TEN

It was rare for Yuri Volkov to drive himself anywhere. Rarer still to do so unaccompanied. Yet here he was steering a silver-grey Audi estate down the M4. The instructions had been clear: go alone, tell no one. But any clarity ended there. Why the Kremlin was interested in two seemingly insignificant addresses in the coastal town of Bridport remained a mystery. One was a private house, the other a community hall. Volkov had been told only that a physical reconnaissance was required.

First, however, he was making a detour to Taunton in Somerset. Bohlin had tipped him off about furniture auctions that might yield pieces for Courtlands. Most of the sales were in London, but some were regional – Taunton among them.

As the miles slipped by along the M4 and he passed road signs for Reading, Newbury and Swindon, Volkov's thoughts wandered. Why would Moscow care about a public hall in an innocuous English town? He'd found out more than enough from Google Street View. More pressing, though, was how he had come to be an errand boy for an establishment that made him increasingly uneasy.

Volkov felt alone. His childhood friend and business partner, Vladimir, was keeping his distance. It left him exposed and wary, as though the ground beneath him was quietly shifting.

Their friendship had always been an enigma. Vladimir, part boyhood best friend, part mystery, had been a commanding presence in his life from the day they met in St. Petersburg. Even as a boy, Vladimir was a force to be reckoned with; his unyielding standards enforced on anyone in his orbit. During arguments with referees on the handball court or fierce martial arts sparring sessions, Vladimir had never backed down.

The two had grown up side by side, navigating the rites of passage together. They'd shared an obsession with spy movies, pop music and chemistry experiments of the explosive kind. But their paths had diverged after school. Volkov went to Moscow, and Vladimir stayed in St. Petersburg, eventually joining the KGB and rising through its ranks.

Years later, their friendship reignited. Vladimir's ascent to political power became a boon for Volkov's fledgling oil company, Oliniya. Together, they amassed staggering wealth. But that closeness was now gone. The instructions to visit Bridport had made it painfully clear – Volkov was a pawn in someone else's game.

By the time he turned onto the M5 at Bristol, the landscape had become unfamiliar. He reached the Taunton auction room about an hour later, blending in with the modest crowd of bidders. For a man accustomed to limousines and private jets, driving an unremarkable car and attending a local auction offered an unfamiliar but surprisingly pleasant sense of anonymity.

From the auction catalogue, Volkov selected a Charles II coffer made from ash – a modest purchase that would find a place in Courtlands and provide cover for his day away. Forty-five minutes later, he revelled in the small thrill of winning the bid. It was a rare feeling of freedom, as was his lunchtime stop at Lyme Regis on his way to Bridport. There he walked the harbour wall made famous by Austen and Fowles and savoured the sea air and the taste of normality.

But freedom was an illusion. The road to Bridport brought him back to reality. The first address, a plain brick house near the main street, offered no answers. The second, a community hall on the town's northern edge, was equally unremarkable. His task was to assess road access and, curiously, routes of escape. Why? What could Moscow possibly want here?

By the time Volkov returned to London, thoughts of the day's idiosyncrasies had been replaced by a growing dread. At the Wigmore Hall, he found solace in music, but not in the company of Maria Mirova. She was as relentless as ever, her agenda clear and ruthless.

After the concert, over dinner at Claridge's, she broached the subject Volkov had been dreading.

'Yuri, you have not yet mentioned the marriage proposal I made to you at Covent Garden?'

Volkov's heart sank. 'I've considered it, but I need to understand the financial implications—'

'You needn't trouble yourself,' Maria interrupted, her voice hard. 'The implications are unquestionably good.'

Good for her, perhaps. Good for the Kremlin. But not for him, Volkov thought. This was no proposal. It was a coup d'état. Marriage to Maria would tighten Moscow's grip on him, eroding his power and wealth until nothing remained. But as things were, refusal was not an option.

Maria's voice softened, but her words cut deeper. 'I thought a reception here at Claridge's would be appropriate.'

Volkov's chest tightened. 'Maria, I must speak to my daughter first. I won't spring this on her.'

Lizabeta had become the only card he had left to play.

Maria's eyes narrowed. 'Very well. But do it soon. We have plans to make. And there's another matter – your friends. Bohlin, his wife, that florist, Roger Strand. I want to know everything about them.'

Volkov bristled. 'Bohlin is my property advisor. His wife is a priest. Strand is my florist. What is there to discuss?'

Maria ignored him. 'Who is the old woman – Bohlin's grandmother?'

'You're asking about an elderly woman?' Volkov asked incredulously.

Maria's smile was chilling. 'I simply want to know everything. Nothing can be left to chance.'

For Volkov, it was clear: his life was no longer his own.

CHAPTER
ELEVEN

'Yuri told me he went to a furniture sale in Taunton yesterday,' Felix told Dimity over a bowl of cornflakes at breakfast.

'And did he buy anything?'

'A coffer.'

'You look concerned.'

Felix laughed. 'Perhaps I'm worried about what he bought.'

'You're always worried about what people put in their houses. Anyway, what did you tell me about Yuri's house in Belgravia?'

'I told you it was beautiful – or what I saw of it was.'

'Well, there you are then. Don't I always tell you to have a little faith? Anyway, I'm still not on the best of terms with you after you sprung the art exhibition on me. Have you any idea how much work it's taking?'

'You have mentioned it... on several occasions. But Bidian thinks it's a good idea.'

'Well bully for Bidian. He isn't the one putting on the show while trying to manage a large church whose egocentric vicar is hellbent on an alternative career in the media.'

'Doesn't managing the church have something to do with the vicar?'

'Not our vicar; he is far too busy writing his next piece for *Thought for the Day* or prepping for the *Moral Maze*. It's a pity he can't find his way out of the maze and give me a hand. Next, he'll be in *I'm a Vicar Get Me Out of Here.*'

Felix smiled and, with a straighter face, said, 'I'm sorry, Mitten.'

'Well, to make amends, you can help me out this morning.'

'What with?'

'I'll show you. So, finish your coffee and let's get going.'

Fifteen minutes later, Dimity led Felix down a flight of stone steps deep into the crypt of St Margaret's church.

'But this is... marvellous, absolutely marvellous...why haven't you shown me this before?' Felix whispered, awed by the amazing rib-vaulted ceiling over his head.

'Because of all the rubbish down here. It's been a dumping ground for years, by the looks of it. Anyway, I thought it would make a good exhibition space – and not just for your secret squirrel stuff. It should bring in lots of people, and I think we could well have several sponsors falling over themselves with money and offers of pieces to display.'

'What will you do with the rubbish?'

'You let me worry about that.'

'I will. But once cleared, with some new lighting and a freshen up, I think it will be a perfect gallery or exhibition space. You could rent it out now and then.'

'That's what I thought. So, you agree?'

'I certainly do. Now, I had better get on.' Heading back up

the steps, Felix called down, 'Don't forget to get in touch with Yuri. I'm sure he will love this space.'

* * *

Felix had some fresh news for his next meeting with Sir Bidian.

'Dimity got in touch with Volkov. He went to see her at St Margaret's. He said that he had always admired the church. She showed him around, told him about the plans for the art show and took him down to the crypt. I went there the other day. It has to be cleared of rubbish, but I must say that with some work, it'll be a great space for the exhibition.

'Volkov had several ideas that Dimity said were very useful. He offered to partly sponsor the show and loan several pictures. He told her he had an admiration for Eastern religious paintings, even though he admitted to having no faith at all. She told him she would try to help him out of that state if he wished. He politely declined but said it would not affect his offer to help with the show. It sounds as if the two of them hit it off.'

'Well, that is a positive development. When does Dimity think she can put on this show?'

'In a few months.'

'That doesn't give Petro and Tiya much time to create a masterpiece. Did you learn anything else from Volkov when you spoke to him?'

'Not really, but he had been to Taunton.'

'Taunton? Why there? Not much oil and gas, unless it's for central heating.'

'I told him about a furniture sale. So, he went.'

'Did he buy anything?'

'A coffer. Why the interest?'

'Just professional curiosity. The man disappeared for a day. I wonder where he went.'

'I told you, Taunton.'

'Perhaps. But did he go anywhere else? For the time being, I like that man where I can see him. That won't change until I am happy he is no longer curious or interesting.'

CHAPTER
TWELVE

Felix, Ellie and Volkov met in Piette, a French-style café on a corner of Sloane Square. Sir Bidian had suggested an informal and relaxed meeting place. Felix had been surprised that Volkov had agreed to meet at the bistro rather than at his house.

When Felix had suggested Piette, Volkov said, 'I know the place well. I sometimes have coffee and read the papers there on Sunday mornings. It is lively, I enjoy the chatter and the people watching, and there is a very good newsstand close by.'

Felix had thought this strange behaviour for an oligarch.

Now Volkov, Ellie and Felix sat on rattan chairs around a small, round table with a crisp white tablecloth.

'Felix tells me that your family were French,' Volkov said to Ellie.

'That's right, and they fled here at the height of the French Revolution. But I think of myself as British, as that line here goes back many generations.'

Volkov nodded his understanding. 'It is a well-worn path.

So many people come to London from all over the world to escape repression and persecution.'

'But you are not escaping repression and persecution, surely?' asked Ellie with an innocent smile.

'No. In my case, I was following a childhood dream, although my departure did coincide with another revolution of sorts – privatisation. But I read much about England when I was young. Now I am older, I can make those early dreams real.'

'And become a major collector of important art?'

'Yes, it is a passion of mine. I am fortunate to be able to indulge it. I now have two passions, one is the art of my motherland and the other, a newer passion, the art of my adopted land.'

'Russian and English?'

'Yes. I have here in London some of the paintings I brought from my Moscow home.'

'Have you specialised in a certain period, Mr Volkov?'

'I like the modernists – Malevich, Kandinsky and Chagall.' Ellie nodded approvingly. 'But I also have Levitan and Shishkin.'

'Wonderful landscapes,' Ellie commented.

'Yes, they are. But now I want to concentrate on English painters for Courtlands.'

'Do you have any particular subject, painter or period in mind?'

'The eighteenth century.'

'Ah, my favourite.'

'Why is that?'

'I think it goes back to my French heritage, and particularly my Parisian roots. It was really only in the eighteenth century that a British painting style developed. But that style undoubtedly originated in France. Hogarth was influenced by others, including Watteau. Then the style of the French portraitist, Jean-Baptiste van Loo, became a touchstone for emerging British painters, principally Gainsborough and Reynolds. Oh, I'm sorry, Mr Volkov, I think I'm getting carried away and beginning to lecture: it is a fault of mine.'

'It is a charming fault, Miss Lydden, I always enjoy listening to an expert. But the influence of France in Russia was also great at this time, in political, social and creative spheres, was it not?'

'It certainly was. Russia owes much to French art.'

Felix had taken a back seat in this conversation. He too enjoyed listening to experts talking about their specialist subjects. But he also knew that Yuri was sounding out Ellie, getting her measure and gauging whether she could be trusted to advise him.

Felix asked Ellie, 'How many genuinely good British eighteenth-century pictures come onto the market these days?'

He was sure the answer to this question was one Yuri should also want to hear.

'Genuinely good pictures?' Ellie said. 'Not that many, to be honest. And of course, the big galleries snap up the major examples. Even if they don't have sufficient funds themselves, they can apply for government grants or public donations, especially if it means preventing an important national picture from going overseas. Of course, this greatly slows down the speed at which one can put together a collection built on quality rather than size.'

'So, what is the answer for private buyers?' Volkov asked.

'Well, that is where people like me come in. We hunt for the hidden gems – the incorrectly attributed pictures that, through enough good investigation, can be identified as genuine.'

'It still sounds like a long process,' Felix said.

'Very often it is. But I have to say, to build an important collection that truly reflects a period, there should be a variety of artists to explore developing techniques and tastes, and also subject matter. Still life, for example, with artists like Beesley and Furguson.'

'I have never heard of these painters,' said Volkov.

Neither have I, thought Felix, but he could see from Volkov's attitude that Ellie was impressing him. Felix was becoming ever more impressed with Ellie himself. On her subject, this rather shy woman became passionate and authoritative. She had command of her field of expertise, and that commanded the attention of others. Her enthusiasm was contagious. Felix could see that Ellie now had all of the Russian's attention.

'Do you think you could help me, Ellie?' Volkov asked.

'I should love to help you, especially on a subject so close to my heart.'

'Good. I think you should work out the financial details with Felix, who is managing the Courtlands project for me. But would a monthly retainer and a bonus of some sort be agreeable?'

'Very agreeable, thank you.' Ellie became flustered at the talk of money.

Volkov then asked Felix about some other issues concerning Courtlands, including bats in the roof that were causing a delay to the works.

Volkov waved to a passing waiter and asked for the bill. Once he had paid, he stood up and shook hands with Ellie and Felix.

'Oh, Felix, I nearly forgot to mention,' Ellie said to him as they were all about to leave. Felix smiled to himself as Ellie started the routine they had rehearsed until they were word-perfect and natural.

'It's a bit of a coincidence under these circumstances, but I've been contacted by a dealer I have done business with in the past. She told me there might be something coming up quietly that could be of interest – a Russian picture. It has no provenance, but she says it seems right for a particular painter.'

Felix could feel Volkov lean in slightly, clearly interested.

'Which painter?' Felix said.

'A man called Saltanov.'

'Excuse me interrupting, but do you mean Bogdan Saltanov?' Volkov asked.

'Who's that?' Felix said on cue.

'Saltanov is a respected Russian painter from the sixteenth century,' Ellie replied.

'His work is very scarce,' Volkov added with a frown.

'That is correct, of course,' said Ellie. 'There is an issue with attribution. But my contact thinks there are questions to be asked with this particular work.'

'What is it your contact has?'

Volkov clearly couldn't resist asking, Felix thought.

'It is a miniature,' Ellie said.

'Who is selling the work?' Volkov asked.

'She hasn't told me. She just asked if I might be interested. I told her I would like to see the piece. She said OK, but first she has to get it here.'

'Where is it?' asked Volkov.

'It's in America, I think.'

'Who is the dealer? I might know her.'

'I'd rather not say, Mr Volkov. But I have implicit trust in her and respect her judgement. Not that she's saying this *is* a Saltanov. I want to make that clear. The dealer just thinks that I might want to take a look.'

'And do you also have specialist knowledge of Russian art?' Volkov asked with a note of scepticism.

'Actually, Mr Volkov, I do. Felix may not have told you, but after St. Andrews, I did my master's degree in history of art at St. Petersburg University. I conducted a great deal of research in Moscow for my dissertation.'

'So, you speak Russian?' Volkov asked with surprise.

'Not as well as you will,' replied Ellie with a smile.

Volkov looked taken aback. 'I would like to see this miniature when it is here. It interests me greatly. Your dealer friend is definitely looking for a buyer?'

'Yes, she is. But she wants to see if I can unearth some evidence that links the miniature with Saltanov. If I can, the piece becomes very valuable indeed.'

'Despite this, I am very interested.'

'Well, I will tell the dealer that if I may?'

'Yes, please do. But do not mention my name.' Turning to Felix, Volkov said, 'I think this has been an excellent meeting.'

Felix and Ellie watched Volkov stroll off in the direction of his home in Eaton Square. After a short while, they followed in the same direction.

'Did I do OK, Felix? I was very nervous.'

'Nervous? You didn't look it. You were fantastic.'

'Was I really?'

'Amazing. I'd say we have Mr Volkov well and truly hooked.'

'I'm shaking.'

THE ART DEPARTMENT

Felix laughed. 'I think you need a drink. I know just the place, The Antelope. It's just up ahead.'

* * *

'It sounds as if Ellie did a good job,' said Sir Bidian later, while on the phone to Felix.

'I should say so. She was entirely believable. She even blushed when Volkov started to talk about money. How's that for authentic? She was entirely in the role. When she was talking to him, I even forgot it was all a ruse for a while.'

'Never lose focus, Felix,' Sir Bidian said in a warning voice.

'No, but this stuff takes a bit of getting used to.'

'You must get used to it,' Sir Bidian said firmly.

'I'll be careful. So, what's the next step?'

'Petro and Tiya produce the work of art. I'm looking forward to hearing the backstory the team has come up with. I will find some time to get down to Somerset House soon to catch up with progress. Meanwhile, we must arrange for you to introduce Volkov to Rani, the art dealer. By that time, we should have fairly good eyes on him.'

CHAPTER
THIRTEEN

'Hello, darling.'

Roger Strand's voice boomed through the showroom.

Felix looked up from his glazed office at the back and smiled. He preferred this transparent box to the more private office he had on the first floor. Even though he didn't get so much done, he felt it helped him stay in touch with the day-to-day goings on of the business. Some interruptions were irritating, but Roger's were to be savoured and enjoyed. Felix stood up and went out to the showroom, where he received an enormous hug, a loud smacker of a kiss on each cheek and a large flower arrangement already in a vase.

'Hello, Roger, to what do I owe this pleasure?'

'Darling, I have never thanked you properly for introducing me to Yuri Volkov.'

Roger thrust the vase and flowers at Felix, but then suddenly pulled them back. 'I am sorry, but I simply must put them on that divine little Regency table in your window, where everyone can see them. I should put a notice by the side of them, shouldn't I? If only I had one. Oh, look, I do have one in my pocket. What a surprise. Who'd have thought? Would you mind? Of course you wouldn't.'

Roger propped the card advertising his floristry business against the ceramic vase so that window shoppers could see it.

'Yuri is such a marvellous new client. Of course, I don't call him Yuri in person: it's always "Mr Volkov, how high should I jump?" in his house. But I have a twice-weekly contract to provide flower arrangements throughout the ground and first floors of his home in Eaton Square, as well as in some of the bedrooms and bathrooms. He has also commissioned us for a large dinner party, and he has even been talking about Courtlands, so hurry up and finish it because that will be another big contract.'

'I shall do my utmost to get it finished for you, Roger, as soon as I possibly can. I'm so pleased to be of service,' said Felix dryly.

'Now, don't be haughty, flower,' said Roger with a laugh, 'it doesn't become you. You know how very appreciative I am. And to show you just how much, I want you to take Dimity off somewhere for a break. Go anywhere you want, darling. It's all on me.' Roger held up his hand as Felix went to speak. 'Stop, I don't want to hear what you have to say unless it is yes.'

'But—'

'No buts, I insist.'

Felix could see that any argument would be futile. 'OK, Roger, that is very generous of you. A few days away would be excellent.'

'That's just what I thought.'

'But I have got a great deal on, so it won't be for a while, I'm afraid.'

'Courtlands?'

'That, and some other complicated projects.'

'Ooh, that sounds intriguing. Might I ask what other complicated projects?'

'Oh, just some things I've got on,' Felix said vaguely.

'You're being very evasive, petal. What's going on? Anyone would think you—'

'I what?'

'You were up to your grandmother's tricks. Are you?'

'Roger, what do you know about my grandmother?'

'Let's talk somewhere more private.'

With a sense of foreboding, Felix led the way back into his office and closed the door behind them. Roger said, 'Look, I may only be a florist, darling, but this one can smell the coffee as well as the flowers.'

'What are you talking about? And what do you mean about Eliza?' said Felix, suddenly concerned about this turn in the conversation.

'Just putting together a few things Eliza said to me. She was in France in her twenties, but that was during the last war. What was that about?'

Felix said nothing.

'Well, I don't know what she was doing, but she was doing something. And by the way, who was the blue Savile Row suit who accompanied Eliza to your wedding? The one with the Old Etonian tie, cut-glass, public-school accent and a prosthetic hand? He had the stamp of establishment – government, military or something like that. And who are Eliza's little household friends, led by that hunk, West? He doesn't look as if his biggest concern in the world is which moisturiser to use, I can tell you. I can smell intrigue a mile off, Felix, and I can smell it here.'

'Roger, whatever it is that you think you know, please don't rely on it as reality. And do me the decency of not digging for answers. Eliza values her privacy very much indeed.'

Roger sighed. 'I won't dig into Eliza's past, flower, but I know when something's up. For instance, why was I asked to do a job at Cheltenham Ladies' College out of the blue? Getting me and several assistants in a van down from London was not the cheapest option for a school. One or two local florists could have done the job – not so well, of course, but adequate for the occasion. Then what do I find when I get to Cheltenham? You and Dimity with Yuri Volkov – one of the wealthiest men in the world and now one of my clients.'

'You have a lively imagination.'

'Don't kid a kidder, Felix,' replied Roger, looking as serious as Felix had ever seen him.

'I can't say a thing to you.'

'Maybe not, but I am intrigued to know why I was in Cheltenham and why I was introduced to Yuri – not that I'm sorry, he's a good client to have. Is that too much to ask?'

'From me, yes.'

'Then perhaps I should ask someone else.'

'Not Eliza, please.'

'Then whom should I question?'

'I don't think this is something one asks about just when one wants.'

'More a question of waiting to be told?'

'I am no expert, but I think that would be correct.'

'So, I wait for the man in the blue Savile Row suit?'

'Could be something like that.'

'Florists hear a great deal, Felix. To many, we are invisible. Clients think we are too absorbed in stems, leaves and petals and only think about displays. Clients are wrong.'

'I understand.'

Roger smiled at Felix and said, 'Enough of this talk. Now, I want you to promise you will tell Dimity about your little break as soon as you see her. I want you both to start planning. Go somewhere fun and stay in a swanky hotel with that ever-so-reassuring little fifth star.

'Now, I had better get back to the shop before my young apprentice does something silly. He might be pretty gorgeous looking, but he's also pretty stupid.'

'Working for you would be a challenge, Roger.'

'If you want to get to the top in my trade, it is a challenge one has to meet. My apprentice, as they say, has set the bar low for himself and has failed to meet it. Now, I'm off. Don't forget what I said – about everything.'

Roger kissed Felix goodbye and left with as much flounce and drama as he had arrived.

That was the strangest conversation I have ever had with Roger, Felix thought to himself as he called Sir Bidian's direct line.

'Hello, Felix, is everything OK? You don't often call on this number.'

'Hello, yes, everything is OK... ish.'

'Tell me.'

'I have just had a visit from Roger. He was on a fishing expedition.'

'Ah.'

'I have to say, I didn't think he would put so much together – Cheltenham, Volkov, Eliza and you.'

'Me?'

'Yes. He described you as a Savile Row suit and

establishment type. He wondered what you were doing escorting Eliza to my wedding. He also has questions about Eliza and her being in France in the early forties.'

'Did you say anything?'

'I was too stunned to do that. I think I gabbled nonsense instead.'

Sir Bidian laughed. 'Well, I suppose we were correct in thinking that Roger would be a reliable pair of ears. As it turns out, it seems he has a great deal between the ears and a good pair of eyes, too. Those are bonuses, and we should take full advantage – if agreeable to Roger.'

'I can't think for a moment that it won't be. What will you do, Bidian?'

'I think I should have a little chat with Mr Strand. Perhaps I will call in and buy some flowers.'

Felix wondered to whom the flowers might be given, if anyone. Bidian's private life was a complete mystery to him and Dimity. But he simply said, 'I have a feeling Roger will be expecting you.'

'From what you say, I imagine he will. I'd better not let him down.'

CHAPTER
FOURTEEN

'So, how are your plans going regarding the forgery?' asked Sir Bidian on his latest visit to The Art Department. The team, including Petro, Ellie, Tiya and Felix, was having one of its morning meetings – utrenya, or matins, as Petro had come to call their fortnightly get-togethers. Rani wasn't there as she was at GCHQ. The meeting was an opportunity for Sir Bidian to catch up with the studio's progress.

'I want to know all the details,' he said. 'For a start, who was Bogdan Saltanov and why are you using him as your artist? I've never even heard of the fellow, but then Russian art is not my strongest suit.'

'Even if it were, I'd be surprised if you knew the name as he's not very famous,' said Ellie. 'But his work is rare, so it's valuable to a collector.'

'But who was he?'

'He was an artist from Persia who ended up in Moscow. Alexis I of Russia became his patron.'

'What period are we talking about?'

'He was born in New Julfa, the Armenian quarter of

Isfahan in Iran, in the 1630s, and he died in Moscow in 1703,' replied Ellie. 'Although one or two of his contemporaries thought he was a second or even third-rate painter, he was well respected enough to be made a noble. He rose to head the painting workshop of the Kremlin Armoury. His work included icons, illuminated manuscripts and portraits.'

'So, you are creating a work from a third-rate artist?' asked Sir Bidian, clearly dubious.

'To be fair, that was the view of his rivals. But there is a method in our madness,' explained Ellie. 'You see, Saltanov is a controversial figure. There are lots of records in the archives about his life in Moscow, but no single piece of art has been indisputably attributed to him. Saltanov never signed his works, which means attribution is only possible through the records kept by court officials at the time. As there is no leading authority on the painter, all opinions on his artistic style are unreliable. But we have one excellent thing to report—'

'That we are unlikely to have someone questioning the work?' Sir Bidian suggested.

'Well, they may question the work, but not from the authority of real scholarship. All we have to do is find something obscure in the archives and attribute the reference to the work we create,' Ellie said.

'Well, that sounds marvellous, apart from one tiny little detail,' said Sir Bidian. 'How on earth are we going to find anything in the archives when they are in Moscow? Nor do we have much time. We could send someone from the embassy, but they wouldn't have a clue what to look for, and what on earth would we do for a cover story?'

'We don't have to send anyone,' Ellie said with a smile. 'We have the records we need here.'

'And how do we have those?'

'Because I still have all the notes from the research I did in the state archives in Moscow. It's one of the reasons we chose Saltanov. I went through my notes and found a reference that should do nicely. We discovered a commission for a miniature, accepted by Saltanov. But we can find no records confirming payment for the job, and fortunately for us, no records of the miniature surviving – or indeed even ever having been executed.'

'So, no one can question the specific work?'

'As long as we create a believable portrait that will stand up to scientific scrutiny.'

'And you think you can do that?'

'Given the correct materials, yes.'

'Why do I think materials might be a problem?' Sir Bidian asked with an arched eyebrow.

'We need some Russian lead,' said Petro.

'Is that some sort of artist's colour, like Prussian Blue?'

Petro smiled. 'No, it's exactly what I said, lead from Russia.'

'Well, I am sure lead shouldn't be a problem to find, even from Russia,' replied Sir Bidian.

'You do not understand, I think. We need lead from sixteenth century,' said Petro.

'Might I ask why from that century? Isn't lead lead?'

'No, lead is not lead,' said Ellie. 'Do you really want to know?'

'Of course. It's my job to know and to make sure your plan is as carefully thought out as possible. So, tell me, why do we need sixteenth-century Russian lead, as opposed to any old lead?'

'Our problem is modern forgery detection techniques,' said Ellie. 'They are advancing so quickly that fakers can't keep up anymore. In this scientific age, forging pictures is becoming a dying art. Techniques that once made a copy practically impossible to detect from the original have been outpaced by modern equipment.

'As fine art becomes more of a stable investment, owners and buyers have to know that pieces are genuine. So, the drive to prove provenance and technique, and the need to prove chemical veracity in the painting materials, is all-important. After all, an old master worth millions today can quickly be worth just hundreds tomorrow if it is found to be a forgery. Do you know that some museums and galleries are worried that twenty per cent of their precious exhibits could be fakes?'

'Twenty per cent? I had no idea,' said Sir Bidian.

'That's the reason technologies for detecting forgeries have developed so quickly. The Courtauld next door is leading the way in isotopic analysis and carbon dating. These cost a great deal of money to develop and use, but the amount is nothing compared to the value lost on a work that is proven to be a fake.'

'I can see that. So, I don't think it is unreasonable to ask that if it is so difficult to get away with a forgery nowadays, why are we trying it?'

'It depends on the period of the painting you are trying to forge,' said Ellie. 'If it is modern, then one can usually get all the correct paints, papers and canvases relatively easily. Even with nineteenth and early twentieth-century work, it's still possible to find most materials. The problem comes with older works, such as old masters. That is why we need the lead.'

'White is the problem,' Petro added.

'Titanium white pigments only became available in the 1920s,' Ellie explained. 'So, to use one on a painting purporting to be earlier than that would be senseless.'

'I do see that.'

'Forgers do not use titanium white,' Petro continued, 'they ferment lead in vinegar and carbon dioxide to make pigment. Until now, it has been an excellent technique.'

'But not anymore?'

'No,' said Ellie. 'Isotopic testing can detect the age of the lead used to produce the paint, thus making the process completely transparent.'

'Ah, now I understand,' said Sir Bidian. 'So, how do we get around it?'

'The best forgers find correct-age lead in churches or coffins,' said Petro.

'Well, that shouldn't be too much of a problem, although it sounds rather dodgy.'

'Much of the time it *is* dodgy, but it might not be such a problem if we were creating an English painting,' Ellie said.

'Ah, but we are creating a Russian one, so we need Russian lead,' said Sir Bidian.

'Yes, we do,' said Petro with a nod.

'I can see that might present a challenge, especially when time is short,' said Sir Bidian. 'How much lead do you need, Petro?'

'Not big: forty grams. We only produce miniature.'

'OK, I'll speak to our technical people. See what they can come up with. Do you have any other concerns?'

'We did,' said Ellie, 'but we have resolved them. First, the vellum on which the miniature will be painted was an issue. We couldn't take any chances. Vellum is prepared from animal skin, preferably calfskin, and the manufacture is a messy business. It involves cleaning, bleaching, stretching, scraping and treating with lime or chalk.

'Fortunately, vellum is durable. If it has been kept in

average humidity, it can last for a thousand years. You probably know British Acts of Parliament are still partly printed on vellum for the archives?'

Sir Bidian nodded his head.

'Most of the finer medieval manuscripts, whether illuminated or not, were written on vellum. Before the use of canvas became widespread, after about 1500, vellum was used for paintings, especially if they needed to be sent long distances. But vellum was still employed for drawings and watercolours during and after the sixteenth century.

'We couldn't guarantee that the process of preparing vellum in the 1670s was the same as elsewhere in Europe. So, we had to find some vellum we knew had come from Moscow, or at least Russia. We could have taken a chance. We know for sure that in the late 1600s, vellum was regularly exported from Moscow to Amsterdam through Astrakhan. So, Russian vellum was widely available. But to be on the safe side, and to avoid raising any suspicion about the material, we wanted some vellum that we were confident came from Russia.

'Luckily, we found some, or at least a small piece that we know came from Moscow at around the date we needed.'

'How on earth did you find that?' Sir Bidian asked.

Ellie smiled. 'The Courtauld knew of someone who collected ancient agreements. He had an original copy of a long-forgotten trade agreement between the court of Charles I and Tsar Alexis I.

'It dates to the time before the exemption of Russian customs duties to the Muscovy Company in London was rescinded.'

'The Muscovy Company – a trading company like the East India and Hudson's Bay?' asked Sir Bidian.

'That's right. However, the Muscovy Company's support of

the Parliamentarians in the English Civil War displeased the Tsar. So, following the execution of Charles I, he expelled nearly all of the English merchants from Russia. We are lucky the dates fit our purpose, and doubly lucky that the document had a long tail of blank vellum.'

'And the collector just let you have a piece of this?'

'The value is in the material with text,' Ellie said. 'The scroll had a long tail with no text beneath the seal. Plus, the Institute seems to have a lot of clout with the collector.'

'Very enterprising,' Sir Bidian said with a nod of his head. 'Is that all?'

'No. There's the frame. But we have that under control,' said Ellie.

'Felix, have you anything to add?'

'Only that everyone is keen to get started.'

'Can we know what this is all about?' Tiya asked.

'It is better for you if you don't know the whole picture,' said Sir Bidian.

'You're turning us into a team of confidence tricksters,' said Ellie.

Sir Bidian chuckled. 'Yes, I suppose it is state-sponsored confidence trickery, and this is a long con only made possible by a few experts.'

'Tiya, the only thing we need to know is that this is important,' said Petro. 'Our job, it is the most difficult. We reach into history and bring back something that did not exist. Now, that is very difficult.' Petro broke into a deep laugh. Tiya joined him, clearly enjoying his joke.

Felix had only ever heard Petro laugh once before. The Ukrainian seemed glad of the opportunity to use some of his intellectual powers, as well as his artistic ones.

'Right then,' Sir Bidian said, smiling at his small coterie, 'that's it. We have a plan. We know how, why and what we must do. All we need now is to bait the hook and hope our gentleman of interest bites.'

'Come, Tiya, let us begin plan creation,' said Petro. Tiya looked at him warmly, and the pair went back to their work stools, now placed side by side at the large worktable that had become the base of their operations – the tall, lanky Ukrainian man and the small Asian girl.

'Now that Petro and Tiya have their project, what do we do next?' Ellie said to Sir Bidian and Felix.

'We have to plan for our next meeting with Volkov.'

'When I introduce Rani?' asked Ellie.

'That's right, and if you don't mind, you could give Dimity a hand with the art show at St Margaret's.'

'Oh, that would be nice. Does she need a hand hanging pictures? I love doing that.'

'I think Dimity needs all the help she can get at the moment,' Felix said. 'She has a case of the missing vicar.'

'What does that mean?'

'I'm sure she will explain.'

* * *

Sir Bidian and Felix returned to Sir Bidian's office.

'I went to see Roger yesterday,' said Sir Bidian.

'Oh, how did you get on?'

Sir Bidian smiled. 'Very well, as it turned out. Lovely shop, and Roger didn't disappoint. He was quite restrained, really. Most unlike the man I met at your wedding. He has a serious side. It was good to see.'

'He was on display at our wedding.'

'I suppose he was. Anyway, I didn't say much... I didn't

have to. I quickly realised that Roger is very good at reading between the lines. After I sort of indicated my position, he asked me if I would like him to be on "receive", as he put it, when visiting certain clients' houses. I told him that was exactly what I wanted. He asked me if it would be dangerous, and I told him no, not unless he was caught on security cameras listening at keyholes or rifling through drawers.'

'I should think Roger was excited.'

'He was, and that's what makes me nervous. This is not a lark, Felix.'

'I know, but I'm sure that whatever there is to hear, Roger will hear it.'

'On balance, I'm inclined to agree,' Sir Bidian replied. 'But he will have to be kept on a tight leash until I'm certain.'

CHAPTER
FIFTEEN

Felix needed to visit Courtlands for a site inspection and called Volkov to let him know about Rani. His lines had been well rehearsed. 'Ellie has been in touch with her art-dealer friend, who will be in Bristol for a few days, trying to track down an early Banksy. I suggested that if you were at Courtlands too, they could join us. It would be a chance for you to speak to them about the miniature they mentioned, and it will allow Ellie to see the size of the task Courtlands presents.'

'That is a good idea,' said Volkov, 'and I would like to go over progress with you. Could you manage this meeting early next week? Perhaps Tuesday?'

'I will make the arrangements,' replied Felix.

The following week, he drove Ellie to Courtlands. The journey gave them a chance to run over their plan of action.

Rani, who had just passed her driving test, was travelling separately from Cheltenham in her new car.

When Felix and Ellie arrived at the grand house, it had just stopped raining, and everything smelled fresh.

'Oh, this is beautiful,' Ellie exclaimed.

'Well, it will be when all the scaffolding is down, and the workers have gone,' Felix replied.

The house swarmed with people. There seemed to be an army of them on the roof. Felix knew that the old roof tiles had been stripped back, so only the rafters showed. Much of the timber had been replaced, new lead furnished the valleys and ridges, and reclaimed roof tiles matching the old ones were being fitted. An over-roof of tarpaulin supported by a framework of scaffolding protected the house and enabled outside work to go ahead in all weathers. It also meant some interior refurbishment could start in parts of the house that had been weatherproofed.

The landscaping was also in full swing. There was now a ha-ha between the front lawn and the narrow public lane that marked Courtlands's front boundary. A grass bank prevented anyone in the house – at least from ground floor level – from seeing passing vehicles or pedestrians, and vice versa. Local stonemasons were making the wall of the ha-ha from Cotswold stone. Along the rest of the boundary, an estate fence would be erected and a hedge of hornbeam planted just behind for further privacy. The lawn was being stripped back and levelled. It would only be a few weeks before it was seeded. Finally, in a corner of the lawn, a cherry orchard was being planted.

Felix found somewhere to park amongst the cars, motorhomes, caravans, vans, trucks and various cranes and digging and bulldozing machines. An enterprising individual had even parked a catering van by the entrance to supply the teams of workers with hot drinks, bottled water and all-day breakfasts. Some of the locals had started to use it to buy a bacon roll while walking their dogs. Several sets of white plastic tables and chairs had been positioned at the front of

THE ART DEPARTMENT

the van, and it looked as if the caterer was doing brisk business. Felix thought it was like a modern version of a nineteenth-century navvy shanty town. He just hoped that it would not come with a period-correct culture of drinking, debauchery and death.

They found Volkov in the drawing room talking to one of the conservationists.

'There you are, Felix,' he said. Felix hadn't expected him to be accompanied by Maria.

Volkov turned to him. 'I am pleased with the progress,' he said, 'but we must not slow down. I need this project finished.'

'I do understand, Yuri. There will be no let-up in our pace, I assure you. I was wondering if Ellie could take a look around while we're talking about structural matters?' Felix could see Volkov's eyes beginning to glaze over. Maria showed no interest at all.

'Feel free, please,' Volkov said to Ellie. 'You can pick up a plan at the contractor's office, if that would help.'

'One of Ellie's contacts will be joining us in about half an hour,' said Felix, not knowing if anything should be mentioned about Rani in front of Maria.

Volkov made eye contact with Felix, nodded, and flicked him a smile without saying anything.

Good, I got that right, Felix thought.

Felix, Volkov and Maria walked around the exterior of the house before returning inside. Felix and Volkov discussed the work, stopping now and again to talk to foremen, craftsmen and young apprentices about progress.

Maria spent most of the time staring out of the windows.

Through an upstairs one, both she and Felix saw a bright red Fiat 500 coming towards the house. 'That will be Rani, I think,' Felix said to Volkov, and they headed downstairs.

Felix didn't know what Volkov was expecting the art dealer to be like, but he was sure it wouldn't be a young woman from the Indian subcontinent.

'Yuri, I should like to introduce Rani Di,' Felix said. 'Rani, this is Mr Volkov and Mrs Mirova.'

Before anyone could say anything else, Volkov turned to Maria and said, 'Rani is working with Ellie on artworks for Courtlands. We are thinking eighteenth-century English examples.'

Volkov shot a look at Felix, confirming any talk of Russian miniatures should be private and not in the hearing of Maria.

'I hadn't expected someone so young,' Volkov said bluntly.

Rani smiled sweetly. 'You are not the first to be surprised, but here I am.'

'I am surprised that someone of your age could have enough experience for success in the art world,' Maria said with equal bluntness.

'I started very young and learnt very fast,' replied Rani, the smile not leaving her face. 'Youth should be no barrier to success, and learning quickly and well avoids failure, don't you think, Mr Volkov? I am sure you started your business with a degree of youth and inexperience but with an eagerness to learn and succeed.'

Maria scowled.

Volkov smiled and said, 'I certainly did, Rani, and do you know about my business?'

'I do, Mr Volkov. What sort of art dealer would I be if I didn't?'

Felix now saw how Rani's years in the Calcutta bazaars and dealing with unscrupulous art collectors had given her a nerve and confidence way beyond her years. Volkov didn't intimidate her. How this young woman could deal with men like him with such ease, having been brought up on city streets and then in an orphanage, was a mystery to Felix. But mystery or not, he could see Rani was already winning over the Russian, if not Maria.

Volkov looked at his watch. It was a little before one o'clock. 'May I suggest we go somewhere more comfortable to talk? We can have some lunch – unless you would like the food from the catering van?' A slight smile appeared on Volkov's face.

The ensuing silence suggested that anywhere other than the van was the group's first choice.

'Good. Then, might I suggest we go to The Duck, the small hotel by the bridge in the village. It will be warmer and drier. I have reserved a table.'

Volkov and Maria elected to be driven to the inn by Volkov's driver. The others agreed they would walk.

By taking the riverside path from Courtlands through the adjacent parish churchyard, Ellie, Rani and Felix reached the hotel in ten minutes. They spent the time reviewing the conversation with Volkov.

'You were amazing, Rani,' Ellie said. 'You didn't give Volkov an inch.'

'I had to structure his expectations.'

Ellie and Felix laughed.

'So, who's the miserable woman with Volkov?' Rani asked.

'That's a good question,' replied Felix. 'I'm not sure where she fits in yet. But did you pick up that he didn't want to talk about the miniature in front of her?'

'I did. So, today seems a bit of a waste.'

'I don't think so. It was important that you and Volkov met. Let's see what happens over lunch.'

Volkov had arranged a table for five by a window that

looked out over the river. It was set slightly apart from the other tables, giving them some extra privacy from the tourists and day trippers who had become a part of daily life in the village.

'I hope you don't mind, but to save time, I have already ordered. I must return to London soon. I have selected vegetable soup with warm rolls to start, and then trout with a green salad. There is a trout farm next door, and the fish is always fresh.'

Everyone nodded in agreement.

'I will use the cloakroom before we eat,' Maria announced.

When she was out of earshot, Volkov said, 'Now, Rani, what can you tell me about this so-called Saltanov miniature? I must say, it seems a far-fetched idea to me. But one must always take care. In art, one never knows.'

'Mr Volkov, I have never said that the miniature *was* by Saltanov,' said Rani. 'I only suggested to Ellie that she should take a look, as the style is worthy of investigation.'

'And why do you think the miniature *could* be by Saltanov?'

'At this stage, only because that is what the seller says it is.'

'What do they know?'

'I don't think he knows anything about art. In fact, I don't think he knows much about anything at all, except perhaps extorting money from people and hurting them. I think he might know a lot about that.'

'Who is your client?' Volkov demanded.

'I shouldn't say.'

'I think you can tell Mr Volkov,' Ellie said gently, repeating her carefully rehearsed line.

'Do you think so? I am a little scared of my client.'

'Mr Volkov, I'm sure you will be discreet, won't you?' Ellie said.

Volkov nodded animatedly.

A waiter arrived with the soup.

'Take the bowls away. Keep the soup hot. Come back in a few minutes,' ordered Volkov, clearly irritated by the interruption.

'Well, if you are sure it will be okay to tell Mr Volkov, Ellie,' Rani said.

'I am sure.'

Rani nodded. 'The miniature comes from the collection of a wealthy Ukrainian man who died over a year ago. I met a man in Miami who was trying to find a buyer for the entire collection, though he was also prepared to break it up.'

'So, who was the collector?' Volkov asked, looking around to make sure that Maria wasn't approaching.

'The man said he was called Chorney.'

'The gangster?'

'The man didn't say who he was or what he did, but he didn't look very nice, and all his clothes were black.'

'It seems to me that most Ukrainian and Russian men wear black clothes,' Volkov scoffed.

'The man I met was scary. He had tattoos on his face. He said his name was Olev.'

'Then that confirms it. Olev is Vasyl Chorney's brother,' said Volkov.

'I understand that Mr Chorney had quite a collection,' Rani continued.

'I have heard the same,' said Volkov. 'But no one seems to know what became of it after his death. I heard that his brother may have spirited it away before he went on the run from the Russian mafia.'

'Do you think the brother was the man I met in Miami?' Rani asked, wide-eyed. 'I have to say, he looked like the sort of gangster you see on television. I convinced him that I would have to spread the net wide, but only to special clients who were interested in miniatures.'

'Miniatures?' Maria asked. She had materialised at the table as if from nowhere.

'I was just asking about the history of miniatures from the British perspective,' said Volkov, quickly collecting himself.

Felix rushed to help. 'There was an exhibition of English miniatures at the National Gallery last year; I don't know if anyone visited?'

'But of course!' Volkov said effusively. 'It was wonderful.' He beamed at Ellie. 'Not Russian but wonderful.'

'It was most instructive,' said Felix. 'It mapped out the development of miniature portraiture from its roots in manuscript illumination.'

'Why do you discuss this?' demanded Maria.

'Ellie was suggesting a collection of miniatures for Courtlands,' lied Volkov smoothly.

'I thought the period of the house would be a perfect fit,' said Ellie. 'You might know that Henry VIII sent Hans Holbein the Younger to paint his possible future bride, Anne of Cleves, in miniature. I suppose today Henry would have sent a photographer, or better still, used Tinder.'

Everyone laughed except Maria, who scowled.

'I can see how miniatures would have been useful,' said Felix.

'You're so right,' replied Ellie. 'Miniatures were a transportable memento or, as Henry VIII found, a convenient reference. Although Holbein flattered Anne on that occasion, and it did not go too well for the king.'

The waiter arrived again. This time, Volkov let him set the soup bowls down.

Felix glanced at Volkov, who looked relieved.

* * *

Later that evening, Volkov called Felix. 'Thank you for your understanding about the miniature. Maria is a friend but also a rival collector. I didn't know she was coming until the last minute. I am sorry we could not speak freely, but I was pleased to meet Miss Di. Were you able to speak to her about the details after I left?'

'Yes, I was.'

'So, how much does the seller want?'

'Rani said he didn't mention a price. He asked her what she could get for it.'

'If I am interested in this miniature, what should we do?' Volkov asked.

'Well, Ellie thinks we should see it first. But Rani said the man she saw would never let it come to England.'

'Where is the artwork now?'

'At first, Rani thought it was in Miami, but apparently, it's still in Russia.'

'Will Ellie go to Russia and look at the piece, do you think? I will pay for all her time and expenses.'

Despite their meticulous planning, Felix was unprepared for this suggestion.

'Oh, well, I'm not sure, Yuri. I think she would be nervous, understandably. Wouldn't dealing with a gangster be dangerous?'

'Not with my name behind her,' Volkov said.

'Still.'

'If you are concerned, why don't you accompany her, Felix? I will also make it well worth your while.'

Taken aback, but not wanting to appear so, Felix blurted out the first words he could think of: 'I have no objection if Ellie is agreeable.'

'Good. Please ask her. It will only be for a few days. While you are there, you could take a look at my Moscow house. I was going to mention it to you anyway. I would appreciate your ideas about changing the layout.'

'But what if the miniature isn't in Moscow but somewhere else in Russia? Or still in Ukraine?'

'If these people are serious, they will get the miniature to Moscow. It isn't as though they have to move a grand piano,' Volkov said with conviction.

'When would you like us to go?'

'As soon as I make plans and Miss Di arranges it with the seller.'

'What shall I do about tickets and accommodation?'

'The way you will be going, you won't need tickets, and my company keeps a large suite at the Lotte Hotel for guests. You can stay there. You will need visas, which I will arrange through the Russian Embassy. It will take a few days.'

* * *

'So, you and Ellie have a trip to Moscow to view a miniature that doesn't exist?' Sir Bidian said when Felix called him to report.

'That's about the size of it,' Felix replied.

'We should have anticipated that. But sometimes the unexpected happens – it's the way things go. So, one has to think on one's feet and adapt. You had to accept the invitation, of course.'

'That's what I thought at the time.'

THE ART DEPARTMENT

'And you are flying there and back in Volkov's private jet?'

'Yes.'

'All expenses paid?'

'Yes.'

'And you will be visiting Volkov's house in Moscow?'

'Yes.'

'And it is OK with Ellie?'

'Yes.'

'Then I would say that was a pretty good day for The Art Department,' Sir Bidian said with a chuckle. 'Have you told Dimity?'

'Yes. She was jealous but excited for me.'

'And have you told Eliza?'

'No.'

'Why not?'

'I thought you would do that.'

'Coward.'

'Correct.'

CHAPTER
SIXTEEN

Dimity had a rare Saturday off from church duties, so Eliza invited her and Felix for lunch at Witch's. She also invited Sir Bidian. There was something he wanted to discuss with her in person. He arrived early and sat with Eliza in the salon.

'We have received a very curious message from Mara,' he said.

'What's so curious about this one?'

'Well, it's not a British code or, as far as we know, a Russian one. Nor is it recent. From what our cryptographers at GCHQ can tell, it dates from the 1920s.'

Eliza frowned and said, 'A hundred years old... isn't it a bit past its sell-by date? But I suppose if nobody's cracked it yet, it doesn't matter how old it is.'

'Apparently, it's similar to messages sent between the IRA headquarters in Dublin and activists in the UK and USA.'

'The IRA?'

'Yes, I must say we were surprised. One or two variations of these codes were found in IRA boss Moss Twomey's effects after he died.'

'What was the message?'

'Basically, it said, "Unit 29155/Nemezida".'

'Nemezida; that's Russian for Nemesis,' said Eliza.

'So, what do you think Nemezida means in this context?'

'I think it is probably what it says: the inescapable agent of someone's downfall.'

'Yes, but whose?'

'Well, in connection with what we already have from Mara, I should say Bezrodny, wouldn't you? Remember what I was saying about Putin and his lust for revenge? This rather puts the tin lid on it. Or it does for me.'

'It could well be about Bezrodny, but who's the inescapable agent?'

'That, Bidian, is what you had better find out – and fast.'

'We're redoubling our efforts.'

'Have you thought about putting Bezrodny and his wife somewhere safe?' Eliza asked.

'It would only tip off the Russians that they have a mole.'

'It is a dangerous game you're playing, Bidian.'

'Aren't all these games dangerous?'

Eliza sighed. 'What forensic information did you get from the dead drop?'

'The usual. The envelope used was a Russian-manufactured, every-day one. It was clean – no DNA or other marks or writing indentations. And our handwriting people can't say if it was written by a male or female.'

'Anything else?'

'Yes, and that's why I really wanted to see you today. The message was written using Middle Irish.'

'Middle Irish? That's about a thousand years old. What is going on, Bidian? This makes no sense at all. Why are we being warned? Why the Irish connection – and indeed Middle Irish?

THE ART DEPARTMENT

And what or who is Nemezida and Unit 29155? I think your first consideration should now be whether this mystery has a direct relationship with the past connection between the IRA and the Soviet Union. Especially during the 1970s, when any link would have been at its height. That could be the key. There may be no connection, but if that's the case, you can at least eliminate that line of enquiry.'

'I wanted to hear your view on that, Eliza.'

'I don't know what I can contribute. The Troubles were a little after my time at MI6, and the Twomey era was before it. Besides, it was more of an MI5 thing.'

'But you ran the Russia desk at MI6, so you might have something from that side of things.'

'All I can tell you is what you will already know. Yuri Andropov, the Soviet president-to-be but at the time head of the KGB, presented a plan to the Central Committee around 1972. It was known as Plan for the Operation of a Shipment of Weapons to the Irish Friends.

'The weapons were transported to Ireland in a spy vessel disguised as a fishing trawler. A boat belonging to the IRA picked up the shipment about fifty miles off the Northern Ireland coast.

'The leader of the Irish Communist Party negotiated the first shipment of arms. Back then, we were naturally very concerned about IRA links with Russia. We weren't wrong. Later, the Russians introduced the IRA to contacts in North Korea and Czechoslovakia.

'It was politically expedient for the Russians. I remember an Irish diplomat in Moscow writing that Ireland provided the Soviets with "a convenient stick with which to beat the West".

'The arms consignments were part of a plan by the KGB to

destabilise Northern Ireland and, in so doing, the rest of the UK.

'According to intelligence files smuggled out of Russia by one of our double agents at the time, several arms shipments were sent by the KGB. They even continued after the IRA had declared a ceasefire. Ironically, British Army intelligence learned the arms were only used in internal feuds between IRA factions.'

Sir Bidian nodded. 'Anything else?'

'Well, one other thing. Some IRA men went to Russia for terrorist training. As far as I know, we never found out how many.'

'This has us all baffled,' Sir Bidian said, shaking his head.

'Your analysts will be on to it no doubt.'

'Night and day, especially with the Russians building up an offensive capability on the Ukraine border.'

'Do you think that is a realistic threat?'

'It might be sabre rattling or a typical bit of Russian destabilisation, but there is some chatter that it could be more serious.'

'An incursion?'

'Worse.'

'A full invasion?'

'That's our fear.'

'So, this business with Bezrodny could be part of a bigger plan?'

'If they bumped him off, it could prove a useful diversion. The press would go wild.'

'And take people's eyes off a major troop build-up.'

'Well, I hope the analysts come up with something before events overtake us.'

THE ART DEPARTMENT

'Me too. But one piece of good news is The Art Department. The team is getting on well.'

'With the fake miniature?'

'Yes, the pieces are coming together. Remember I mentioned an issue with Russian lead?'

'I do.'

'Well, our quartermaster seems to have solved that problem, and we have some on its way now in a diplomatic pouch.'

'How on earth did you get it?' Eliza asked.

Sir Bidian laughed. 'All it took was one phone call. It's coming from Sweden. The Swedish Army Museum in Stockholm, to be precise.'

'Why Sweden?'

'The quartermaster thought that a musket ball or two should provide the amount of lead needed. Apparently, the earliest Russian lead we have is from the Seven Years' War, which ended in 1763. So, he got in touch with a pal of his in the Swedish Security Service and asked him if he could get his hands on a musket ball from the Livonian War between Swedish Estonia and Tsar Ivan the Terrible in 1558. I always did wonder how a degree in history would help him. Now I know. It seems the Swedish museum had several rather out-of-shape musket balls and thought they could do without a couple of them. No doubt we will have to reciprocate at some stage. Send them something from the Anglo-Swedish War, perhaps.'

'I didn't know there was an Anglo-Swedish War,' Eliza said with a chuckle.

'Nor did I. It was in 1810, apparently. Bloodless, I understand. We occupied a Swedish island, which they somewhat understandably took exception to. But we're friends now.'

'Have you told the team the good news?'

'Yes, and they're excited about getting on with some practical work after all these weeks of theory.'

'Theory is important, Bidian.'

'A point I stress at every opportunity.'

Eliza smiled. 'I should try to remember you are not my trainee any longer.'

'Old habits die hard, Eliza.'

'They certainly do. Now, how are we getting on with our other Russian mystery, Mr Volkov?'

'He's either a shrewd one or he is completely innocent. We are at a bit of a loss at the moment. If he has something to hide, he hasn't put a foot wrong as far as we can make out.'

'But you still think there is something?'

'It's a gut thing.'

'Sometimes gut feelings are all we have to go on.'

'I know. Since the Sergei Skripal affair, we're all a bit on edge.'

Just then, Felix and Dimity came into the room.

'Sorry to interrupt,' said Dimity, 'but Cairo says lunch will be ready in about half an hour.'

'Thank you, my dear,' said Eliza. 'Why don't you two join us for a while? I'll call West for whiskey sours. Bidian and I were just talking about the Russians and how they have everyone off balance.' Eliza turned to Sir Bidian and said, 'I don't need to tell you that is exactly what Mr Putin wants. He is KGB-trained to put enemies on the wrong foot. But it goes deeper than that with him.'

'What do you mean?'

'I mean enmity. Putin has enemies, and he has traitors. He

treats enemies without mercy but also with a kind of grudging professional respect. On the other hand, he treats traitors – enemies of the state – without mercy or respect and, as far as I can tell, with a vindictive zeal that would have impressed Stalin.'

Sir Bidian nodded in agreement. 'Perhaps that's seeped down the generations. Did you know Putin's grandfather was a cook to both Lenin and Stalin?'

'I didn't know that,' said Dimity.

'Nor I,' added Felix.

Eliza tutted at the digression. 'Well, be that as it may, since Putin was elected president, he has steadily gained political strength. It has only accelerated since the sinking of the *Kursk* in 2000 and the St. Petersburg G8 meeting in '06. Before we know it, he will be president for life, and then where will we all be? He will be free to do all his mopping up with impunity.'

'I fear he has pretty much all the impunity he needs right now,' Sir Bidian said.

'That may very well be the case,' Eliza agreed. 'That's what happens when you make someone from the KGB president. The Russian masses thought they were saving themselves from communism, and it would be OK to elect Putin. They didn't understand the power of security men or that they would get Putinism.

'For goodness' sake, that man will quash anyone who says anything against him or the state: just think of that young journalist, Anna Politkovskaya, who was assassinated in 2006. She had no chance. Nor, it seems, does anyone else. And that is the message Putin wants everyone to hear loud and clear. He has created imbalance, confusion and fear around the globe.'

'Of course you are quite correct, Eliza,' Sir Bidian said. 'I hate to say it, but right now, it's hard to tell the wood from the trees.'

'Those Russian forests are very dense. I speak from bitter experience,' Eliza said with a shudder.

'I know,' Sir Bidian said, 'it's just that there are so many Russians in London – a good number of them set up camp within a mile of Harrods. They thought it was a safe haven, an island where they could build their new, gold-leaf Eden.'

'But are they safe?' Dimity asked.

'No, they aren't,' Sir Bidian replied. 'Litvinenko's horrible and public death by polonium and Boris Berezovsky's questionable suicide saw to that. Since then, some of the oligarchs have decamped to Switzerland or the South of France, where they shelter in palaces overlooking Lake Geneva or the Mediterranean. They surround themselves with manicured lawns, high fences and heavily armed security people with large dogs.'

'Even then, it won't stop Putin if he has put his mind to revenge,' said Eliza, 'and the oligarchs know that.'

'But are there still plenty of wealthy Russians in London?' Dimity asked.

'Dozens of them,' Sir Bidian replied. 'Their children are at the best schools. They shop in the best shops, eat in the best restaurants and enjoy London as a glittering home-away-from-home. And therein lies our problem.'

'What do you mean?' Felix asked.

'Well, we fear that not all of them are running from the Kremlin. There might be some acting as stool pigeons.'

'What, Kremlin-backed people hiding amongst the exiles?' Dimity asked.

'It's a certainty, I'd say.'

'And you think that Volkov could be one of them?' Dimity said.

'It's feasible.'

'But you don't know for sure?' Felix asked.

'No. And that is what our scrutiny has become all about. At first, we were just curious. But things have become more urgent.'

'Why?' Felix asked.

'Because we have received some intelligence that we don't fully understand, but enough to make us think that something might be in the wind.'

'Intelligence from where?'

'I'm afraid I can't tell you that, Felix.'

'So, what will you do?'

'The only thing we *can* do for the time being: wait and watch. But watch very closely.'

'And you are watching Yuri Volkov?'

'Among others, including his girlfriend Maria Mirova, but Volkov concerns us. Not just because we now know his history with Putin. But also, because we can't find any behaviour that would put him into the traitor category and make him a target for Putin. You see, after Volkov set up his company, Oliniya, it went through a period of rapid growth. No one seemed to notice at the time. There was so much going on, so many changes within Russia when Putin came to power. But Rosneft, a state-owned oil company, began directing a high proportion of its oil exports through Oliniya. Then Gazprom, the state-controlled gas and oil company, started awarding large contracts to it too.

'One by one, other Russian oil giants began to follow suit. It seemed they were keen to pay court to the Kremlin, or, more particularly, to Putin. These were the Yeltsin old guard; fearful of the Kremlin's increasing grip on power, the men who, when they eventually lost control of their companies, fled to London with their families and their cash – or as much cash as they could get away with, which was still an enormous amount of money. Unfortunately, back then, we didn't have in place the statutory powers we now have to stop money laundering, nor to seize dirty and non-attributable money brought into the UK from overseas.'

'So where did all the money go?' Dimity asked.

Sir Bidian laughed. 'As well as on luxury goods, it went on property outside their own country, particularly in London – otherwise known as Londongrad. At one point, about fifty per cent of London houses worth over five million pounds were being sold to Russians.'

'And what of Volkov?' Felix asked.

'Indeed, what of Volkov – and what of Oliniya? It wasn't long before the company began handling up to forty per cent of Russia's seaborne oil exports, and since then it has become the world's fourth largest oil trader. That we do know. What we don't know is how the profits are divided and who, besides Volkov, are the beneficiaries. Officially, Volkov owns the company, but we think the identity of another shareholder, perhaps even the major one, is being shielded. I don't think it takes a genius to guess who that could be.'

'Vladimir Putin?' Felix suggested.

'Who else has the clout to influence so much state-controlled business going to Oliniya?'

'Making the Russian president potentially a very, very wealthy man,' Dimity said.

'Oh, I don't think there is much doubt about Putin's wealth, regardless of Oliniya,' Eliza said. 'I'm sure he has his fingers in lots of cash pies – perhaps all of them. But I'm not sure it's about wealth with Putin. It's more about power, absolute power. But take your pick; it possibly makes Volkov banker to the Russian president, his international fixer or, at the very least, his puppet.'

'Or all or none of the above,' Sir Bidian added. 'We just don't know.' He looked directly at Eliza. 'But like the things of which we spoke earlier, we must find out.'

West came through the door, looked at them all without expression or grace, and said flatly, 'Lunch is almost on the table.'

Sir Bidian and Eliza exchanged glances and smiled at each other.

Felix and Dimity headed towards the kitchen.

Eliza rose from her chair and asked, 'What do you think about Volkov in all this, Bidian?'

'We are still working on it, but we're getting closer. We have Volkov going to the exhibition at St Margaret's next week. Then Felix and Ellie are going to Moscow the week after. Volkov is sniffing at the miniature bait. But there are still plenty of unanswered questions.'

'Why do you say that?'

'He went walkabout a week or so ago. He told Felix he was driving to Taunton to a chattels sale to buy some furniture.'

'And did he buy some?'

'Yes, a chest.'

'So, what are you worried about?'

'He drove down on the M4 and then the M5. We checked the traffic cameras. A credit card payment shows he went to a garage in Taunton to refuel, but he didn't return the way he came. We picked him up again from the cameras on the M3. He was heading back to London. That night, he went to a concert followed by dinner with Maria Mirova. But we aren't sure where he was between Taunton and the M3.'

'Perhaps he came back up the A303 past Stonehenge for a bit of sightseeing. But then he could also have taken a more southerly route along the Dorset coast...'

Eliza suddenly caught her breath and said, 'Oh, Bidian!'

'What is it?'

'Where does Bezrodny live?'

'Bridport.'

'Bridport on the Dorset coast is on the southern route back to London.'

'A coincidence?'

'I trained you not to believe in coincidence, Bidian.'

CHAPTER
SEVENTEEN

Felix and Dimity arrived early at St Margaret's for the opening of the art exhibition. Felix hadn't been to the crypt since he'd first seen it several months earlier. Now cleared of ecclesiastical detritus, the undercroft revealed Hakewill's simple and elegant design. The rib-vaulted ceiling rising from square brick pillars gave the space a blend of grandeur and intimacy that perfectly suited its purpose for the evening's event.

The flagstone floor in the mid-brown tones of London Stone had been cleared, swept, washed and polished. The exposed brick walls looked fresh, and Felix thought about how much brushing and sealing it must have taken to get them that way. The plasterwork to the ceiling gleamed with fresh white paint.

'This is wonderful, Mitten. How on earth did you manage it in such a short space of time?'

'Isn't one of your methods to throw dozens or hundreds of people at a project?'

'Well, yes, but this must have taken a lot of people a great deal of time.'

'We put out an appeal. It was like that television show *DIY SOS*, except this was *Church SOS*. The response was amazing. Tradespeople and helpers turned up from all over the place. I wanted to surprise you.'

'Well, you have, and the result is incredible.'

'It is, but it's not just for the art exhibition. We can use this space for lots of events and meetings and make some much-needed money for the church.'

'How is your vicar about it now?'

'Oh, he's talking and acting as if it were his idea all along. He has been busy trying to get the Beeb to cover the transformation – with him taking the credit, of course. I think he sees himself on the *BBC Breakfast* sofa or, better still, presenting a series on church restoration and reuse.'

'When it was all started by Bidian.'

'Don't rub it in. Is he coming tonight?'

'No, he says he should stay out of sight. Personally, I don't think he dares to meet Roger again. But he did ask if he could have a private view sometime.'

'That's the least I can do for him,' Dimity said. 'Actually, the bishop should be arriving soon, so I had better put on the exhibition lighting.'

For a moment, the crypt was thrown into darkness. Then, seconds later, it was transformed into a space of intense atmosphere. Felix stood open-mouthed.

'I take it you approve?' Dimity said with a smile.

'Approve? It's fantastic, Mitten.'

The two ranks of brick piers had been uplit from lamps set into the floor. The effect was to cast light up the rough brick pillars and onto the newly painted ceiling. It added to the crypt's magnificence. Each picture in the exhibit was individually lit from above.

'I have to say, I'm extremely pleased,' Dimity said. 'I had no idea it would end up like this.'

'Lots of hard work has done the trick, but some good architecture also helps,' said Felix, 'and lighting. How did you get that so expertly done?'

Dimity laughed. 'Well, we had some *expert* help. A lighting company on the King's Road. You know, one of those trendy firms that advertise in the top-end interiors magazines you read. They got in touch with us and said they had some lighting left over from a major museum project and wondered if we would like it. They delivered and even installed it for us. It took them several days, and they refused any payment. So, we agreed on a year's free advertising in the parish magazine, a permanent plaque of thanks down here and acknowledgements wherever and whenever we had the chance.'

'Worth every mention, I should say,' Felix said. 'It's utterly brilliant.'

'I'm glad you think so. Oh, did you know that Petro and Tiya came here this afternoon?'

'No.'

'Bidian thought they should see the show.'

'That was good of him.'

'Yes, it was. And I must say that Ellie has been a great help. She hung most of the pictures. I can see us becoming friends.'

By now, several more people had entered the crypt. Two men were setting up a bar while a third was checking a microphone. Felix heard a familiar commotion outside, and then Roger Strand arrived with two female assistants and a rather foppish-looking young man whom Felix knew to be

Roger's apprentice. With them came huge vases of flowers and metal stands.

'Hello, darlings,' Roger boomed as he swept Dimity up in a huge hug. 'Isn't this amazing?'

Felix wasn't sure which was more incredible, the room or Roger's clothes. The shirt was a loud Versace number in a blue-and-yellow paisley pattern. The trousers were a matching yellow, and to accompany them a pair of mid-blue suede shoes with red laces.

'Oh, I love the look, Roger,' Dimity said approvingly.

'Do you, petal? I'm so pleased. It has to make up for your ecclesiastical garb. You are looking so – what can I say? – clerical.'

'I don't need to remind you that I am a cleric, Roger. This is my work uniform, and I am in my place of work.'

'I am going to take you in hand, darling. I need to introduce you to my shirt maker. He'll add a little gayness to your drab, bible-black wardrobe.'

Dimity laughed.

'How about you, Felix?' Roger said. 'Can I add a little gayness into your life?'

'I think Felix has quite enough on at the moment, thank you, Roger,' Dimity jumped in.

'You can't blame a boy for trying.'

'In front of his wife?'

'I take your point, darling. Naughty Roger.'

'By the way, Felix,' Roger said in a hushed tone. 'I had a visit from the blue Savile Row suit.'

'He told me.'

'Mum's the word.'

'Yes.'

'It's exhilarating.'

'I thought you would think so.'
'Is he coming tonight?'
'No'
'Shame. What about our mutual client?'
'He *is* coming.'

Roger touched his nose twice with his forefinger and accompanied this with a stage wink.

'Roger, please stop it,' Felix said.

Roger smiled and then shouted, 'Not there, Quentin, put the flowers where the ladies and gentlemen can see them. And what did I tell you about *not* putting the displays in front of the nice pictures so the ladies and gentlemen *can't* see them? Be a love and try thinking, will you? You'll discover it's surprising how much of a difference it can make.'

Roger turned back to Felix and Dimity, and said, 'Darlings, I think I had better supervise, don't you?'

'That poor boy,' Dimity said when Roger was out of earshot. But she was prevented from saying anything further by the vicar, who was concerned he wouldn't have enough lighting at the microphone when he gave his vote of thanks.

The guests began to arrive and stood in admiration at the sight of the crypt. Then they made their way to the bar, collected a glass of wine and wandered around the exhibition.

The bishop appeared with his wife, shortly followed by Yuri Volkov and Maria Mirova.

'Oh lord, he's come with that woman again. I wasn't expecting her,' Felix said.

Dimity and Felix greeted the pair, and Dimity steered them to the bishop. 'I should like to introduce Mr Yuri Volkov,' she said. 'Mr Volkov has been an important benefactor of this event. Frankly, we would not have been able to put it on without him.'

The bishop shook Volkov's hand warmly and engaged him in a polite conversation about religion in art. Dimity and Felix left them to talk while they circulated.

A little later, the bishop came up to Dimity and Felix and said, 'Dimity, I think I should say a few words. Then I shall ask you to add any thanks you need to make.'

'I thought our vicar was going to do that, Bishop,' said Dimity.

'Oh, I think protocol and form demand that I say something, don't you? Then we should hear from the person who has done all the hard work,' he added with a smile. He walked up to the microphone, welcomed the crowd, thanked them for coming, and praised the venue before introducing Dimity. Felix looked over to the vicar and saw that he had a face like thunder. If it was the bishop's intention to take him down a peg or two then it had certainly worked.

'Thank you, Bishop, there are so many people to thank – too many to mention individually,' Dimity said. 'But I must say that without Elexetera, who have fitted this fabulous lighting free of charge, this gallery space would not have been possible. Please go to them for all your lighting needs – although I'm afraid you will have to pay.'

The audience laughed and applauded while the owner of Elexetera took a bow.

'And I also want to thank our good friend, Yuri Volkov, for his support; not just financially but also for the loan of several important pictures here.'

There was more loud applause.

'Now, I'd better hand you back to the bishop.'

'Well said,' whispered Felix to Dimity, 'although the vicar doesn't look too pleased.'

'I'll be in the doghouse, but I'm glad that's all over. Now, I think I had better go and mingle.'

Felix enjoyed walking around the exhibits. At one point, he noticed Dimity and Maria deep in conversation. It didn't look like the friendliest of exchanges.

Volkov came up to Felix, looking particularly pleased with himself. 'I have had an excellent talk with the bishop,' he said. 'A good man, I think. Also, the vicar has asked me if I would consider sitting on the church's finance committee. I said that I would think about it. This has been a fine evening. I have been thinking, I would like you and Dimity to come to dinner at my home and meet some of my Russian friends. I am sure you will like them.'

'Yuri, that would be lovely,' Felix replied. 'We should be delighted to get to know some of your countrymen and women.'

'Then I will arrange something and check some dates with you. Roger Strand can do the flowers. Perhaps we can make time in two weeks, after you have been to Moscow with Miss Lydden. Then you can tell me all about your visit to my homeland.'

* * *

After the exhibition, Felix and Dimity walked back to their flat. It was a dry and mild evening. 'We don't often get time for a walk on our own these days, do we?' Dimity said, slipping her hand into Felix's.

'No, we're both so busy with everything that is not about us.'

'Do you mind?'

'A little, but it certainly makes for an interesting life. It would be nice to have some downtime, and on that note, Roger wants us to have a few days away on him as a thank you for the Yuri introduction.'

'That would be lovely, but when will we have the time?'

'And to add still more to our busy lives, Yuri has invited us to dinner. I've been dying to tell you. He suggested in a couple of weeks.'

'Well, that should be interesting, especially in view of what Maria told me this evening.'

'I saw you two talking.'

'It was more of a lecture than a conversation.'

'A lecture about what?'

'About not getting too close to Yuri.'

'You were being warned off?'

'*We* were being warned off.'

'Why? How?'

'I have the feeling that Maria treats Yuri as her private property. She gave me the impression she would like to make her relationship with him official. The theme of the lecture seemed to be not to make ourselves too comfortable, as changes will be made.'

'Does she mean marriage to Yuri?'

'That was what I took it to mean.'

'I wonder how Yuri feels about that?'

'I'm not sure... if he knows at all. But I don't think Maria will be pleased to find out we are to be dinner guests, if she doesn't know already.'

'It sounds like a fun evening.'

'At least Bidian will be pleased.'

'He's not the one who has to go to the dinner. Did Maria say anything else?'

'She asked again about your background.'

'She's digging.'

'Yes, she is. And there's more. She made it clear Roger would be one of her future changes.'

'That's bad. She could be a one-woman wrecking machine. I had better alert Bidian. Thinking about it, you don't think Maria actually suspects anything, do you? Perhaps we should try to get out of this dinner.'

'I'm not sure she does,' said Dimity, 'but she is being extra careful about us. As for the dinner invitation, it's a bit late to decline now. And besides, isn't this the sort of thing Bidian wants to happen?'

'It's exactly what he wants and what Eliza was concerned about – our getting too involved.'

'Why do you suppose Maria wants marriage?' asked Dimity.

'Perhaps because it would make her one of the wealthiest women in the world.'

'Surely, she isn't doing it for the money; she must have more than enough already. And I'm pretty certain it's not for love.'

'It might not be Maria who wants Yuri's wealth. Bidian thinks there's a fair chance Moscow would like to gain control of it. He says it could be easier for them to access the money if Maria is involved. Of course, Putin could just bump Yuri off, but the international fallout could be counterproductive.'

Dimity sighed. 'This is getting complicated, isn't it? But then I suppose that is the nature of these things.'

'I'm afraid I have another slight complication for you,' Felix said.

'What now?'

'Your vicar asked Yuri onto the church finance committee.'

'He did what?'

CHAPTER
EIGHTEEN

A week after the art show, one of Volkov's staff picked up Ellie and then Felix in a grey Audi estate and drove them to Luton Airport.

Avoiding the main terminal and instead drawing up at the airport's private facilities was a new and enjoyable experience for them both.

The departure formalities were over quickly, and they were driven to Volkov's private jet. The interior was fitted out with white leather seats, deep carpet and polished walnut detailing. A smartly groomed and uniformed flight attendant offered Ellie and Felix glasses of champagne or Bucks Fizz, along with a plate of blinis with sour cream and caviar. Before they knew it, they were airborne and flying high over the east of England on their way to Moscow.

Ellie raised a glass to Felix and said, 'This is the way to travel.'

'It is, but it's all a bit surreal, isn't it? Especially when one is more used to Luton's main terminal; I'll never want to go back to that.' Felix laughed.

The flight took about four hours, and they landed at Vnukovo Airport just before 3pm Moscow time. Clearing immigration using the visas obtained with the help of Volkov, a driver in a large, black BMW then picked them up from the plane.

The 17 miles from the airport to the centre of Moscow took the better part of two hours in heavy traffic. Still, it gave Felix, a first-time visitor to the Russian capital, the opportunity to see some of the city's outskirts and suburbs. At first, he spotted the usual car dealerships that cling to most big city arterial roads the world over. Then there were offices and shopping centres. Finally, as they approached the centre of Moscow, vast blocks of flats dominated the landscape.

Felix and Ellie had decided they should not talk much in front of the driver. They didn't know if anything would filter back to Volkov. Bidian also warned about casual surveillance by Volkov's staff, although he suggested this would probably be through curiosity rather than suspicion.

But for Felix, this was a fascinating drive. 'I've been looking forward to seeing these suburbs,' he said to Ellie.

'Why on earth do you want to see them? Aren't they brutally ugly?'

'Well, they're not Hampstead Garden Suburb, if that's what you mean, but they are architecturally interesting. Although, come to think of it, I suppose these suburbs are like any others – places of aspirations and failed dreams, good ideas that start well and then, as likely as not, slowly crumble. I read somewhere that these suburbs would be great for a six-year-old but boring for a teenager.'

'Gosh, Felix, you're not going to get all deep, morbid and philosophical on me for the next few days, are you? You sound

THE ART DEPARTMENT

as if you're turning into a Russian already, and we've only been here five minutes.'

Felix laughed. 'I promise not to, but it was an interesting social experiment. There were hundreds of thousands of blocks like these all across the Soviet Union.'

'Yes, the Russians call them "mikrorajón" – sleeping districts,' said Ellie. 'I stayed in a place like this when I was here for a few months. The apartments are not much more than cubicles to come home to at the end of the day, but in summer, when it doesn't get dark until midnight, the locals hardly seem to want to go home, and the whole city appears to live in outdoor cafés.'

'So, where are the expensive seats?'

'If you mean the better housing, it's within the inner city or the trendy enclaves of Chistye Prudy or Gorky Park.

'Look, we are coming up to the Moskva River. The Kremlin is up there on the left,' Ellie added, pointing north.

Ten minutes later, the car swept up to the hotel entrance.

'I can see how being one of the wealthiest people in the world has its perks,' said Ellie, as she took in the hotel foyer with approval.

A smartly dressed man approached them and said, 'Ms Lydden, Mr Bohlin? Welcome to the Lotte Hotel, Moscow. My name is Andreyev; I am the assistant manager. Your driver called to say you were arriving. The general manager is so sorry not to be here to welcome you personally. He is detained on another matter away from the hotel. But his losing is my winning. Let me escort you to your suite. We can then deal with the formalities in private.'

Smooth, thought Felix.

'Mr Volkov's private suite is a replica of our royal one,' Andreyev explained as they rode non-stop to the top floor in the lift. 'But I have to say, I think Mr Volkov's bathrooms are even better.'

The assistant manager opened the door to a palace of rooms. 'Your bags will be here soon. Meanwhile, let me show you the suite, which covers 490 square metres.'

Andreyev showed his new guests the winter garden, the VIP waiting room and a separate study, library and kitchen. 'The living room has a grand piano,' he said. 'Do you play?'

Felix and Ellie shook their heads.

'Shall I have someone come and play for you? As you are in Russia, some Tchaikovsky or Prokofiev perhaps?'

Felix and Ellie politely declined.

They reached the bedroom, and Felix noticed the slightly horrified look on Ellie's face. 'I had taken it that there was more than one bedroom, Andreyev,' he said.

'And so there is, Mr Bohlin. Let me show you the adjacent guest suite.'

Felix and Ellie laughed in relief.

'I'll take the guest suite,' said Felix. 'You should get to live like royalty, as befits your ancestry.'

'Will there be anything else I can do for you?' the assistant manager asked. 'Tickets for the Bolshoi, perhaps – or a private tour of the Kremlin or the Tretyakov Gallery? Just let me know; it will be a great honour for me to make your stay as pleasurable as possible.'

Andreyev took out two business cards and presented one each to Felix and Ellie. 'Now, I will let you relax after your long journey. As your luggage has arrived, would you like us to unpack for you?'

Ellie and Felix again declined.

'Please let me know if we can arrange dinner reservations. Of course, our hotel restaurants are world-class. Ovo offers contemporary Italian gastronomy, and my favourite, MEGUmi, has superb modern Japanese cuisine. But if you would prefer something more relaxed, the hotel lounge provides excellent international dishes.'

'The product of a Swiss hotel school, I have no doubt,' Felix said to Ellie once Andreyev had left.

'Well, I'm sure I wouldn't know,' Ellie replied. 'I don't think Swiss hotel schools have had much to do with the places where I usually stay.'

Felix laughed. 'What about some rest then supper in the lounge and an early night? Tomorrow should be a long day.'

'That suits me fine,' Ellie said. 'I want a long, hot soak in that magnificent bath. But tomorrow night, I will show you two-star Russia; that is unless you want the Bolshoi?'

'Both are equally tempting,' Felix said with a smile before he disappeared through the door to the adjoining suite.

* * *

Next morning, over a room-service breakfast of coffee and fresh orange juice, with muesli for Ellie and a bagel with cream cheese for Felix, they discussed the coming day.

'I think we should walk to Red Square and let you get a look at the Kremlin and St. Basil's,' Ellie suggested.

'I'd love that,' Felix replied.

'Good. Afterwards, we can have coffee by Red Square. The GUM store has a wonderful café. Then we can head off to the gallery.'

'Where's that in relation to Red Square?'

'It's across the river, to the south. As it's a good day, it should make for a nice walk. It takes about twenty-five minutes. You can soak up some Moscow atmosphere. Then I will head for the library and archives, and you can look round the galleries. They are amazing. You will understand much more about Russian art by the time you have finished.'

'How long will you need?'

'Most of the afternoon, I should think. Things move slowly here. Will you be all right? I can text you when I've finished.'

* * *

After breakfast, Ellie and Felix went down to the foyer and walked out to the street.

'I'm looking out for suspicious men in trench coats and fedoras,' said Ellie.

'Please don't get paranoid. I'm sure we look innocent.'

'But we're not innocent, are we? We're here to look at a picture that doesn't exist, brought to us by a man who doesn't exist. We're just play-acting.'

'I know. It's odd, like everything else going on right now, but it's not all a farce. Volkov's house may provide me with a new commission, and it gives you time in the archives to make sure we have our story straight about Saltanov.'

'I still think we are under surveillance. Look, haven't we seen that dirty grey car before?'

'For goodness' sake, Ellie, am I going to have this from you for the rest of our trip?'

'It depends if I keep seeing the same car. Then I will know we are being followed by SMERSH.'

'I wondered how long it would take before you brought that up.'

'Well, you never know. Remember, I've been to Moscow before.'

'And were you followed by SMERSH then?'

THE ART DEPARTMENT

'Well, no – or at least I don't think so.'

'There you are, then.'

'But what shall we say about this meeting that isn't going to happen?'

'We say what we have been prepped to say by Sir Bidian's people.'

'And what about our not using Volkov's or the hotel's car – won't that look suspicious?'

'We will say we wanted to explore on foot to see more of Moscow. To make doubly sure and put your mind at rest, we will keep our eyes open for suspicious cars and men in trench coats.'

'And fedoras. Then we will have to lose our tail.'

'You have been reading too many spy stories, Ellie.'

'I've been reading nothing else since this caper began. By the way, do you think the hotel suites are bugged?'

'That hadn't crossed my mind. But now you mention it, I suppose we should be careful. If Volkov puts up business clients here, it would be useful to know what they are saying in private. So, we could be being watched or listened to for all we know.'

* * *

When they reached Red Square, Felix said, 'Everything is so close together; I had no idea.'

'I know,' replied Ellie. 'It comes as a big surprise when you first see it. But by the time you leave, you'll have walked through centuries of Russian history in an oddly intimate way. What would you like to see most before we go to the gallery?'

Felix fixed his gaze on the striped, swirled and gloriously

colourful spires and onion domes of St. Basil's Cathedral. Pointing, he said, 'That.'

They paid for entrance tickets and spent a fascinating hour admiring intricate frescoes and icons, exploring the chapels and navigating the narrow passages and stairways.

Afterwards, they ambled to the gallery, where they parted company. With a smile, Ellie told Felix to keep his eyes open and not to talk to strangers.

Felix studied the gallery guide and map. He had already decided on several must-sees – the *Portrait of an Unknown Woman* by Ivan Kramskoi and Andrei Rublev's *Trinity*.

Before long, he was absorbed in the art that charted so much of Russia's creative history. He wandered through the galleries, choosing pictures he wanted to spend extra time studying. Then he sat on the central benches and enjoyed examining their colours, technique and style.

A group of young French students led by a tutor came into the gallery, where they were joined by a museum guide. They stopped by Shishkin's *Morning in a Pine Forest,* a realist painting of a family of bears playing in a misty forest glade. The guide spoke in French. Felix listened as she explained that the picture had become so popular that some commercial enterprises reproduced it on packaging for various products, including Clumsy Bear chocolate. According to one poll, Felix heard, the painting was the second most popular in Russia behind Vasnetsov's *Bogatyrs*, which was also in the gallery.

When the group moved off, Felix went in search of Vasnetsov's famous painting. Standing before it, he couldn't help thinking how much one of the characters reminded him of Gimli from the film version of *The Lord of the Rings.*

Later, Ellie sent a text to say she would be another hour.

So, Felix took out his sketchbook and, to pass the time, started to draw a marble sculpture of a throned Ivan the Terrible.

Fully immersed in his task at hand, he didn't notice that someone had come up behind him.

A voice said something in Russian. Felix looked around. It was the guide he had seen earlier. He gazed into penetrating blue eyes.

'I'm sorry, I don't speak Russian,' he said in French.

'You're French?'

'No, British. I studied in France for a while.'

'Ah... I was admiring your drawing,' the guide said in fluent English.

Felix was surprised by the sudden switch in language. 'Oh, well, thank you. I saw you earlier. You were explaining about *Morning in the Pine Forest*. I enjoyed your talk, although I felt a little guilty as I had not paid for your expertise.'

The woman laughed and then, looking at her watch, said, 'Oh, I must go. I have another group. It was good speaking to you.'

'And you,' Felix said.

The woman turned towards the next gallery.

'Excuse me,' he called as quietly as he could while still making himself heard.

The guide turned around and said, 'Yes?'

Felix carefully tore the drawing from his sketchbook, stood up and walked over to the woman. 'I should like you to have this,' he said. 'Call it a thank you for your knowledge.'

The woman seemed touched by the gesture. 'That's lovely of you,' she said. Looking again at the drawing, she added, 'But you haven't signed it.'

Felix took out his pencil and signed, F. Bohlin.

'Might I ask what the F stands for?'

'Felix.'

For a moment, the woman seemed to lose concentration. Finally, she said, 'Thank you, Felix,' and walked away again. Then, pausing by the exit, she turned and looked back. Felix met her eye, lifted a hand and waved. She waved back.

'How did you get on?' Felix asked Ellie when they met shortly afterwards.

'Fine. I've managed to confirm various things and have made copies of some records that should be useful. It makes for some very compelling evidence for our fake picture. So, tell me how *you* got on.'

'I have had a perfect day. You're right; I now know a great deal more about Russian art than I did before.'

'So, if there were a fire, which painting would you save?'

Felix thought for a moment. 'The *Bogatyrs*.'

'Why?'

'It makes me laugh.'

'It's not meant to make you do that.'

'I know. I'll explain over dinner.'

'What would you like to do now?' Ellie asked.

'I think I would like to see the Metro.'

'That's easy; we can go from here back to Red Square. We can get a drink there if you like?'

'Sounds good to me. Then how about your two-star restaurant?'

* * *

Felix and Ellie returned to the hotel shortly before ten o'clock. They had enjoyed a good meal in a busy restaurant that Ellie had frequented as a student.

When they reached the lobby, Andreyev was behind the

front desk. He came round to greet them. 'Mr Bohlin, Ms Lydden; you have had a good day, I hope?'

'We have, thank you, Andreyev,' Felix said.

Andreyev lowered his voice. 'Er, there is a gentleman waiting for you in the bar.'

'Us? We are not expecting anyone,' said Felix.

'He has been here for some time.'

Felix looked at Ellie, then returned his attention to Andreyev. 'Would you take us to him, please?' he asked.

'Perhaps it's one of Volkov's people making sure we are comfortable,' Felix whispered to Ellie as they walked.

'Or checking on us,' Ellie replied, looking concerned.

Andreyev led the pair to a corner table in the bar. A clean-shaven, mature man in a well-tailored dark suit stood up. Felix guessed he was in his late sixties. 'I hope you will forgive this interruption to your visit,' he said.

'How can we help you?' Felix asked.

'I am an officer in the state security services, and I would like to ask you some questions.' The man showed his identity card. Felix recognised the photograph but none of the details.

'Questions?' Felix said, suddenly feeling anxious.

The man smiled. 'I don't think you have anything to worry about, Mr Bohlin. But when one of our most high-profile citizens invites guests here, we routinely like to make sure that they – and we – are comfortable. I take it that your visit is for more than sightseeing?'

'Yes,' Felix said. 'I am here to look at Mr Volkov's Moscow house. I am his property advisor, and he has asked me to give him some ideas about a new internal layout.'

'And I am an art historian. I'm researching a Russian artist,' Ellie said.

'Which artist is that?'

'Bogdan Saltanov.'

'I don't know that name. But then I am no art historian or connoisseur. So, this is a working trip for you both?'

'And seeing the sights,' Felix said honestly. 'It is my first time in Moscow, although Ellie has been before. I have to say, I am enjoying the city immensely.'

'I am pleased, Mr Bohlin. But you are no stranger to my country, Ms Lydden.' This was a statement rather than a question.

'No, I'm not a stranger. I stayed here for some months.'

'Ah, while you were studying at St. Petersburg?'

'You know about that?'

'Of course. We like to know about all our visitors.'

'Might I ask what these questions are for?' Felix said.

'In my country, it is better not to ask. You plan to leave the day after tomorrow, Mr Bohlin?'

'That is correct.'

'Well, then let me wish you a good rest of your stay in our city and a safe journey back to London.'

Feeling relieved that the questioning had stopped, Felix said, 'Thank you, Mr... I'm sorry, you didn't mention your name.'

'No, I didn't. Just one other thing, Mr Bohlin, Ms Lydden: it would be unwise to tell Mr Volkov that we had this conversation. It would be very unwise indeed. Do I make myself clear?'

'Very,' Felix said.

'Good, then I will wish you goodbye, Mr Bohlin. Dasvidaniya, Ms Lydden.'

'Dasvidaniya,' Ellie replied.

With that, the man stood up, nodded his head at Felix and Ellie, and turned and left them.

'He knew I spoke Russian,' said Ellie.

'A reasonable guess, as you studied here.'

'I suppose so, but what on earth was that all about?'

'I have no idea. Perhaps Bidian will have some thoughts.'

'You're not going to contact him from here, are you?'

'Lord no. I think we have to assume that for one reason or another, we are under some sort of surveillance.'

'But we're not guilty of anything.'

'I'm not sure that makes much difference in Russia.'

'Well, I suppose we *are* here under false pretences.'

'But there's no reason that man would know this, and what we're doing is hardly a national security issue. He's not the police, so why should he care?'

'It is like some kind of spy plot.'

'Ellie,' Felix said in a whisper. 'I'm beginning to think it might well *be* some kind of spy plot.'

'It doesn't add up,' Ellie said.

'What doesn't?'

'He wasn't wearing a trench coat or a fedora – that's sneaky.'

* * *

The following morning, Andreyev was at his post behind the front desk. 'Mr Bohlin, Ms Lydden, how may I help you today?' he asked. 'Perhaps with transportation? The hotel limousine and driver are at your disposal.'

'Actually, that would be very helpful, Andreyev,' Felix said. 'We have to go to Mr Volkov's home. His housekeeper is expecting us.'

Andreyev picked up the phone.

'I thought we weren't going to use the hotel car,' Ellie whispered to Felix.

'I've been thinking; it would seem a bit odd if we didn't accept a lift at all.'

'I suppose you're right.'

'The car will be at the front momentarily, Ms Lydden, Mr Bohlin,' Andreyev told them. 'Please call me when you are ready to return to the hotel or to travel anywhere else. Is there anything else I can do for you?'

Felix suddenly had an idea. 'You mentioned the Bolshoi. Can you arrange seats for us tonight by any chance?'

'Tonight, there will undoubtedly be a full house. The performance is *Sleeping Beauty*. But I am sure that as friends of Mr Volkov and The Lotte Hotel, the concierge will be able to arrange seats for you. The tickets will be waiting for you at the theatre box office this evening.'

'Thank you, Andreyev,' Felix replied, suddenly tasting the power of real wealth. Turning, he said, 'As you say, Ellie, one could get used to this. Dimity is going to be green.'

'You will just have to make it up to her.'

'How do you make up for missing out on *Sleeping Beauty* in Moscow, at the Bolshoi?'

'I see your point.'

Volkov's house was just a few blocks from the Kremlin.

Bidian would be thrilled that he had been allowed free rein to snoop around, Felix thought, before remembering there could be cameras and microphones everywhere.

'I'm not surprised he wants a revamp; there's an awful lot of theatrical gold and glitter,' Ellie said.

Felix put a finger up to his lips. Ellie grimaced and mouthed sorry. Felix then spent several enjoyable hours making drawings and taking photos with a clear conscience –

after all, it was what he had been asked to do. Meanwhile, Ellie admired the art collection.

The evening at the Bolshoi was another gold and glittering experience that passed in an unforgettable blur of glorious colour, movement and sublime sound. After the ballet, and forgetting all about tails and surveillance, Felix and Ellie strolled back to the hotel, excitedly talking about the performance as they walked.

They had almost reached the hotel when a dirty grey car pulled up alongside them. The driver lowered the window. It was the security man they had met the previous evening.

'Have you had a good evening?' he asked.

'Er, yes, we have. We've been to the ballet,' said Felix.

'And you have completed your research, Ms Lydden?'

'Oh, yes,' said Ellie.

'I am pleased. May I wish you a safe journey back to London tomorrow. Also, please be careful with your new friend.'

'Mr Volkov?'

'Be careful, Mr Bohlin. I want you to take that message back with you.'

The window closed, and the car moved slowly off.

'What was that all about?' Ellie said.

'I have no idea. But Sir Bidian will need to know.'

CHAPTER
NINETEEN

Róisín found a table towards the back of the small eatery she went to when she wanted to avoid bumping into anyone she knew. It was an intimate, basic and busy café-cum-restaurant outside the Golden Circle, Moscow's inner peripheral road. It was out of the way and well beyond the central area of government offices, expensive apartments, shops and national landmarks.

She took off her hat and scarf and draped her coat over the back of a chair. As usual, the restaurant was full of noisy locals. No one paid her any attention.

Only minutes after she had taken her seat, she saw her dinner companion enter the establishment. He carefully looked around, taking in all the diners. Having spotted Róisín, he walked towards her.

She watched him weave between the crowded tables. He still looked elegant. For as long as she had known Nicolai Rykov, who was now in his late sixties, he had kept himself trim. He was just under six feet tall, and his hair was now almost white. Róisín had always thought he had a kind face – unlike most of the heavy-set FSB men with whom he worked. Róisín admired the way he wore clothes. She knew he used a fourth-generation, back-street tailor who turned out well-made, fashionable suits copied from photos cut from Western magazines.

'Good evening, darling,' Nicolai said fondly to Róisín in English before kissing her on the cheeks three times in turn. It was their habit to speak in English; partly because Róisín knew Nicolai liked to practise the language, but also because there was less chance of being understood if overheard.

'Good evening, Nicolai. It's good to see you. How is Eva?' Róisín asked, referring to Nicolai's wife.

'She is well. Thank you for asking.'

'And your boys?'

'They are both fine, too. How about you?'

'Oh, not much to tell. Just the usual things.'

A waiter came over and offered two menus. 'We don't need those,' said Nicolai, reverting to his native language. 'We will have two bottles of beer – Baltika, Number 9, with glasses – and to eat, we will both have kotlety. And bring some bread.'

Róisín smiled. There had been no reference to her in the curt order, but after all these years, there didn't need to be. They always ate and drank the same things in this restaurant.

'You look tired,' said Nicolai.

'That's not a very flattering thing to say, but to tell you the truth, I am feeling tired. Perhaps it's my age, but I think I've finally become weary of Moscow. My heart isn't here any longer, Nicolai.'

'Where do you think it is?'

Róisín laughed. 'That is a very good question.'

'You always told me that home is where the heart is.'

'My heart has been with you. You were in Moscow, so it became my home. Now I don't know. I just think it's not in Moscow anymore.'

'I am sorry, darling.'

'There is nothing to be sorry about, Nicolai. We both made the decision about us a long time ago. Staying with your family was the right thing to do then, and it is still the right thing to have done.'

'Do you really think so?'

'Think of your boys. That is answer enough.'

'Yes. But you have not had a family.'

At first, Róisín didn't reply. When she did, she said, 'That part of life seems to have cheated me. Not by choice.'

'By circumstance?'

'Something like that.'

A waiter brought over a wooden platter of black rye bread.

'Mmm, apart from the company, the bread is the best thing about this place,' said Nicolai, before returning to the conversation. 'You are very unhappy.'

'Yes, I am.'

'Is it time?'

'Time for what?'

'Time to leave Russia.'

'You know I can't do that.'

'Do I?'

'What do you mean, "do I", Nicolai? I can't go back to Belfast after all these years. Your people would never let me go. Plus, I have no passport and no chance of getting one.'

'There are ways. You must know that.'

'I don't know that. Anyway, what is there for me in Ireland anymore? The Troubles ended a long time ago. No one would welcome me back. I am dead to everyone, even myself. Where would I go?'

'To another place.'

'What other place?'

Nicolai smiled and said, 'You will know better than I do.'

Róisín let the remark slide and replied, 'I'm not even sure who I am any longer.'

'I have often thought that about you.'

'You have?'

'You speak English with an Irish accent, but then occasionally an English one takes over. It happens when you are relaxed. Where do you think you belong?'

It was a question Róisín didn't have to answer as the waiter appeared with the beers and the food – mashed potatoes and meatballs made from minced beef.

'What would you miss most about Moscow?' Nicolai asked.

Róisín thought for a moment. 'I would miss how tough Moscow makes me feel. It has an energy that invigorates me. I enjoy the language and the music. I have even come to like nineteenth-century Russian novels – something I never thought possible.'

'It makes a difference to read them in Russian.'

'You taught me that, Nicolai.'

'And what about Muscovites, would you miss them?'

'I would miss their creative sarcasm and their clever sense of humour.'

'What wouldn't you miss?'

Róisín laughed. 'I wouldn't miss the aggression and rudeness of strangers. Nor how miserable Moscow can make me feel.'

THE ART DEPARTMENT

'If things had been different, do you think you would have felt settled here?'

'If things had been different between us and we had been together, do you mean?'

'Yes.'

'We shouldn't look back like that. I have no idea. But I'm sure I wouldn't have wanted to leave as I do now.'

'Well, that is honest.'

'Honesty is all you and I have left.'

'Are we both being honest with each other?' Nicolai said, looking Róisín in the eye.

'What do you mean?'

'I think perhaps that is a subject for another time and place. But what has brought all this on? You seemed happy enough last time we met.'

'Perhaps I've become more of a Muscovite than I thought. I've become ironic. Look at these Soviet-era posters on the walls. Once, it was the art of propaganda. Now it's the art of nostalgia. This feeling has been creeping up on me for some time. But it was something small and very recent that convinced me. It happened at the gallery last week. I met a man – he was English and a lot younger than me. He gave me a finely drawn sketch he had made because I commented on it. It was such a kind gesture, and it touched me. I suddenly felt at home somehow – a strange feeling. I was drawn to him, or at least to the place he represented. It left me both confused and sad.'

'We both seem to have met Englishmen last week,' said Nicolai.

'You too?'

'Yes.'

'Through your work?'

'Allied to it. He said he had been sent here by Yuri Volkov. He was with a woman carrying out some research on a painter called Saltanov. Do you know of this artist?'

'Yes, I do. What was the man doing here? Did he say?'

'He told me he was advising on Yuri Volkov's house.'

'Do you think it was the same person I met?'

'It would seem to be a coincidence if it was, but more of a coincidence if it wasn't. Did this man tell you his name, Róisín?'

'Yes. Bohlin, Felix Bohlin.'

'Then it is the same person.'

'How strange. Is the FSB interested in him?'

'No. I just wanted to tell him that Yuri Volkov might not be all that he seems.'

'Why would you tell him that?'

'He might need to know.'

'Nicolai, you wouldn't just do that. What else is going on?'

'You know I can't tell you.'

'But you are telling me something.'

'I told him to be careful of Volkov, that's all,' said Nicolai, failing to answer Róisín's question.

'Why?'

'I'm not sure whose side Volkov is on – ours, his own or someone else's.'

'Wouldn't you know if he was on your side?'

'These days, I'm not so sure.'

'So, you wanted this man to know that?'

'And anyone else that he might know.'

'Do you think he knows anyone else?'

'I hope so. It wouldn't be good if Volkov turned out to be a nemesis, would it? I think there are people who will want to know about him.'

THE ART DEPARTMENT

At the word nemesis, Róisín was caught off guard for a moment. It was a word that seemed out of place in the conversation, as though it had been planted intentionally. It was a word she had encrypted just a few days ago. Recovering quickly, she said, 'There is much, even after all these years, that I don't know about you, Nicolai.'

'I can say the same about you, darling.'

CHAPTER
TWENTY

'Are you sure that was exactly what the man said to you?' Sir Bidian asked, his tone serious.

Felix had finally been summoned to Sir Bidian's office in the Vauxhall MI6 headquarters, but any preconceived ideas of its resembling the one M occupied in the early James Bond films were quickly dispelled. This light and airy room overlooking the River Thames was furnished with smart, modern furniture, while around the walls were a colourful collection of John Piper lithographs.

'I'm certain that's what he said,' Felix replied. 'He said, "I want you to take that message back with you".'

'And what do you think he meant by that?'

'At the time, I took it to be a figure of speech; that we should remember to be careful of Volkov when we got home. Do you think it meant something different?'

'Why did he say message? He could have said warning. You don't think he meant you to take that message back to someone in particular?'

'Back to whom?'

'To me, for instance.'

'You, Bidian? How could he know about you?'

'That's what I'd like to know.'

'It was nothing Ellie, or I, said – I can assure you.'

'No, I'm sure it wasn't.'

'Could it be that Volkov knows something about me?'

'I don't believe that either. From what you say, the man you met doesn't seem to be on Volkov's side. The problem is, I'm not sure *whose* side he is on. Like a number of other things at the moment, it makes no sense. It certainly doesn't make sense that you were warned not to trust Volkov and were told to bring that message back.'

'Are you sure he meant that, Bidian?'

'Well, I can't be sure, but the language of espionage is both about what is said and what is *not* said. If you had been told to remember something, then that would have been the instruction. As it was, the direction was to take a message back with you. It seems to imply that there was someone to whom you should relay that message.

'This is a concern. So, first, we need to establish the identity of the man you met. That's why you are here. I am going to ask you to go through photographs of all the known Moscow security people we have on file. If that doesn't work, we will need to create a facial composite and see if we can get recognition through our people in Moscow. But I warn you, the photographs could take a long time to go through.'

'This has just got serious, hasn't it?' Felix said.

'Yes, I'm afraid it has. This is no longer an intelligence exercise in social and cultural assimilation. It has become a full-blown, counter-espionage security issue.'

THE ART DEPARTMENT

'Do you want The Art Department out of the picture, so to speak?'

'Ideally, yes, I do. But withdrawing you now may set off alarms, and we don't want that. It might do more harm than good.'

'So, what *do* you want us to do?'

'Carry on as usual, for a little while at least, until we can get a grip on what is going on. First, help us by trying to identify the person you met in Moscow, then go to Volkov's dinner party and find out anything you can. After that, we will assess where we are.'

* * *

It was almost four hours later, when Felix was beginning to think he had seen quite enough of the MI6 building, that he recognised the man he had met in Moscow.

The grainy photograph was of an officer in army uniform under a large and high-peaked hat. The man was much younger in the picture, but there was no doubt in Felix's mind that this was the person he and Ellie had encountered.

Felix reported his findings to Sir Bidian.

'Then the man you met is Lieutenant General Nicolai Rykov. He is very senior, which gives us more questions than answers.'

'Such as?' Felix asked.

'Such as why is an officer of such high rank meeting you... and alone? Why was he by himself? Didn't he want anyone else to know he had met you, and twice? Why show himself to you, knowing that he could be recognised? Why would he want to be remembered?

'Here's what I think. He was acting alone, and he wanted

to be known – but only after you had left the country. If he had just wanted to scare you, then he had plenty of people who could do that. I don't think Rykov wanted to frighten you, but he did want to make a point in no uncertain terms. This is interesting; we've never had Rykov down as a hardliner. If anything, he's the opposite. So, he must have kept his nose clean with whatever goes for the politburo these days. It would be interesting to have his take on what is going on at the moment.'

'What, the build-up of troops near the Ukraine border?'

'Quite so.'

'Are you concerned about that, Bidian?'

'Extremely. FSB top brass potentially creating a channel is an intriguing prospect.'

'Is that what you would do if you had doubts?'

'It's certainly one of the options I should think about. So, I want to know why Rykov talked to you personally.'

'What will you do?'

'I'm not sure yet, but it won't be easy.'

'And what happens if Volkov asks if Ellie or I met or spoke to anyone? Perhaps the whole thing was a test.'

'Somehow, I don't think so, but you are going to have to be as ambiguous as possible, and we will see where it ends. Have you been in contact with Volkov since you and Ellie returned?'

'Yes. I spoke to him on the phone, thanked him for his hospitality and told him the visit had been a success. I suggested that we meet him on Sunday back in Sloane Square.'

'Very good. Now, you had better get back to the studio and see how the team is doing.'

* * *

THE ART DEPARTMENT

At Somerset House, Petro and Tiya had made all their colour pigments, including white, using the lead from Sweden, and had almost finished the likeness.

'We have been fortunate with the frame,' Petro explained to Felix. 'The Courtauld Institute contacted the National Portrait Gallery. They have a fifteenth-century miniature frame. The wood of frame was correct. It is in poor condition, which is good, yes? The badness of frame makes portrait look right.'

Petro took hold of the corner of a cloth lying on his workbench and slowly drew it back to unveil a miniature.

Felix looked at it for a moment and said, 'But that is utterly amazing.'

Looking up at Felix was a male figure holding a sceptre and wearing a jewelled crown.

'Meet Saltanov's patron, Tsar Alexis I, also known as Alexei Mikhailovich the Quietest,' said Ellie. 'As he was tsar during Saltanov's time, Saltanov would almost certainly have painted his portrait.'

'But how did you get the likeness – I take it this is a genuine likeness?' asked Felix.

'There are several contemporaneous portraits of the tsar by unknown artists, so we were able to use those to give us facial characteristics,' said Ellie. 'We then sent copies to the University of Dundee. They have a superb forensic art and facial imaging section within their School of Science and Engineering. They sent us back a 3D computer rendering. Alexis died when he was only forty-six, but we had his reign of thirty-one years to work within. The specialists in Dundee gave us an image of a man of about forty. We painted the portrait from that. The Victoria and Albert Museum advised on the robes and regalia.'

'It looks as if the miniature has had a hard life and not been protected in a collection for hundreds of years,' said Felix.

'It was important to give the piece character. We wanted to lead eye from frame to portrait and let miniature tell its story. We made picture dirty and then cleaned it as if it had been cleaned many years ago,' Petro explained.

'Won't cleaning materials give away the age?' Felix asked.

'We used urine,' Petro replied.

'We didn't want a museum-quality piece,' added Ellie. 'We wanted it to appear to be the cherished possession of generations of owners.'

'A group that Volkov will want to join?'

'That's the idea,' said Ellie.

'I'd say that Petro and Tiya have just become two of the world's leading forgers,' said Felix with a smile.

'I not proud,' said Petro glumly, although Felix could see he was pleased with the outcome.

'But if you're as good as I think,' said Felix, 'no one will ever know that you and Tiya are behind this. No one will question the originality of the miniature – or the provenance that Ellie has been able to piece together. It is impossible to see where reality ends and fiction begins. It will be interesting to see what Volkov thinks.'

* * *

Felix and Ellie met Volkov again at the bistro in Sloane Square.

'I have some layouts of your Moscow house to show you,' said Felix. 'They were done by our design team from my sketches. And of course, we have much to tell you about the Saltanov miniature.'

'I am most interested in what you have to say on both.

Perhaps we will leave the miniature until after you've told me about your thoughts on my house.'

'Well, first, Yuri, both Ellie and I should like to thank you for your overwhelming hospitality. Your hotel suite was beyond anything we had experienced before, as were the flights. But we must pay you for the Bolshoi tickets that went on the hotel account.'

'Please, it is my gift to you,' said Volkov. 'I am delighted that you were able to go to the Bolshoi. It is a special experience.'

'That is very generous, thank you, Yuri,' said Felix.

Ellie added her thanks.

'Now, I have given a great deal of thought to the layout of your house,' said Felix, producing several of his sketches. 'I should like you to go over these in more detail when you have a chance. To the modern eye, there is a great deal of wasted space. By taking out some walls, smaller rooms and connecting corridors, we have been able to add some interesting features. For instance, I was taken by the winter garden in your hotel suite, so we have found a way of introducing the same sort of feature in your house. It is perfect for the Russian climate. Also, we have designed an enfilade, which creates a more palatial air. The suggested changes will also introduce more light into the interior; a major consideration in Moscow, I have learnt.'

'That sounds very interesting. I look forward to studying them further.

'Now, Ms Lydden, how did you get on with your research in Moscow?'

Ellie gave Volkov a review of her findings and introduced some more details from the archives that helped further support the miniature's provenance. Volkov nodded his understanding.

But why wouldn't he? thought Felix. The evidence that Ellie put forward was compelling.

'And what about acquiring the miniature?' Volkov asked eventually.

Felix and Ellie had rehearsed the account they were about to give repeatedly with one of Sir Bidian's cover experts, establishing where their fictitious meeting had taken place and with whom, until they were word perfect.

'The man we met was no art dealer, and he had no idea what he was showing us,' Ellie said.

'And what did he show you?' Volkov asked.

Ellie took several photographs from her handbag that had been shot and printed that morning in the studio. Volkov pored over them.

'Whose portrait is this?' he asked.

'As far as we can ascertain from the archives and other contemporary portraits, it is almost certainly Tsar Alexis I,' said Ellie.

'That is very good. When will you know this for certain?'

Felix and Ellie had agreed it was essential to downplay their views while retaining Volkov's interest.

'We will probably never know more than we do now, Mr Volkov,' said Ellie. 'It is not like checking the veracity of a French Impressionist painting with the Wildenstein Institute. For Russian art, there is no final arbiter.

'We have done all we can to confirm this is genuine. Perhaps if we do further analysis on the style and technique, we might learn more, but I don't think it will throw up any surprises. In my view – and it is only my view – this is a miniature of Alexis I, probably given to his wife, Maria

Ilyinichna Miloslavskaya, and almost certainly painted by Bogdan Saltanov.'

'What about the frame?' asked Volkov. 'That doesn't look as if it was made for a tsar.'

'That is an excellent question,' said Ellie. 'I have questions about the frame myself, and I confess that I am confused. One would think that a miniature of an important person, especially a tsar, would have warranted something more fitting. This frame is very plain, I agree. I can only suggest that it was changed at some point, and for some good reason. Perhaps the original frame, if there was one, was damaged beyond repair or was used for something else. We will never know. But this miniature's frame is helpful in that we can date the wood if we choose to.'

'But dating the wood would not guarantee it was made at the same time as the painting,' said Volkov.

'That is correct, but to be fair, neither would any other frame. I think we would just feel more comfortable if it were embellished with jewels and precious metals.'

'I would like to acquire this,' said Volkov abruptly.

'Then I will tell Rani and ask her how much her client wants for it,' said Ellie coolly.

'How much should I pay?' Volkov asked Ellie.

'The value of miniatures, like other portraits, depends on the condition and the importance of the sitter. Because early miniatures were painted in watercolour on vellum, they were delicate items. In general, many have not survived in the same way that an oil painting on oak board might have done. Later miniatures painted on ivory fared much better. So, we are fortunate that this portrait of Alexis has weathered so well.

'The value, as you will know, also depends on the pool of potential buyers. Because the miniature is of a tsar, there will be interest from major galleries and museums, other Russian collectors and perhaps Russian institutions, such as the Kremlin Museum.'

'I anticipate there will be significant interest, and also from those with a great deal of money,' said Volkov. 'But the seller can't go to official institutions or museums, can he?'

'I agree it would be difficult without the seller having first established some form of freedom of prosecution – an amnesty,' said Ellie. 'As for the price, it is a specialised market, and as such is difficult to predict. We should start at the top for a guide. Perhaps the most notable miniature painter was Nicholas Hilliard. He painted Elizabeth I. Today, a Hilliard miniature could reach over a quarter of a million pounds. We are not in this price bracket, but I should imagine we could be thinking up to a hundred thousand pounds on a good day in the open market.'

'But this is not going to be on the open market, is it?' Volkov said. 'This picture, because of its last owner, is on the *black* market. So, I think we should offer a black market price – ten thousand pounds sterling, in cash.'

Ellie nodded. 'I will let Rani know.'

'Good. Now, it sounds as if you have both had a very worthwhile trip to Moscow. Tell me, did you enjoy the city, Felix?'

'I did very much. I was able to see many of the things I wished to see.'

'That is good. And did you meet anyone of interest while you were there?'

Here it is, thought Felix, the moment of truth. But he couldn't tell if this was just an innocent, off-the-cuff question or one that was far more loaded. Had Andreyev from the hotel said anything to Volkov about the security man? Felix hoped not.

'Well, I must say that all the people we met seemed interesting and polite, Yuri. But we didn't have much time for meeting people, just those in the hotel and passing by in the street. It was so useful that Ellie speaks Russian. But I did meet a nice woman at the gallery. She was a guide. I gave her one of my drawings.'

'Why did you do that?'

'She generously complimented me on a sketch I had done, and I gave it to her as a gift. She seemed pleased.'

'I am sure she was. Now, what is next?'

'Next, we contact Rani and try to get a deal for you.'

'Good. Please keep me informed. And what about Courtlands?'

'I have to go down there tomorrow. But I understand that the roof restoration is complete and we can move to finishing the windows and rainwater goods.'

'And the interior?'

'I will let you know after tomorrow, when I have spoken to the interior project manager. But I am sure I will be told they are pressing ahead with restoring the ornate ceiling plasterwork and the wooden panelling. Before long, we will need to discuss further lighting and plumbing, and the kitchen and bathrooms.'

'Good. Now, I wanted to know if you and your wife would like to join me for dinner on Thursday?'

'Oh, well, thank you, Yuri, we should love to. I'm sure that it will be OK. But I will speak to Dimity and make sure she has no parish work on that evening. May I get back to you later today?'

'Of course, I look forward to your call. Now, I am afraid I must leave. I have another meeting to attend.'

After leaving the bistro, Felix and Ellie went to the Antelope to debrief.

'How do you feel?' Ellie asked.

'Like we are getting more and more drawn into something over which we have no control,' Felix replied.

'I feel the same,' said Ellie.

CHAPTER
TWENTY-ONE

'You look amazing, Mitten,' Felix said as Dimity appeared in their small sitting room. 'You remind me of Audrey Hepburn.'

'Kind of you to say, but I hardly think so.'

'Well, you do to me. Helped by a certain glamorous retro chic.'

'I borrowed the dress from Eliza. She told me she had this "old thing" hanging up in the back of her wardrobe that was doing nothing. Old thing indeed. It's a 1961 vintage Givenchy – an original little black dress. Eliza said she had only worn it once. Do you think it will do for tonight?'

'It's perfect.'

'You should see what other clothes Eliza has. There was quite a choice, but they were all of an era.'

'I take it that wasn't the only thing you borrowed? Or have you emptied the bank account or taken out a huge loan from a dodgy money lender?'

Dimity laughed. 'The necklace and bracelet?' She held out her bejewelled wrist for inspection. 'Eliza said they would set the dress off. She told me that a Russian banquet is quite a thing, and everyone goes dolled up to the nines. Eliza seemed to know quite a lot about Russian dinner parties. I didn't ask her why.

'Apparently, these pieces belonged to your great-great-great-grandmother. They were a gift from a maharajah. Aren't they beautiful? Cornflower blue sapphires – the best – and diamonds set in twenty-four carat gold. Eliza told me that your forebear's husband was up to his eyes in some opium deal for the British Government.'

'Sounds like the old boy,' Felix said ironically, knowing next to nothing about this ancestor. 'Anyway, you look sensational. Good old great-great-great-grandmama.'

'Eliza told me to enjoy them, but not to lose them. But I have to say, you don't look so shabby yourself.'

'I don't look too James Bond in this dinner jacket, do I?'

Dimity laughed. 'Felix, how could any man look *too* James Bond?'

'I don't want to look like a spy.'

'I can assure you that you don't. But you do look very dashing. Now, are we OK for time?'

'The cab will be here in about ten minutes.'

'Are we ready for this?' Dimity asked.

'To tell you the truth, I am more than a little anxious about this evening.'

'I'm glad it's not just me. I'm scared that I'll say something I shouldn't – that I'll give the game away somehow. This won't be a fun evening, Felix. If Yuri is up to no good and has suspicions about us, it could quickly become dangerous. We have Eliza to think about. And what if Mrs Mirova is there? I don't like her at all.'

'I know how you feel. We will just have to be extra careful

about what we say. We'll keep on safe ground and avoid anything contentious.'

* * *

An English butler in white tie and tails opened the door of Volkov's house to Felix and Dimity. He bade them good evening and led them up the main staircase to the magnificent first floor drawing room, where he announced them.

'That's a first,' whispered Felix to Dimity.

'Welcome to my home,' said Volkov, kissing Dimity on each cheek and warmly shaking Felix's hand. 'Of course, you know Maria.'

'We meet again,' she said. Felix thought this sounded more like an accusation than a welcome.

Volkov then introduced Dimity and Felix to his other guests. There were nine couples, all Russian. Some of the women were dressed in full-length gowns, with lots of expensive jewellery on display. Felix noticed several of them, including Maria, eyeing up Dimity's bracelet and necklace.

The butler brought over glasses of champagne on a silver tray.

Felix took in the interior of the drawing room. The mirrored, chandeliered and gilded room was full of beautiful art and French-style gilded furniture with chairs upholstered in red velvet.

'Can you tell us about the history of this house, Yuri?' Felix said, opening up the conversation on a safe subject.

'Yes, of course. It was built for a landowner whose family in later generations could not keep up the maintenance. A South African diamond magnate was the next owner – he was, I think your expression is, a Randlord. He kept the house as his London base for a few years. After that, a South American bank owned it. They used it as a corporate office and accommodation for visiting directors. Then they moved their offices to Canary Wharf and put their directors up in hotels instead. The house fell into disuse for many years. It was much like Courtlands in that way. I purchased it from the bank during the last downturn. They wanted it off their books as soon as possible. I helped them out for a cheap price.

'The house is about forty thousand square feet and has fifteen bedrooms. It did have more before some rationalisation and other improvements were made.'

Just then, the butler came into the room and struck the small hand gong. 'Ladies and gentlemen, dinner is served,' he announced.

Volkov offered Dimity his arm and led the party through a top-lit, marble-columned picture gallery towards the dining room. Felix escorted Mrs Mirova, who wore a billowing, brilliant-white gown. Felix smiled to himself as he imagined what Roger would make of the outfit. He imagined him likening Mrs Mirova to a snowplough.

The walls of the gallery were in a beautiful shade of distressed, natural-pigment red; the type of colour Felix knew from Roman murals in places like Pompeii. Lining the gallery were pictures from Volkov's collection of Russian art, including several exceptional icons.

Between the pictures on pretty side tables was an eclectic collection of fascinating objects. Felix stopped at one, a small bronze of a ballerina.

Volkov looked back. 'It is by Degas. Like many Russians, I adore the ballet. Look here...' Volkov pointed to a glass case. Inside, beautifully displayed and lit was a pair of worn pointe shoes, the satin covers threadbare at the toes. 'They belonged to Pavlova, who wore them to dance *The Dying Swan* in St. Petersburg in 1905. Sergei Diaghilev once owned them.'

At the end of the gallery, looking spectacular under a bright spotlight, was a magnificent ethnic saddle. All the fittings appeared to be silver, and the long straps that hung down on either side were tightly woven, tasselled cords of silk. Deep yellow, brocaded silk, woven in a dragon-rondel pattern, covered the seat, side skirts and stirrup pads.

'This is stunning. Is there a story about this saddle?' asked Dimity.

'Only that it is so beautiful. The Khalkha people of Outer Mongolia valued saddles by their number of silver ornaments, called whites. A saddle could be eight whites, ten whites or, as here, twelve whites – that's the highest category. Notice the eight straps hanging down. They were used to hold equipment or to secure game after the hunt. But they held another significance. The horsemen recited an incantation over them before setting out. It is said to be a custom initiated by Genghis Khan. The Manchu emperors bestowed the right to use silk of this colour and weave on saddles. It was a mark of the highest favour.'

'It's ravishing,' said Dimity.

'I enjoy collecting these beautiful things, especially from in and around my native Russia. It is far from easy. After the Revolution, many Russian treasures were lost, stolen or sold and then scattered across the world. I have been fortunate to gather back some of the precious objects owned by tsars, tsarinas, princes, overlords and wealthy merchants from the extremities of the Russian Empire and beyond.'

Volkov looked about him and lowered his voice. 'That is why I am so interested in the miniature.'

'What about Fabergé?' Felix asked with a smile.

'Ah, the elusive egg. Of the original sixty-nine, fifty-seven are known about. I am in perpetual search of at least one of the twelve unaccounted for. It would be the centrepiece of my collection.'

Volkov led his guests into the glittering dining room. 'Please, Dimity,' he said. 'I would like you to sit to my right, and Felix on my left. The other guests circled the table looking for their place cards. It struck Felix that they weren't new to this.

The table was magnificent. Crystal glasses danced in candlelight, and the china tableware and silver cutlery shone upon a dazzling white damask tablecloth.

Felix picked up the menu card in front of him and was pleased to find it written in English.

Champagne
1990 Krug

Red caviar with blinis, king prawns and oysters
2007 Riesling Schoelhammer Hugel

Beetroot salad, pickled vegetables, duck pâté, salmon gravlax and sliced meats
2015 Chevalier-Montrachet, Grand Cru, Domaine Leflaive

Mushroom blinchiki and beef piroshky
1990 Ch. Margaux

Rack of lamb and prawn cutlets
1982 Petrus, Pomerol

Russian cream with strawberries Romanoff
2009 Ch. d'Yquem, Sauternes

Coffee or tea

Port
1994 Warre's

Vodka
Jewel of Russia Ultra

Once everyone had sat down, Volkov clinked a glass with a knife. 'I would like to welcome you all here tonight. It is a special occasion, as we can offer some Russian hospitality to our new English friends.' There was a murmur of agreement from around the table. 'I don't know what you know of Russian hospitality, Felix and Dimity, but we hope to do it some justice tonight.'

'You have already, I can assure you,' Felix said.

'You have made us feel very welcome, Yuri,' added Dimity. 'Although I have to admit, I have had experience of warm Russian hospitality before.'

'You have?' Volkov asked.

'Yes, it was in a tent halfway up Everest. We were snowed in for days. Countrymen and women of yours made up another expedition. They looked after me very well. They didn't have much food, but they did have a lot of vodka.'

Everyone laughed, and Volkov clapped his hands. 'And you will have more vodka tonight, Dimity. I didn't know you were a mountaineer?'

'In my younger days, but I should love to know more about Russian hospitality.'

'Well, what can I tell you? Ivan the Terrible, despite his infamous reputation, was very hospitable to guests. Lunch would last for three or four hours. Dinner went on until after midnight.

'Other tsars were also excellent hosts. Meals might include swan, crane and fried peacock, as well as all possible varieties of blinis and pastries.

'I'm sorry to tell you we are not eating quite on that scale tonight – nor for as long, I suspect.'

Everyone laughed.

'But I have to say, Peter the Great had more modest tastes. He liked cabbage soup. Catherine the Great also ate simply. Her favourite dish was boiled beef with pickled cucumbers.'

Volkov paused.

'Oh, do go on,' said Dimity.

Felix could see she was enjoying the descriptions. Volkov was an excellent raconteur and seemed well versed in his country's imperial history.

'Well, Alexander II enjoyed eating but was strict on the duration of breakfasts and lunches. Both were to take no more than fifty minutes. This rule was from time to time made more difficult because the tsar would change where he wanted to eat at the last moment. Sometimes, the venue was so far from the kitchens that the staff found it impossible to get all the food to the table on time while still hot. In the end, they came up with the idea of using large hot water bottles to keep the food warm.'

'What did they drink?' Dimity asked.

'That is an excellent question. Vodka, of course, but it was

Alexander II's son, Emperor Alexander III, who started Russian winemaking.'

'I didn't know there was much winemaking in Russia,' said Felix.

There was a ripple of laughter around the table.

'What is so funny?' asked Felix good-naturedly.

'Felix, you weren't to know, I think. Russian wine is not up to the standard of most other winemaking countries. The Crimea is the only area that has good soil for vines – although the republic is now, for many, a touchy subject and not a good topic for tonight. But some Russians joke that it was re-occupied for the Kremlin's wine cellar.'

'So, where else did Russia look to for wine?' asked Felix.

'Traditionally, Moldova. Wine has been produced there for over two thousand years. They have perfect conditions and more vines per capita than anywhere else in the world. Moldovan white wines are particularly good. But now Russia has banned the importation of wine as the relationship between the two countries has become complicated. But then the relationship with Russia and everywhere else in the world is complicated.'

The butler and an under-butler arrived and busily set to work putting food onto plates at the sideboard. Once they had done so, they served the first course.

Volkov turned to Dimity and explained, 'It is our custom to serve food à la russe. This means it's portioned on the plate by servers before being given to the diners. There are no serving plates or tureens on the table, as in the French style.'

'I didn't know about that,' said Dimity to Volkov. 'This table looks so beautiful. The flowers are just gorgeous.'

'You have your friend, Roger Strand, to thank for those.'

'I hope you won't think me rude, Yuri, but may I ask you about your china?' Dimity said.

Felix admired his wife's social ease with a tinge of envy.

'Of course you can,' said Volkov. 'It comes from the Imperial Porcelain Manufactory in St. Petersburg and features the two-headed eagle emblem of Nicholas II. For many years, production was almost exclusively for the ruling Romanov family and the Russian Imperial Court. This service was used at the Winter Palace in St. Petersburg. Only a thousand pieces of service made around the time of the coronation in 1896 survived the Revolution.

'I was lucky to acquire the service. A Qatari prince I know through business owned these pieces, but the pattern didn't contain enough gold for him.' Volkov laughed and added, 'We Russians love our gold, but I have to say our Arab friends do so more. In the end, the prince sold the service to me. He didn't know what he had. But then I don't think he would have cared if he had known – it still didn't have enough gold.'

'What a wonderful story,' said Dimity. 'I can't imagine how big the original service must have been.'

'Many, many thousands of pieces,' said Volkov, who chatted on until the butlers took away the empty dishes and served the second course.

To catch the attention of the table, Volkov said in a loud voice, 'Now, Felix, I am sure we would like to hear something about your great London houses.'

'What would you like to know?'

'Well, I was telling you about the history of this house earlier; it would be interesting to know about that in the context of the social history of your country.'

Felix noticed the faces around the table all looking at him expectantly. He thought for a moment and said, 'The downfall of the English country house and its London cousin was almost an extinction event. It certainly was in London. The families that owned both vast country and London houses derived most of their wealth from their land in the provinces, particularly land that produced wool, coal, iron and tin – the mainstays of the Industrial Revolution. The London house didn't contribute to family wealth. Instead, it drained it. In those days, it was a vanity, and a very expensive one.

'One by one, the great houses of Central London fell into disuse, as they were only really occupied during the social season. Demolition followed, and the land was used for redevelopment. Most of those houses not sold by the time the Second World War began succumbed to the Blitz.

'You may be interested to know that many of London's rich decamped to the Dorchester Hotel after their houses were bombed. The building, constructed in concrete, was the most bombproof of all the city's hotels at the time. It was said that it was Mayfair's best air-raid shelter.'

Everyone laughed.

'At the Dorchester, and at many other luxury hotels in the area, the good life continued. While most of the population was being rationed, the very rich did not go short. Oysters, caviar and lobster escaped regulation. At the Dorchester, some of the wealthier guests even brought produce such as salmon, game and eggs from their country estates. Lady Cunard, who set up home in the hotel, gave weekly dinner parties for favoured friends. One saying that the wealthy used at the time was, "To hell with the Blitz, we're off to the Ritz!"'

Everyone laughed again. 'This is most interesting and entertaining, Felix,' said Volkov, 'wartime life here in London doesn't sound as bad as Stalingrad.'

'I'm sure it wasn't. But after the war, any great houses left were taken over by embassies or used as flats, clubs and offices. The only grand houses to survive in some reasonable condition in the heart of London were the Duke of Wellington's Apsley House by Hyde Park Corner and Spencer House in St. James's, the original London home of Princess Diana's family, although it had been requisitioned during the war and badly treated. Buckingham Palace was damaged by bombs, as well as some other royal houses such as Clarence House, home of the Queen Mother before she died.

'Such was the economic and social impact of the war, it has taken about fifty years for us to see the rebirth of the grand London townhouse, but this time, the resurgence has been created through a great deal of overseas wealth. You, Yuri, and your countrymen and women are helping to re-establish a grand tradition in our capital. I think it is good for conserving our architectural heritage. So, thank you. You have played an important part in bringing back the full glory of this grand London house.'

The dinner guests applauded as the mushroom blinchiki and beef piroshky arrived.

The lively conversation continued over the next course. Felix was left talking one to one with Volkov.

'I was interested in what you were saying about the wealthy in London living well during the war,' said Volkov. 'May I ask how you feel about that?'

'As opposed to the rest of the population?'

'Yes.'

'That was then, and this is another time.'

'We Russians did something about inequality.'

'The Revolution?'

'Yes.'

'But even though Britain didn't have a revolution, we all

seem to have arrived at the same place now, haven't we? The wealthy are living in grand houses while poorer people are, in one way or another, still rationed. Doesn't everything seem to go around in circles?'

'Felix, I think you are a philosopher. Are you sure you don't have Russian blood?'

Felix laughed. 'Not that I know of, Yuri, but I must say, I try and keep away from politics, especially as far as my clients are concerned. Oh, I am sorry, I didn't mean that to sound like a rebuke.'

'I assure you, I didn't take it as one. It is an excellent rule. But politics aside, do you approve of the use of wealth for what might be seen as frivolous reasons?'

'How can I disapprove? It is how I make my living. Without patrons and the employment of artists, craftspeople and even architects, we would not have the flowering of creativity that has enriched humankind since it was decorating caves. It is just the caves that have changed, not the artistic urge.'

'You put it well, Felix. We will put politics aside and talk instead of artistry.'

'But tell me one thing, Yuri.'

'Ask it.'

'You may find it an impolite or even an impertinent question.'

'Ask it anyway.'

'You obviously like England—'

'But why haven't I stayed in Russia?'

'I was only wondering.'

'It is a fair question. I do love this country. And I do love my homeland.' Volkov lowered his voice. 'But life for me in Russia is complicated. Recently, much has changed.'

'Many of your countrymen have moved from Russia, some to London,' Felix prompted.

'That is correct. We have created an anklav.'

'An anklav?'

'An enclave. We live like Russians – or rather, we live like privileged Russians in another beautiful country and magnificent city. But I have another important reason to want to be here.'

'Would that be your daughter?'

'Yes, of course. Where my daughter is, I want to be.'

The rack of lamb and prawn cutlets were served.

During a slight lull in conversation, Volkov turned to address Dimity. 'I am sure we are all interested to know about your mountaineering,' he said.

Dimity gave the party several stories of her climbing experiences, but not of her last, when she so nearly lost her life. Felix found himself feeling proud again. Many questions followed from the guests, which Dimity fielded with charm, honesty and self-deprecation.

'Yuri, I must tell you, I have never tasted wine as good as this,' said Felix.

Volkov bowed his head in acceptance of the compliment, and said, 'Wine is another passion of mine – as long as it isn't Russian!'

The butlers removed the empty plates and replaced them with the dessert.

There was a warm hum of chatter around the table, the sort that any host or hostess would be pleased to hear. It signified a successful fusion of food, drink, ambience, service and amiable guests.

The butlers served the port, followed by the coffee and tea, and the chatter continued over delicious petit fours and vodka, until the guests began to express their thanks to Volkov and take their leave.

'Yuri, this has been such a lovely evening; it could not have been better,' said Dimity.

'Well, I must thank you for being such charming and entertaining guests. Let us hope this evening is the first of many.'

A taxi that had not been ordered by Felix or Dimity arrived to take them home.

'I have to say,' Dimity said once they were in the cab, 'much against my fears, that was a lovely evening. Perfect host, delicious food and delightful guests – apart from Maria.'

'You're still not keen on her?'

'She asked me if my necklace and bracelet were an heirloom. She looked as if she would rip them off my body.'

'What did you say?'

'I told her they are from your side of the family. I tried to laugh it off. I said I was really a jeans and T-shirt sort of girl – that or my clerical garb. But she was fishing. Why do you think she was doing that again? Do you think she suspects something?'

'I'm not sure, but it makes me uncomfortable. I'll report back to Bidian in the morning.'

'But let's not let it spoil our perfect evening.'

'Was it too perfect?'

'Cynic.'

'I love you, Mitten.'

'What prompted that?'

'This evening.'

CHAPTER
TWENTY-TWO

The following morning, Roger Strand dropped in early to Felix and Dimity's flat. He had just been south of the river on a buying trip to the flower market and then to his centre of operations, where his group of talented florists made the magic happen, supported by four vans and their drivers.

'I just had to know how last night went, darlings.'

'You were much in evidence, Roger. The flowers were glorious,' said Dimity.

'I think you have a job for life there,' said Felix.

Roger snorted. 'Let's hope it isn't a short one.'

'What, your job or your life?' asked Felix.

'Both.'

'I'm sure they won't be. You tend to keep your clients and have managed to avoid premature death by ghastly means over the past twenty years – or so you tell me,' said Felix.

'You're right, petal, and I have to say it wasn't without trying sometimes. But fortunately, I'm still here to die another day – isn't that what they say in the trade?'

'Which trade are you talking about, Roger?'

'Well, I'm not talking floristry, that's for sure.'

'I for one am very pleased that you are still with us,' said Dimity.

'Are you, flower? That's nice of you to say so.'

'Otherwise, what would we do for flowers here in the flat if we didn't have your cast-offs?'

'You can be a very cynical cleric sometimes.'

'I accused Felix of cynicism last night.'

'Oh, he's a cynic, of course. But talking of last night – spill.'

'I am not sure there is a lot to spill. It was a charming evening. Volkov was a perfect host. By the way, do you know anything about Mrs Mirova?'

'Apart from her hating the sight of me? She's a widow. Her husband made tractors in Russia – all the tractors in Russia. He died in a car accident on the French Riviera and left his wife loaded. They only had one child, a son. He's a heroin addict and lives with Mirova in Kensington Palace Gardens. She's another big collector of Russian art, I was told. I'm not sure what the connection is between her and Yuri. It is all a tad curious. But she shows up at most of his dinners, and if he is going to social events anywhere else, he often takes her. They go to the ballet at Covent Garden a great deal. Volkov has a box, or she does. I think she would like to be more than friends, but she doesn't seem Yuri's type.'

'What is Yuri's type?' asked Felix

'I'm still trying to work that out.'

'How on earth did you find out that much in such a short space of time, Roger?' Dimity asked.

'It was not easy. Aside from the English butlers and the head chef and sous chef, who are both French, the staff are mostly Russian. All the household staff working above stairs try to go about unnoticed. It's the same for my florists. We can't publicly arrange flowers in the house. So, we have developed a sort of hit-and-run process when we know the coast is clear.'

'Still, you have found out things,' Felix said.

'Well, I would, wouldn't I? Oh, one more thing I did find out—'

'What was that?' Dimity asked, clearly enjoying the gossip.

'Volkov owns the house next door, and a smaller one around the corner in Chester Row – the sort of house Noel Coward called a Baby Grand. Volkov doesn't seem to be in the next-door house much – it's used for large parties of guests, but apparently, he does visit Chester Row quite often.'

'Perhaps that's where he entertains Mrs Miniver,' Dimity observed.

'Mrs Mirova,' Roger corrected. 'But she sounds just as tragic.

'Anyway, it has to be said that Volkov keeps his life highly compartmentalised. Are you going to see the Savile Row suit soon, Felix?'

'I am. Later this morning, in fact, to let him know about last night.'

'Well, tell him what I said about Mrs Mirova, will you? And tell him to come and buy some more flowers. A bit of intrigue is good for the blooms.'

* * *

Felix met Sir Bidian at Somerset House. All the portraits in his office had gone, revealing bare walls in need of a fresh coat of paint.

'Great pity about the pictures,' said Felix. 'Did they rehang them in the gallery?'

'Yes, and it's a great comedown,' replied Sir Bidian, looking mournful. 'I'm disinclined to invite anyone here at the moment. Still, they will start decorating another gallery soon, so who knows what might turn up here then? They have dozens of good Impressionists. Perhaps they will hang some in here. A Pissarro would be good: his *Lordship Lane Station* would remind me of Dulwich, where I grew up. I have always loved how Pissarro paints light – although I am no expert; I haven't a clue how he did it. But when I am here with the walls full of wonderful pictures, it almost makes me think I am at Witch's.'

Felix laughed. 'It's amazing how quickly the pictures at Witch's fade into the background if you are there for some time. I have to shake myself sometimes to remember how extraordinary they are and how lucky I am.'

'I'm sure. Now, Felix, tell me about last night.'

'Well, I have to say, it was a fabulous evening. The food was delicious, and the wine was out of this world.'

'How out of this world as a matter of personal interest?'

'Chevalier-Montrachet, Margaux, Petrus, Château d'Yquem and Krug.'

'That out of this world? I'm envious.'

'Yes, it was magical. All the other guests were Russians. Like Volkov, they were living the billionaire exile life. Maria was there. She seems a fixture. I'm not sure if it is worth mentioning, but she was digging a bit again last night.'

'Could just be idle curiosity. But we can't take any chances.'

'I'm not sure about her, Bidian. Roger says she lost her husband in a car accident in the South of France. She lives in Kensington Palace Gardens amid another amazing collection of Russian art.'

'That we know – the house is near the Russian Embassy. I'll look into the car accident. Do carry on, Felix.'

'The table chat was the usual dinner party stuff. Nobody said anything contentious as far as I could make out. I had a short one to one with Volkov over dinner.'

'Tell me about that if you would.'

'We talked about wealth coming back to London from overseas and re-establishing London's grand houses.'

'You were for the motion, I imagine?'

'I could hardly have said I wasn't.'

'True. What else?'

'I asked Volkov why he wanted to live here rather than in Russia.'

'That was a bold question.'

'The opportunity presented itself.'

'And how did that go?'

'He said that they – the Russians – had created an annexe in London. He called it an anklav.'

'That's an interesting way of putting it.'

'He also said that life in Russia was complicated. Much had changed.'

'But he didn't say if he thought that was good or bad or why it was complicated for him particularly?'

'No.'

'Nothing about Russian troop movements?'

'No.'

'Go on.'

'He said they lived as privileged Russians in another beautiful country. The other reason he gave for being here was his daughter.'

'Is that all?'

'I think so. Oh, he told me the relationship between Russia and everywhere else in the world is complicated.'

'He's not wrong there.'

'I'm sure there is nothing else. Roger told me more about Volkov's life this morning than I think I learned last night. Did you know Volkov owns the house next door?'

'Yes, I did.'

'What about the one in Chester Row?'

'Yes, that one too. But it sounds as if I should have another word with Roger.'

'He thinks so. He says that you should go and buy more flowers. He's getting his information from Volkov's staff. Domestic life in Chateau Volkov sounds pretty strange, from what Roger says.'

'You're getting a good feel for this work, Felix.'

'What can I say? I'm an Arrow. So, what's next?'

'I'll go and buy some flowers, we'll look into Chester Row and the car accident, and I have one or two other things I'm working on. Meanwhile, you carry on with our Volkov programme and arrange for Ellie and Rani to deliver the miniature.'

CHAPTER
TWENTY-THREE

'Although we have no cameras or microphones inside Volkov's house, I can safely say we have good eyes on him, Eliza,' said Sir Bidian at their next meeting.

'Did the Volkov dinner party flush anything out?'

'Not really.'

'What about the dinner guests?'

'We ran checks on everyone. The other guests were all ex-pat Russians who left about the same time as Volkov. All are very wealthy. One owns a premier division football club.'

'And Maria?'

'The Treasury are all over her finances, and our Moscow people are digging into her past in Russia. We called the French police about her husband's death. There is an open verdict over the cause of the accident. The police questioned whether the brakes on his car might have been tampered with. But they have never found anything conclusive or a culprit, although they did question Maria. Otherwise, we're doing what we can at this end. But there's not much to go on yet. She lives quietly but grandly in a Kensington mansion with her adult son and a staff of about ten. Apart from her events with Volkov, she never seems to go out much – never to Harrods or the Knightsbridge restaurants favoured by many wealthy Russians in London. Apparently, she has an art collection to rival Volkov's.

'One thing that does concern me is that Maria was questioning Dimity about her jewels and where she got them from. I think your generous loan may have backfired a bit, Eliza. Dimity managed to laugh it off, but we should be extra vigilant and try not to encourage Mirova to be more inquisitive than she already is. If she has the right contacts, she could trace things back here. I'll have a word with West, Cairo and Frankie before I go and ensure they are on full alert.'

'They are always on full alert, Bidian.'

'I'm sure they are, but some good intel came from Roger Strand.'

'Now, why doesn't that surprise me?'

Bidian smiled. 'Strand mentioned a house in Chester Row. It's not directly owned by Volkov, but we traced the title through the Cayman Islands to an offshore company owned by Oliniya. There were all sorts of companies and blind trusts, and we had to call in a huge favour for the information.'

'Why so well hidden, do you think?' asked Eliza.

'I'm not sure. But it's a nice house – double fronted with two upper storeys and a basement.'

'So, how about Felix and Dimity?'

'Felix said Dimity was excellent at drawing out Volkov. I think they are cementing themselves into Volkov's outer circle. But I am sure they will never be in the inner one. Besides, Maria warned off Dimity in no uncertain terms about getting too close.'

'Well, we don't want Dimity and Felix in the inner circle. It would be far too close for their own good. They could easily find themselves in situations they can't handle. They're not trained for that sort of undercover work, Bidian.'

'I know, Eliza. We won't let them get in too deep.'

'I hope not. Now, what did Volkov say?'

'Volkov gently sounded Felix out on his political leanings.'

'Felix doesn't have any political leanings.'

'I know. I think he managed to convey that quite well.'

'Good. But are we any closer to finding out where Volkov's sympathies lie?'

'I'm afraid not. Felix said he remains neutral on the subject. He couldn't tell if he was for or against Putin. But he did say he thought Volkov was extremely proud of Mother Russia.'

'Well, I can't think Volkov leans towards the old Soviet regime. That would make no sense. But the question about Putin is an interesting one.'

'What do you mean?'

'If Volkov isn't for Putin, whom does he support? The only alternative is another leader – a regime change. I can't see that happening any time soon. But Volkov could be beginning to worry that Putin has become the nearest thing to a tsar for a hundred years.'

'But not a name on the Kremlin hit list?'

'For now, I can't think why he should be. Which leads me back to the stool pigeon theory.'

Sir Bidian sighed. 'We're going round in circles. Volkov might have been a fully paid-up member of the Putin squad, but is now wavering. There could be some, even in Moscow and perhaps working close to Putin, who are not so committed to the current Kremlin global strategy of superpower military buildup, territorial gains and even individual retribution.

Especially when so many of the people in the country are on or near the breadline. We are becoming seriously concerned about Putin's ambitions for Ukraine and indeed some, if not all, of the states that made up the Soviet Block. We think there must be some in the Kremlin who privately worry about this, too. I'm talking about Russians who may be prepared to do more than worry.'

'You don't mean a coup d'état?'

'No, but small, conscience-salving, single acts of personal rebellion that create the foundation of regime change.'

'That's an interesting hypothesis. Where does it come from?'

'It comes from the fact that the traffic we have been getting from our mole is becoming more frequent. Something is going on, and someone is warning us. And I'm still wondering about Nicolai Rykov.'

'You don't think the mole and he are connected, do you?'

'I'm not sure what to think.'

'Has there been another communication?'

'Another message arrived yesterday. It was in the same code as the previous one.'

'What was it?'

'It reads more like a sign-off. I wanted to ask you about it. It was sent by Mara, who referred to him or herself as "The Irish Friend".'

'The Irish friend? Do we have any Irish friends?'

'We do have one or two, but none in Moscow that we know about.'

'It seems to me there are a lot of people in Moscow we don't know about.'

'That might well be true. But what about this one?'

'The Irish friend is an interesting term. Apart from being

an innocent-sounding expression, it is a slight corruption of the phrase used by the Russians regarding their agreement to support and supply arms to the IRA. If you remember, it was called Plan for the Operation of a Shipment of Weapons to the Irish Friends.'

'Our mole used the definite article: it wasn't *an* Irish friend, but *the* Irish friend. So, who is that? A Russian? After all, it was originally a Russian phrase. Or is this person Irish? And if so, are they republican or loyalist? Or none of the above?' Sir Bidian said.

'I think the time is fast approaching when you should ask that question.'

'I agree. But there is something else. Inside the envelope, drawn in a corner, was a circle and possibly the faintest dot within it – although it is so faint it could be nothing. But what could the circle mean?'

Eliza thought for a while about spycraft, and about symbols and shapes. But the circle meant nothing to her. She thought of fieldcraft and everything she knew about messages and signals. Fields made her think of woods and woods made her think of people who spent time in them. Not farmers but perhaps gipsies or tinkers.

'Boy Scouts.'

'Sorry, Eliza?'

'Boy Scouts.'

'What about Boy Scouts?'

'Tracking messages: a circle of stones with a stone in the middle. It means gone or going home.'

'You think that is what it is?'

'I can't think what else it could be.'

'Occam's razor – the simplest explanation is usually the right one.'

'That's always a good place to start.'
'Could it be as simple as that?'
'Bidian, weren't you in the Boy Scouts?'
'Sadly, no.'
'Then you missed out on your backwoodsman badge.'
'A remarkable gap in my early education.'
'Evidently. But what is the greater message?'
'That's the sixty-four-thousand-dollar question, Bidian. 'If the message sender is Russian, then they wouldn't have gone home or want to go home. They are already home. Plus, I'm not sure if tracking was part of the Young Pioneers' training, as it was in the Boy Scouts. If the sender isn't Russian, then presumably they are getting their information from someone who is. So, is that information given freely, innocently or through force, blackmail or other coercion?

'We could be dealing with two people working together. Or one person gaining information from an unaware source.'

'Or someone being fed information,' Sir Bidian offered.

'From a Russian?'

'The permutations are many and varied.'

'Too many and too varied, I fear,' said Eliza. 'You will need to narrow the options. But it seems to me the first thing to find out is if your mole is a Russian or Irish double agent.'

'Or someone completely random?'

'Back to Occam's razor, Bidian. You ought to start there. But I am intrigued by the symbol. I wonder if this means our mole has gone home and we won't hear from them again, as he or she was signing off. Or does our mole want or mean to come home?'

'So, you think the symbol could be a request?'

'Possibly. Perhaps the mole is on their way home physically or has decided that is what he or she wants to do.'

THE ART DEPARTMENT

'Come in from the cold. Could that be it?'

'This matter could have just become far more complicated.'

'Yes, it could. Now we need to decide what to do with our mole.'

'Have you thought about how you are going to respond?'

'I have some ideas. But I also wanted to ask your opinion.'

'Well, we don't know with whom we are dealing. We could be being played. I think a non-committal but leading response would be best. In which case, I think I have a suggestion.'

CHAPTER
TWENTY-FOUR

'I bring this meeting to order,' said the woman at the head of the table in a loud and commanding voice.

Twelve eyes turned to Maria Mirova, and the room fell silent.

'We only have one item on the agenda this evening, and it is the matter of Kazimir Bezrodny.'

Yuri Volkov addressed the chair. 'Madam Secretary, are we to hope that we have now received final instructions from Moscow?'

'That is correct, Mr Vice Secretary.'

'Madam Secretary, will we be receiving friends from Moscow to carry out this operation?'

'No, Mr Vice Secretary, we will not.'

The twelve eyes narrowed.

'Then, Madam Secretary, may I ask what instructions we have received?'

'We have been told to go ahead with our chairman's wishes on our own.'

There followed a murmur of voices around the table.

'Silence, I will have silence,' said the chair sharply.

If she had possessed a gavel, she might have used it violently. As it was, she slammed the table with her open hand. A hush descended on the room once again.

'Madam Secretary, are we then given to believe that our chairman' – no one on the committee ever directly used the name of their ultimate leader – 'wants this committee to execute his plan on behalf of the department?'

'That is correct.'

'With great respect to you, Madam Secretary, and to our chairman, no one on our committee is trained for such a mission. We are businesspeople, here to support the department in an advisory, logistical and financial capacity.'

There was a whisper of agreement around the table.

'And with my greatest respect, Mr Vice Secretary, and speaking on behalf of our chairman, those are our orders. Bezrodny is now our "business". We will carry out our orders to the letter, regardless of the difficulty, the cost, or whether or not you or any other members of the committee find the mission distasteful. May I remind you of the price of disobeying our chairman's orders?'

None of the six other committee members questioned the authority or the ruthless commitment the secretary held for the chairman's and the department's aims. All of them had heard the rumour that Madam Secretary had tampered with the brakes of her husband's car. An alternative one was that she had drugged her husband before he drove his beloved classic 1952 navy Maserati Spyder along the torturous Corniche. Most committee members believed the third rumour, that she had done both, just to make sure the job was done properly. Madam Secretary's husband, it was generally accepted, had taken more than he gave in the national cause. It

THE ART DEPARTMENT

was generally held that a great deal of her husband's fortune had found its way to the Kremlin.

Now all eyes looked down at the table, Volkov's included. But none, it seemed to him, wanted to catch the eye of the secretary. No one was itching to carry out whatever task Madam Secretary had in mind.

There was an empty feeling in the pit of Volkov's stomach. It was he who had been chosen to visit Bridport ahead of the operation. He had been happy and eager to do so as an information-gathering exercise. It had turned out to be a great day out. But now he had the dreadful feeling he would be involved again, but to a much more sinister extent.

'Mr Vice Secretary?'

All eyes lifted from the table – five pairs in hope, one in concealed trepidation.

'Yes, Madam Secretary?'

'It is to you that this great honour falls.'

'Me, Madam Secretary?'

'Yes. You alone have been given the distinction of eliminating a traitor to the Motherland. You will become a hero of Russia – to those who know of such things.'

'That is indeed a distinction,' said Volkov, trying hard to look pleased. But he was far from pleased. He had no training for this work. Nor was it his inclination to do – what was the horrible expression? – "wet work". Volkov was a businessman not an assassin. He would only admit it to himself, but one of the reasons he hadn't signed up for the KGB after he left school was that he was squeamish. He knew many of his classmates went on to work for the agency, and one in particular, who liked the idea of dispensing anxiety, fear, pain and even death to enemies of the state. Volkov had no such desires.

The secretary continued. 'Our planners in the department

have come up with an excellent but simple scheme that only requires one committee member to carry it out successfully. The chairman thinks that because of Salisbury, someone already based in the UK should carry out the operation – someone disassociated with the Embassy and beyond reproach or suspicion. Then there is no danger of British immigration identifying operatives entering or leaving the country, as happened last time. Our chairman wants the world to know that no traitor is safe, wherever he or she cowers in the world. But he does not want another failure either. That would make Russia appear weak and disorganised. We are not weak or disorganised, are we?'

'No,' cried the rest of the committee. Volkov fancied most of them looked relieved that they had not been singled out for the task.

'Mr Vice Secretary?'

'Yes, Madam Secretary.'

'You will be given further orders. Remember, the reputation of this committee and Russia is at stake.'

'Thank you, Madam Secretary. May I ask when this operation must take place?'

'Our chairman wishes it to be carried out in seven weeks, when a sale of the contents of a large mansion not far from Bridport is to be held. The details are in the envelope. The sale is something in which you will be most interested, I imagine.'

'Undoubtedly, Madam Secretary.'

'Excellent, business with pleasure – or should that be pleasure with business? It gives you, Mr Vice Secretary, the perfect cover on the day. It also provides you with the chance to run through the plan beforehand, as there will be public viewings in the days leading up to it. The date of the sale also coincides with the weekly meeting of the Bridport Chess Society.'

'The target of our attention is a member of a chess society, Madam Secretary?'

'Need you ask that question?'

'No, Madam Secretary,' said Volkov, feeling both chastened and annoyed. He was not used to this level of subservience and felt alone and vulnerable.

'That concludes our meeting at Moscow House this evening,' the secretary said. She then rang a handbell and added, 'It only leaves me to wish our vice secretary success in his mission to eliminate the traitor. We will be behind him every step of the way.'

Volkov understood the hooded but literal meaning of this last remark.

The other committee members all wished Volkov well. A waiter came through a door and carried to the table a tray of small glasses and an opened bottle of vodka. He poured out seven measures. When he had gone, each committee member stood up and held his or her charged glass.

'Comrades, a toast – to Nemizeda,' said Madam Secretary.

The members of the committee raised their glasses and together said, 'To Nemizeda.' Then they all downed their vodkas in one.

Volkov looked at Maria, who seemed extremely pleased with herself.

He felt sick.

* * *

That morning, Róisín had received a question about an item she had put up for sale on the market. It meant there was a message for her at the dead drop. This was unusual. Communication was almost entirely outgoing from her, although there had been one or two exceptions over the years.

Róisín had designed her request carefully. She had enciphered a message containing Nicolai's warning about Volkov and written it on the inside of an envelope, as usual. Then she had pencil-drawn a tiny circle and put a hardly discernible dot within it. She hadn't wanted to send a normal coded request, so she whimsically used a Boy Scout tracking sign. It was an enormous risk, but one she felt she had to take. She wasn't sure if this was because she was frightened that the Russians might find her out or that she might receive a refusal. But at least this way she could always tell herself that the symbol hadn't been noticed or understood.

How she felt about passing on information given to her by Nicolai was a question Róisín had asked herself many times over the years. But as he had never discussed it and yet kept up the stream of intelligence, she felt he was complicit. She didn't have the same qualms about repeating confidences gleaned from Russian acquaintances. But since she and Nicolai had last met, she kept going back to something he said. She didn't know what he had meant by honesty, and she hadn't wanted to ask. Nor did she know why he had said there were ways of getting home 'for people like us'. The restaurant hadn't been the place to ask. Did he want her to go?

* * *

Volkov sat in the back of his black Mercedes-Benz limousine and raised the glass screen between the driver and passenger compartments. Whenever he felt cornered in life, he sought the comfort of a soft cocoon. He felt boxed in now and shrank into his deep leather seat. He didn't understand what had just happened. He usually had the ear of his business partner in Moscow. But lately, he had only been able to communicate with him through a business administrator. Now this. He knew the mission was a test. Perhaps it was also the cost of not readily agreeing to Maria Mirova's marriage proposal. But Volkov also knew it was time for him to pay his dues. He needed to return the debt he owed for all his success, riches and indulgences. He had expected to receive the bill sometime, just not in this currency.

He pulled a mobile phone from his pocket and dialled a number. 'Are you free this evening?' he asked. 'I need some company... in half an hour? Good. I will see you at the usual place.'

Tonight, he wanted to be with someone in whom he could confide – as much as he could confide in anyone these days. Volkov needed to talk to someone who would understand his mood.

He used to confide in his wife; that was, until his extramarital lifestyle embarrassed and angered her beyond breaking point. Most people assumed he was a widower. He found it useful for them to think so. Now his ex-wife lived in splendid isolation in his dacha outside Moscow – when she wasn't travelling the world in lavish style. He hadn't seen her for years, although he heard about her through Lizabeta.

The Mercedes weaved its way through the busy nighttime London traffic.

Volkov pressed the car's intercom button and said, 'Take me to the house in Chester Row.'

This smaller property gave Volkov some separation from his more public life in Eaton Square. Here, he could enjoy the other side of his existence – a life that was more difficult to live in Russia. In London, there were far more freedoms.

The front door opened without Volkov having to let himself in. A tall and slim young man with a sweep of blond hair welcomed him and closed the door behind him. 'I am expecting a guest soon,' Volkov said, before adding, 'Bring me vodka; I'll be in the drawing room.'

The house was exquisite, and like his main home, had been decorated by Tamerlan. But this interior leaned slightly more to the decorator's strong Persian influences than the house in Eaton Square. The air was thick with the smell of tuberose and pomegranate. Everywhere there were fresh flowers in the most beautiful cut-glass or ancient, Islamic-patterned ceramic vases.

Volkov went into the drawing room and sank into a comfortable sofa covered in plain yellow, linen velvet. Behind it, rising to the full height of the room, was a giant tapestry overhung with a pair of ornate, gilt-framed mirrors with candle sconces. On the floor was a vibrant rug based on a nineteenth-century Persian design. A large, glass-topped coffee table supported oversized volumes on art. Side tables, either covered in Suzani fabrics or left bare to expose beautifully grained wood or marble, held pretty dishes of candies and fruit. These were grouped with miniature bronzes, low piles of leather-bound books and marble busts or figurines. The lighting was low and subtle, but pinpointed beams of light were carefully directed for reading. Everything was to hand in a most comfortable way.

This house was another of Volkov's cocoons. Patterned fabrics balanced plain ones; beautiful objects were not restricted to one era or another but represented many different centuries, cultures and styles. All had beauty in common, and each object worked in perfect harmony with its neighbours.

Volkov heard the front doorbell ring and the soft step of the housekeeper crossing the marble-tiled floor to the front door. Moments later, he appeared at the drawing-room doorway and announced, 'Your guest has arrived, Mr Volkov.'

* * *

Róisín put on her warm outdoor clothing and began the journey to Kolomenskoye Park. It was what she termed an "iron day". The sky, the city, the people and even the mood were grey. There were too many days like these for her in Moscow now. She longed for the blue skies of springtime, when she felt uplifted by the weather. A vision of the Lakeland fells, complete with lambs and daffodils, flashed across her mind.

The Metro ride took just under an hour. Afterwards, Róisín caught a trolley bus down Andropova Avenue and, after several stops, got off, walked through a pedestrian subway under the busy dual carriageway and entered the park.

Although there were a few people about, the park felt empty and joyless, and the ravine seemed to have lost all its mystery.

She had made her decision. She didn't want to live out her last years in Moscow. It wasn't her city, nor was Russia her country. Age had caught up with her. She had considered the options and the dangers, and she still wanted to go home.

But she had no money to speak of and no passport. By land, the nearest boundary with Russia was Belarus, but the two countries were too closely aligned. Ukraine was also too much of a risk, especially considering the fast-gathering tensions with Russia. There was little about the troop build-up in the Russian media, but Róisín knew from chatter that there was cause for concern. She could go to Romania and then on to Turkey. But that was twelve hundred miles. If she had been thirty years younger, she might have tried, but not now. That left Estonia, Latvia or Finland.

The only money she did have outside Russia was hidden in a tin box buried beneath the stone floor of a barn in County Antrim. It wasn't much, although it could be a start. But first, she had to get there.

The only other options were to be sent home by the Russians or be brought in from the cold by another actor – whoever that may be. The first was fanciful thinking. As for the second, was she worth bringing home after all these years? Her communications continued to be accepted, which gave her a glimmer of hope that she was still considered of value. She knew being recovered was her only realistic chance of escape.

Assisted exfiltration would mean she might not need a passport or money. But it was still hazardous. Róisín knew that she couldn't expect Nicolai to help her. She wouldn't dream of asking him. It was more than his life was worth. Plus, if she were caught trying to escape, her future would be in prison, slaving at a sewing machine in a rat-infested, hellhole sweatshop for the remainder of her life. No, she was on her own – as she always had been.

Róisín came to the path that led to the boulder where she might find out her future.

She trudged on. It had stopped raining, but the drips from overhanging boughs soaked her hat and the shoulders of her coat. She walked carefully down the long flights of slippery

THE ART DEPARTMENT

wooden steps that reached the floor of the ravine. There was no one on the path to the stone.

The nearer Róisín got, the more nervous she became. For goodness' sake, she thought, after living on the edge for so long, why is this so different? She rounded the corner of the path. She could see the stone. She lifted her head and picked up her step, resolving to get a grip.

She was ten yards from her destination when a movement from the other side of the path made her start. A man, dressed in a fur hat, a thick scarf that covered his lower face and a heavy coat with its collar turned up, came out from behind a tree and walked towards her.

Róisín was caught off guard. She glanced at the man, who looked ominously official. Her blood ran cold.

At Chester Row, the housekeeper stepped away to reveal Volkov's guest.

'Oh, I am pleased you are here,' he said. 'I am so deeply pleased that you are here.'

'Of course, petal, you look as if you've had a bad day. Pour some vodka and tell Roger all about it.'

Róisín's head swam. 'Nicolai, what are you doing here?'

'I might ask you the same question.'

At least I am not at the dead drop, Róisín thought. She hadn't entirely been caught red-handed.

'I often come here,' she said. 'It is where I usually walk and think. What's your reason, Nicolai?'

'I wanted to talk to you.'

'How did you know I would be here?'

'Because this is where you usually walk.'

'You know about that?'

'Yes, and more.'

'Nicolai—'

'Let me stop you there, Róisín.' Nicolai took a hand from his pocket and held out a crumpled envelope. 'I think you are here for this.'

Róisín's heart sank. 'Litter?' she said, struggling for composure.

'Ah, so you come here to exchange litter?'

Róisín knew the game was up. 'Is this what you meant by honesty?'

'Yes, it was. You have never been totally honest with me.'

'Nor you with me, it seems.'

'No,' Nicolai replied with a nod.

'I was honest with you – about you,' Róisín said.

'I know. As I was about you.'

'But why did you keep telling me things you shouldn't?'

'Don't you know?'

Róisín frowned. 'Because you wanted me to know those things?'

'It started when I needed to know more about you. All the IRA people who came here were under scrutiny. But you were different from the others. The others were just killers, but your connections were with the IRA high command. Even then, I suspected you might not be all you seemed. That made you not just a double agent, but once you were in Russia, possibly a triple agent. I was impressed.'

'Then why didn't you do something?'

'I did. I shielded you.'

'Why?'

'I thought I could be as useful to you as you could be to me – as a channel.'

'But you didn't tell anyone else?'

'No.'

'That was very dangerous. It amounts to treason. It makes you a spy.'

'I know.'

'So why?'

'Apart from our relationship, I needed a conduit.'

'For what?'

'For occasional information I wanted to share. Róisín, I love Russia, but I do not agree with some things that are happening in her name.'

'Do you know what you are saying?'

'What I am saying makes us equal. It makes us reliant on one another. You want to go home, but I still need a channel. And because I am the only one who can help you.'

'It looks like we will have to trust each other.' Róisín looked searchingly at Nicolai and added, 'How long have you known?'

'Almost from the beginning.'

'Yet you entered into an affair with me?'

'I fell in love with you.'

Róisín exhaled. 'So, what now?'

'First, I think you should open the envelope.'

'Why didn't you let me collect it myself?'

'Because that would have been cruel to a friend.'

'Do you know what's inside?'

'No.'

'You haven't looked?'

'No. I thought I would wait for you.'

'How did you know I was coming here today?'

'I didn't. I followed you.'

'You've followed me before?'

'Yes. Shall we see what's inside the envelope?'

Nicolai handed her the crumpled object.

Róisín, numbed by the past few minutes, grasped the envelope, straightened it and peered inside for a message.

She stared at three characters: q, o and p. They made no sense to her. She turned the envelope upside down. Now the characters read d, o and b, which made no sense either. She handed the envelope back to Nicolai.

'What does this mean?' he asked.

'I genuinely have no idea.'

As she was hit by a wave of disappointment, Nicolai put his arms around her and held her for a while. Eventually, he said, 'What are you thinking?'

'I don't know. Perhaps it's not worth recovering me.'

'That is not correct.'

'You think so?'

'I know so. But first of all, I should get you back home.'

He handed the envelope back to Róisín. 'Come, let's go to the car. It's starting to rain again.'

They travelled back mostly in silence. Nicolai dropped Róisín off at a Metro station two stops from her flat.

'We will find a way,' was all he said as she got out of the car.

After arriving home, changing out of her wet clothes and making a cup of tea, Róisín laid out the envelope on her kitchen table. She sat down and inspected the inside again.

She spent the evening trying to work out what the marks meant and applying all the cryptology knowledge she had. Still, she was no nearer to any understanding. Finally, mentally exhausted, she went to bed and eventually fell asleep.

It was in the early hours of the morning that she woke with a start and sat up. Something had prodded her mind: dob. It made no sense, but it was nevertheless nagging at her. Dob, why was that familiar? What went with dob? Suddenly, she laughed out loud. How stupid of her. Dyb – dyb – dyb – dyb; dob – dob – dob – dob. Someone had a sense of humour. She had sent a Boy Scouts' tracking symbol as an exfiltration request, and they had sent back the Cub Scouts' motto, DOB – Do Our Best. A shiver went down her spine; a shiver that came from reprieve and knowing that somebody, somewhere, thought as she did. She had a friend, but who?

CHAPTER
TWENTY-FIVE

'What on earth has happened?' Felix asked. It was nine o'clock in the morning, and he had answered the prolonged buzzer of the entry phone.

Roger Strand arrived upstairs looking somewhat shellshocked and unshaven. Not fashionably, stubbly unshaven, but unshowered, been-up-or-out-all-night unshaven.

'Coffee,' Roger demanded.

'Who is it?' Dimity called from the bedroom.

'It's Roger.'

'Good morning, darling,' Roger said to Dimity as she entered the room. 'I must say, you look particularly priestly this morning. A good thing too; I have a confession.'

'You look as if you haven't slept,' Dimity said.

'After the night I've just had, I should say so. I've just spent it with someone of particular interest. It was wonderful in a way, and I must say very enlightening.'

'Oh, that's more like it, Roger. Are you going to tell us who it was?'

Felix could see Dimity was agog for some salacious news. At times and at odds with her vocation, Felix often thought his wife could happily follow the calling of a sleaze-hungry newspaper reporter.

'Was it scandalous? A film star, royalty or a politician? Perhaps more than one politician?'

'Darling, that's not scandalous, that's normal.'

Dimity laughed. 'I stand corrected, Roger. But who was it?'

'Are you sitting down?'

'You can see we are. Come on, Roger, who was it?'

'Yuri Volkov.'

'Yuri Volkov?' Felix and Dimity repeated in unison.

'The very same.'

'Where were you?'

'At his beautiful Chester Row house. It smells of roses.'

'I didn't know Yuri was gay,' said Felix. 'When did you find out?'

'I had my suspicion – the old gaydar, you know. It all started a few weeks ago. I was seeing to the flowers in Eaton Square. My florist, who usually works there, was off sick. We are supposed to be discreet, but Yuri came into the room where I was working, and we just began talking. Talking led to drinks and drinks led to supper. It was nice, but nothing happened. I should be too old for him, and he should be far too old for me. But we sort of hit it off. He's quite a shy man, really, and I'm, well, me. I thought it was a one off, a bit of bicuriosity on his part. But we've seen each other on a few occasions since. Nothing was said, but I think we both knew it was heading upstairs.'

'You never said anything,' said Felix.

'There was nothing to tell until last night. It was none of anyone else's business. But now I need to tell someone. Now it *is* someone else's business. Not about whatever is or is not going on between Yuri and me so much, but what was said. I need to see the Savile Row suit.'

Felix could tell this was important. He picked up his phone and dialled Sir Bidian, who answered within six rings.

'Hello, Felix.'

'Bidian, Dimity and I are at our flat with Roger. He has some news – about Volkov. He says it won't wait.'

'I'm in the car, on the way to the office. I could stop by.'

'I think that would be best.'

'Good. Then I will see you in twenty minutes or so.'

Felix clicked off and said, 'He'll be here soon. We'd better give you that coffee, Roger.'

'And you might like to freshen up and wash away any vestiges of last night's pleasure,' suggested Dimity.

Roger laughed. 'You are a very naughty priest – something which I imagine Felix is extremely pleased about.'

'I know he is,' said Dimity.

A short while later, Felix answered the entry buzzer for the second time that morning.

'This sounds urgent,' Sir Bidian said. 'What's going on?'

'Roger will explain. Come on up.'

Dimity gave Sir Bidian a cup of coffee. 'Do you want us to go?' she asked.

'Not if Roger doesn't mind,' Sir Bidian replied.

Roger looked at Dimity and said teasingly, 'Recently, I seem to be as up to date with their goings-on as they are with mine, so I don't mind if no one else does.'

'Well, you'd better get on with it then,' Sir Bidian said impatiently.

Roger explained how he had received a call inviting him to

Chester Row. He then gave a rundown of the night, omitting only the more intimate details.

'So, would you say Volkov was highly agitated?' Sir Bidian asked.

'I would say he was very agitated indeed. When he called me from the car, he sounded distraught. I think he had been to some sort of meeting. His driver brought me back this morning and told me he had been in Fitzrovia the evening before.

'As the night went on and Yuri drank more vodka, he gave more away. He stayed sober enough not to disclose any real details, but he said enough.'

'Such as?' Sir Bidian asked.

'He said he wished he had never become involved, but there was nothing he could do. He said he was trapped – no, cornered was the actual word he used. He said he felt lonely and isolated. That was why he called me.'

'What else?' coaxed Sir Bidian.

'He said he couldn't reach one of his business colleagues in Moscow. Oh, and at one point in the middle of the night, he was saying something about "that bloody woman". He said he hated her but couldn't do anything.'

'What did you take that to mean?'

'I'm not sure. That Yuri felt he was being coerced, pushed into something he didn't agree with, perhaps. At one point, I think I heard him crying, but I can't be too sure. It was all rather intense. But I needn't go into that,' Roger added.

'Did you get the name of the woman Volkov was talking about?' asked Sir Bidian.

'No, I didn't. Look, was I wrong getting involved with Yuri, under the circumstances?'

Sir Bidian thought for a moment and then said, 'I'm sure it

THE ART DEPARTMENT

just happened, as these things sometimes do. But you should have said something before. As it is, the circumstances are beginning to look critical. I can't deny that this new situation could be a useful step forward for us, but it's a dangerous one for you. I have to say, I hadn't expected our assimilation programme to be quite as personal as this. Actions have consequences, and I have to ask, Roger, how much of a compromising position does this put you in with Volkov now?'

'I have thought about that. I have had a long night to think about it. I like Yuri. He has a ruthless side, but I suppose you don't get to be one of the richest men in the world without a streak of ruthlessness. However, and I could be wrong, I think he is, at heart, a good man. But now he seems to be on a bit of a sticky wicket.'

'And what about you... emotionally?' Sir Bidian asked.

'I know he is outrageously wealthy, and we live in totally different worlds, but I understand his desires and proclivities, and we do get on surprisingly well. I think I can continue this because I want to try and help him out of whatever scrape he is in.'

'Scrape might be rather an understatement, Roger.'

'I want to know what sort of trouble Yuri has got himself into. Perhaps I could press him carefully and gently question his domestic staff – if he keeps me around long enough.'

'You could, but you would possibly be putting yourself in harm's way,' Sir Bidian said. 'This matter is escalating dangerously, and we may not be able to protect you all the time.'

'Oh, I think I can handle it. It wouldn't be the first time,' said Roger.

'This is serious,' Sir Bidian replied. 'I don't want you getting out of your depth. There could be some very nasty people involved. The consequences of being discovered could be extremely unpleasant, and that's putting it mildly.'

'I know, or I think I know. But I don't think Yuri is dangerous; he doesn't seem the type. Maybe others are. I think we can help him. That's why I want to continue.'

'You really like this man, Roger,' Dimity said.

'Yes, I do. More than anyone for a very long time.'

'Personally, I have found Yuri perfectly nice,' said Dimity.

'Me too,' said Felix.

'And I've met terrorists who were seemingly nice on the surface – before they sent someone in a suicide vest to kill hundreds of innocent people,' Sir Bidian said pointedly. 'And what if you find out Volkov is not all that you think he is?'

'Very few people are,' said Roger.

Sir Bidian laughed. 'Roger, you're a philosopher.'

'I'm a florist, what's the difference?'

'But will you be able to help us if you find out it may harm Yuri?'

'Call me an old romantic, but I don't think this action will harm him. Something else could, though. If I can help, then that is what I want to do.'

'OK, Roger, follow your instincts and let us know each step. I am going to put a small team on this to support you, and I will give you fresh contact details, especially if there is an emergency and you need assistance. We will give you a special secure mobile phone as well.'

'Then I'm on the team?'

'I rather think you are.'

'I don't have a special secure mobile phone,' said Felix dryly.

'You're not sleeping with Volkov,' replied Sir Bidian.

THE ART DEPARTMENT

'And nor are you going to,' said Dimity. 'You can have a new phone for sleeping with me.'

'Sounds good to me,' said Felix, brightening.

'Look, I want you all to know that whatever this is with Yuri and me, it isn't a big thing at the moment,' said Roger. 'It may never be a big thing. It's a gay thing. Yuri has his own life, and I have mine. We live in very different worlds. He works in the oil business, and I work in the flower business. He has no budget, and I work on the tightest of margins. We are two gay men of a certain age in a group obsessed with youth. We have our appetites. We are promiscuous or have been. But I harm no one, and I don't believe Yuri does either – consenting adults, that sort of thing. You might think it sad. If so, I agree with you. Being gay sometimes is sad. Especially when forgoing the companionship of an amiable and supportive mature partner for a hot one-night stand. But I think my days and nights of debauchery in Ibiza – and London for that matter – are behind me. And I think they are for Yuri.'

'Roger, I've never heard you speak like this,' said Dimity.

'I'm a gay man, flower. I am very emotional, and I think about these things deeply, but I don't often talk about them. I have regrets, like not having a family, but mostly, for the sake of sanity, I try and ignore all those thoughts and get on with my life.'

'So, what's happened?' Dimity asked.

'What has happened is that I have met a man, roughly my age, who is not only at the same stage of life but is asking the same questions and realising there are things that may have to – or should – change. What has happened is that Yuri and I like each other – and he's not so bad for his age.'

'Do you think you have found a soulmate?' asked Dimity.

'Don't even go there, petal. Yuri was not part of my plan.

Especially given he doesn't look like a twenty-year-old Greek god and is being pursued by MI6.'

'So, I come back to my original question, Roger,' Sir Bidian said. 'How will you feel if Volkov turns out *not* to be the person you thought or hoped he would be?'

Roger thought for a moment. 'Yuri will have to take his chances. If he wants to live here in the UK, then he must play by UK rules. If he doesn't want to do that, then I don't want anything to do with him. He will have to suffer the consequences.'

'And you can carry this through without warning Volkov or interfering with our surveillance?' Sir Bidian asked.

'If you haven't noticed, Sir B, *I* am your surveillance. But I believe I can see this through. It's for the greater good, whichever way you look at it. Now, if you have all you need, I'd better get back to work. Flowers don't arrange themselves, you know.'

Felix showed Roger out and went back to Dimity and Sir Bidian.

'What do you make of that?' he asked them.

'I think it changes some things but not others,' said Sir Bidian. 'Perhaps Volkov is not so much of a threat here. Our surveillance might have led us to the real truth. But, as it stands, he is still part of the overall danger.'

'So, what will you do?' asked Felix.

'We must start with what Volkov said to Roger about "that bloody woman".'

'Who's that, do you imagine?' said Dimity.

'I think we know her,' replied Felix slowly.

'I think you do,' said Sir Bidian. 'Mrs Mirova.'

CHAPTER
TWENTY-SIX

'We have just received another communication from the dead drop following the DOB message,' said Sir Bidian to Eliza over the phone.

'What was it?'

'All it said was "six men".'

'And that was it?'

'Yes. Have you any idea what that means?'

Eliza thought for a moment, then laughed and said, 'The only six men I know in this context are all honest serving men. It's Kipling – "I keep six honest serving-men, they taught me all I knew. Their names are What and Why and When and How and Where and Who".'

'As simple as that?'

'As simple as that. To me, it's a clear confirmation that Mara wants to come in, although I'm not sure how you exfiltrate someone you don't know, especially when one's not quite clear whose mole this is anyway.'

'I'm not sure either, but the mole has to be ours.'

'So, how are you going to find out who it is?'

'Not without great difficulty.'

'Why?'

'Because our Irish friend will ask if we want personal details or foreign intelligence. I would.'

'Foreign intelligence,' said Eliza emphatically.

'Quite so.'

'But that means springing an unknown. If it all went badly wrong, goodness knows what fox you could let into the hen house.'

'I know, which is why I would value your thoughts.'

'Well, a false passport is out of the question by the sounds of it – at least until you know with whom you are dealing. From the start, to stop any intelligence contamination, you are going to have to contain and isolate. But you are also going to have to find out whether you are dealing with a male or a female, and I think you ought to establish exactly how long in the tooth this mole is – if only for logistical reasons. That will determine if it should be a soft or a hard exfiltration. It's no good setting up a cross-country extraction for someone who can't climb a short flight of stairs without having a heart attack. How hot will the mole be? Is there a chance they are under suspicion or surveillance? So, if it were me, I'd say no gender, no age, no deal. I should also ask about hobbies and interests. That will possibly help you get a cover organised if you need it, which you probably will. But then I shouldn't need to tell you any of that with your training,' Eliza added with a smile.

Sir Bidian returned the gesture and said, 'It seems a lot of work when we have no real idea of what we are getting.'

'Oh, I don't know, Bidian, when one thinks about it, the debrief alone could be very valuable.'

Sir Bidian sighed and took out a notebook. 'I'm sure you

are right, Eliza. You usually are. But I think we should at least ask some questions through eBay first. It will be quicker to find answers that way, and it could give us something to go on.

'I've been thinking about what questions to ask, such as how old is the item? Is it collection only?'

'We are happy to pay for express delivery. Do you prefer first- or second-class post?' Eliza added with a smile.

'In what sort of condition is the item?' Sir Bidian said.

Eliza laughed. 'Does it come in pink or blue?'

'Will there be a guarantee?' Sir Bidian suggested, also warming to the theme.

'Are there any other details about the item – imperfections, etc?' Eliza added.

'Will there be any import/export documents required for onward shipping? There, that should do it for the time being,' Sir Bidian said. 'I'll get our Russian desk to translate and send the questions... unless you want to translate them, Eliza?'

'Gosh, no, my Russian is far too rusty. I haven't used it for years.'

'I'm sure it is more than serviceable,' Sir Bidian replied.

* * *

Several days after the meeting between Eliza and Sir Bidian, Róisín logged on to eBay to find a message from a buyer. She read the list of questions with mounting excitement.

Is it collection only?

No, I can ship easily to the export representative, Róisín typed in reply.

How old is the item?

About seventy years.

Do you prefer first- or second-class post?

I prefer first class.

In what sort of condition is the item?

Róisín smiled to herself and typed, Good for age.

Does the item come in pink or blue?

Róisín laughed out loud. There seemed to be two people asking these questions: one was business-like, the other more light-hearted – perhaps the person who thought of using the Boy Scout tracking sign and understood who the six men were. Róisín hesitated. In all these years, she had avoided giving away her gender for security reasons. Now she answered pink.

Will there be a guarantee?

The item will have to be accepted sight unseen and as per the description.

Will there be any import/export documents required?

No export documents. Buyer will need to supply import documentation.

Are there any other details about the item – imperfections, etc?

The item has the usual imperfections for age and will need to be handled carefully, Róisín typed in reply with a grin.

Any concerns that these questions were anything other than genuine were almost dispelled. They might have been asked in perfectly written Russian, but one thing seemed clear: the humour certainly wasn't Slavic.

* * *

Sir Bidian called Eliza. 'We have heard from our Irish friend.'

'Good. What do you have?'

'Well, in answer to the pink or blue question, it was pink, and the age given is around seventy.'

'So, female. But she's a bit long in the tooth to do this sort of thing – unless it's a spy swap.'

'Which it won't be. That could take years. Our friend intimates that she can get herself to a point, but has no passport.'

'What about the question on imperfections?'

Sir Bidian laughed and said, 'Mara responded, "The usual imperfections for age. Will need to be handled carefully".'

'Ha, I think I like this woman, whoever she is. Even at what must be a stressful and dangerous time, she displays a sense of humour. That's an encouraging sign, I always think, don't you? It shows a certain confidence,' said Eliza. 'I admire that. Did Mara offer any form of assurances?'

'No.'

'That is all well and good, but you should have something.'

'I agree,' Sir Bidian said, 'but I think we will have to ask for that through the dead drop. We can't overuse the eBay route.'

'So, what do you think about exfiltration, now that you know all this?' Eliza asked.

'I had a word with the planning department. Basically, any remote border crossing is out of the question on account of the age of the package. And any derring-do, snatch or smuggle-and-run stuff is risky for the same reason. As far as I can tell from her replies, there doesn't seem to be any suspicion or surveillance, which means the package isn't hot. What do you think, Eliza?'

'Well, that's a help. The package, as you put it, seems to be at an age where she would prefer to be comfortable, I imagine, rather than packed into the boot of a car, as I had to do with Bezrodny. She doesn't seem to be in imminent danger, and there appears to be no issue with time, so you could use a slow extraction.'

'That's what planning thought. They suggested we ask Mara where she goes for sea and sand holidays.'

* * *

Two weeks later, Sir Bidian called Eliza again.

'We've had something from the dead drop. Mara likes Russian literature and art and goes to the Black Sea for her holidays.'

'That could help things along,' said Eliza. 'What about a guarantee?'

'That was interesting. We got back, "Be not inhospitable to strangers, lest they be angels in disguise".'

'That is vaguely familiar, where do I know that from?'

'It's WB Yeats, but a variation of a biblical passage.'

'Of course. Yeats, Irish, Republican... beautiful. But I've been thinking, if Mara was IRA and had changed allegiance, would that be so bad?'

'What do you mean?'

'Well, she's been sending us good and useful intelligence all these years. If she had anything to do with the IRA, she might still give us some useful information. Perhaps it might answer some lingering questions we have from the Troubles. With the IRA disbanded, it's not as though she could stir up much trouble – especially with you breathing down her neck, Bidian.'

'I know what you mean, Eliza. So, you agree with me that we should take the risk?'

'I think you have more to gain than lose.'

'That's what I thought. Now, as we have the holiday hot spot question answered, and we know Mara's interests, we can let planning come up with a scheme.'

'One other thing, Bidian. Have you heard anything more about Mrs Mirova and her digging?'

'No, all quiet on that front.'

CHAPTER
TWENTY-SEVEN

'It'll be a cruise ship – that's how they'll take you out,' said Nicolai.

Róisín and her former lover were sitting together in a dirty, noisy basement bar in Moscow's unfashionable Basmanny district. It was the sort of place in which, Nicolai had assured Róisín, no government employee would be seen dead.

'They can't fly you out of Russia. You don't have a passport, and it would be too dangerous for you to use a false one – even I can't help you with that.'

'I wouldn't expect you to. And you're right, if I went for a black market passport, it might not pass inspection, and that really would be the end. You wouldn't be able to help me then either.'

'But this sounds like an interesting plan. You told them you visit the Black Sea coast. If you're not going out by air – and Sochi or similar isn't exactly on the road to anywhere – then it must be by boat – ship.'

'I can't see me being picked up in a submarine, can you?'

'I hardly think so. And it doesn't sound as if it would be a merchant ship. You did ask for first class, after all. That leaves a cruise liner. Many stop off in Sochi while sailing the Black Sea in the summer months.'

'I wonder how they would get me on board.'

'I'm sure they will have worked that out. The plan sounds – what is your word?'

'Ingenious?'

'Yes, ingenious. If it is to be a cruise ship, they sail around the Black Sea to and from Istanbul. It will be a British-registered one, I imagine. Once you are on board – with nowhere to run – MI6 have four or five days to interrogate you. If they are satisfied, they can organise a passport and your onward journey. If not, they will send you back to Russia or—'

'Feed me to the fishes.'

'There is always that,' Nicolai agreed with a grin.

'I don't know why *you're* smiling; you're not the one doing this,' Róisín said.

'I am sure it won't come to that. It is a good plan. If our authorities discover that you have fled, which I don't think they will, as I'm the only one watching you, they will have to find you and then stop, board and search a foreign vessel, possibly outside Russian territorial waters, and risk an international incident. Even then, MI6 will have worked out where they will hide you in an emergency.'

'So, you think I'll have to get to the Black Sea?'

'That would be my guess. Perhaps it's time for you to take a holiday in the sun.'

'I wonder how long I will have to wait.'

'Possibly only until there is a suitable ship docking in Sochi or similar.'

'If it all goes horribly wrong, I'll be thrown in the gulags. I'd be a lot safer staying here.'

'When were you last safe, Róisín?'
'Over fifty years ago.'

* * *

Five weeks later, Róisín sat with Nicolai in his car, which was parked on a side road outside the airport. She had with her a medium-sized, cheap suitcase that held the only belongings she had to take with her. There weren't many things to show for all her years in Moscow, she had thought as she packed.

'I want you to have this, Nicolai,' she said, handing him a neatly wrapped parcel.

'What is it?'

'Well, you gave me Russian literature. Now I'm giving you Irish literature. Do open it, please.'

Nicolai carefully unwrapped the gift.

'It's Yeats,' said Róisín. 'But it's in Russian. It's the only work by him in your language. Only twenty of these handmade copies were produced. The poems are about love, life and death. I think Yeats speaks to Russians just as we have spoken to each other. I will never forget you, Nicolai.'

'Thank you, Róisín. I will treasure it, and I will never forget you either. But how can I? It is our destiny not to forget each other.'

'Will you forgive me?'

'Forgive you for what?'

'There are things I haven't told you. Things I can't tell anyone.'

'I know. Or rather, I don't know. But I think I understand.'

'You have never asked difficult questions. Why not?'

'Would you have told me?' Nicolai asked, smiling. 'I would only have been asking you to lie to me. You are very good at lying, Róisín. I think I know the world's best spy that no one has ever heard of – even her own people, it seems.' Nicolai laughed and added, 'That is real talent. Now, before you go, my little enigma, I have two things for *you*.'

Nicolai handed Róisín a small package. 'Don't open it now. Hide it well somewhere and only unwrap it after you've reached Sochi. You do not want anyone to discover it. It is not as romantic as your present to me, but it might be useful. The other gift is a name.'

'What name?'

'Moscow House. It's in London.'

'What is it?'

'Just a name for someone to investigate. Take it with you, as it might come in useful, along with my other gift. Now, we need to leave, Róisín. You must go and find your home, your peace and your happiness. Just don't forget to write.'

Róisín laughed. 'You too, Nicolai. Shall we use the old address?'

'I don't see why not for the time being. Then we may figure out something more in the moment. But for now, I will have a walk through the ravine with good memories to keep me company.'

'And I can imagine you there,' said Róisín,

'And where should I imagine you being?' Nicolai asked, raising an eyebrow.

'Ah, well, that comes under the title of difficult questions,' Róisín replied.

* * *

Róisín caught her flight. It was only ninety minutes late taking off, and the plane landed in Sochi about two and a half hours later. She took a bus rather than a taxi to the centre of town, then another bus to a stop by a block of self-catering holiday apartments, where she had reserved a second-floor unit for three nights. Along the route, she could see the cruise ships docked in the port area. That evening, they would continue their journeys. Tomorrow, other ships would arrive, and one of those could be carrying her from Russia to a different future.

Róisín had stayed in these apartments on several occasions while holidaying in Sochi. As far as she knew, there was nothing to draw her to anyone's attention, and she would make sure it stayed that way. She had already paid for the apartment in full. She wasn't sure how long she'd be staying, and to allay suspicion, she had told the property manager she might be called back to Moscow at any time on urgent business. She didn't want anyone asking awkward questions, but if the process took a few days longer, she would either stay on for more nights at the apartment or make alternative arrangements.

The style and decoration of the flat hadn't changed since Róisín was last there. The principal colour scheme was red and white. There was a kitchen/dining area, a sitting room and a shower room. The bedroom, with its beige wallpaper, carpet and quilted bed cover, gave the only respite from the strawberries-and-cream palette. Off the living area, a narrow balcony, just large enough for two plastic chairs and a table, gave a partial view alongside the building and through a forest of cypress trees and tower cranes to the sea.

Róisín arranged her clothes and sorted through her other belongings. From the lining of her case, she withdrew the small package that Nicolai had given her. She took a kitchen knife to the sealing tape and sliced open the wrapping. She took out a small, worn, black leather identity wallet and opened it. She stared in amazement at the photograph in a laminated card. The picture was of her, but the identity was not. This woman was called Svetlana Navka, and she held the rank of colonel in the Federal Security Service. This was such a precious gift, Róisín thought. Within Russia, it was more valuable than a passport. But it was also a death warrant if she were to be caught.

The following morning, Róisín had a pre-arranged meeting in a beachfront café. She had been given a four-line identity routine to follow, in which she was told to wear holiday clothes and carry the latest issue of Russian *Vogue*. Her handler would have a Leica camera around his neck. For the first time, Róisín allowed herself a tinge of hope. She wondered if she was at last going back.

* * *

Wearing a floral sundress, sandals, a woven straw hat and sunglasses, all of which she had bought online, Róisín sauntered along the beachfront. A raffia bag with jaunty blue-and-yellow stripes hung from her shoulder.

Stopping outside various cafes, she affected an inspection of the menus on display. Finally, she found the café she was looking for. Speaking in English free from any Russian accent, she asked a bored-looking waiter standing by the street entrance if she could have an outside table for two.

At eleven o'clock precisely, a tall man walked up to Róisín's table and sat down. Róisín thought he looked about her age – that was clever, she thought; they had sent someone she could identify with. He was casually but elegantly dressed in worn but polished tan deck shoes, beige chinos and a loose, perfectly ironed blue linen shirt. A Leica camera hung from his neck. He wore no hat, and his hair was a well-cut, distinguished silver-grey. He looked as if he had just walked off a cruise ship.

'I nearly didn't make it, I almost missed the bus,' the man said.

'Then I would have had to go on without you,' Róisín responded, as she had been instructed.

'That would have been a shame.'

'Yes, you would have missed the Sochi Arboretum.'

'It's good to meet you, Mara. My name is David.'

Róisín was in no doubt whatsoever that this man's name was not David, any more than she was called Mara – or Róisín for that matter.

'All being well, I'm here to escort you home.'

'All being well?'

'First, we should like to know some details.'

'Such as?'

'When you came here and where you came from.'

'Came to Russia or Sochi?'

A look of impatience crossed the man's face. 'Russia.'

'I've already said I won't reveal that until I'm far away from here.'

The man sighed. 'What about your source?'

'My sources,' corrected Róisín. 'My answer is the same as the last one, and even then, I will need certain assurances.'

'You're not in much of a bargaining position. Not telling me might jeopardise getting home.'

'Then I have a return ticket to Moscow, and the flow of interesting information stops. I have given up plenty over the years. Is this all the thanks I'm going to get?'

'We have to be sure.'

'So do I.'

The man nodded.

The waiter finally arrived to take their order. 'Coffee with hot milk and a glass of orange juice, please,' Róisín said.

'I'll have the same, please,' said the man.

When the waiter had left, Róisín said, 'So, what's the plan, David?'

'Once I have the go-ahead, you are going on a voyage. You did ask for first class.'

'I did.'

'You are taking the homeward leg of a Black Sea cruise.'

'I guessed as much. To Istanbul?'

'No, Piraeus, Greece. It's safer than Turkey.'

Róisín nodded. 'And you get longer to interrogate me.'

'To get to know you.'

'And then?'

'Either direct to London Heathrow on a commercial flight or indirectly via Cyprus on an RAF flight to Northolt or Brize Norton. It will depend on the paperwork and how we get on.'

'What about getting me on board the ship?'

'There are two issues. The first is entering the port area. We must get you past the immigration people without a passport. Then there is the ship. We have some control over that, but not so much if there are more immigration people by the gangplank.'

'It sounds a bit hit and miss to me.'

'The alternatives would not have been first class. You will join the chef and his team, collecting some fresh produce, and taking it back to the ship. The security is usually heavier for the passengers than for the ships' crews, who come and go all the time. For the crews, security is more casual, and corners are often cut. The locals appreciate the business the ships bring. It's good for the economy, and they like euros.'

'Do I have a cover story on the ship?'

'Yes. You are a specialist in Russian art and will be lecturing on that subject to the passengers tomorrow night in the theatre.'

'So, no pressure there, then?'

'We assumed it would be OK with you.'

'You assumed. Wasn't that rash?'

'Won't it be OK?'

'It will be fine.'

'Sadly, the previous lecturer came down with food poisoning and had to stay in Batumi in Georgia – the ship's last stop before Sochi. But I understand she has made a full recovery. Now she is looking forward to an exhilarating performance of Georgian song and dance by the State Assembly. Not to mention a fortnight's all-expenses paid stay in a five-star hotel with a great pool and restaurants until the next ship picks her up.'

Róisín relaxed a little. 'Who would want to miss music and dance from the State Assembly?'

'Indeed,' said the man, with the briefest smile.

The waiter arrived with the coffee and orange juice.

'Where and when do we next meet?' Róisín asked.

'Take any baggage you have to the Ostrova Hotel. I take it you are travelling light?'

Róisín nodded.

'Be there at the front at five o'clock precisely. You will be picked up in a minibus. I'll be there. Is there anything else you want or need to know at this stage?'

'No. What do we do now?'

'Talk about the weather while we have our drinks and then go our separate ways.'

* * *

Róisín changed into white trousers, navy slip-on shoes and a navy jacket. It was the type of outfit she wore to work at the gallery in the summer months – age-appropriate and respectful of her audience, but relaxed and casual enough in a warm climate and arty environment. This, she judged, would be a suitable look for the hours ahead before the ship left port.

Avoiding the main desk at her apartment block, she slipped out of a side door and, trailing her wheeled suitcase behind her, walked for ten minutes to the Ostrova Hotel. At five o'clock, she handed her case to one of the passengers of a white minibus that drew up in front of the hotel. She climbed inside. Besides the driver, there were five other occupants. One of them was David, who introduced her as the replacement lecturer.

'Let me give you this,' he said to Róisín. 'It's a boarding pass. You won't get onto the ship without it.'

The minibus reached the service entry road to the port with ease, but came to a halt in a long line of traffic.

'I wonder what is going on here,' said David.

'It looks like spot check by our border force.'

'Is that normal here?'

Róisín could hear the slight concern in David's voice.

'Not so much here at service entrance, but they like to flex muscle every month or two,' said the driver.

'Could you go and check, please? We don't have much time. The ship will be leaving soon.'

The driver shrugged, got out of the van and walked quickly in the direction of the security gates.

'This doesn't feel good,' whispered Róisín.

'No, I thought we would be waved through. I'm told that is what usually happens.'

'Well, it isn't happening today,' snapped Róisín.

'Not by the looks of it.'

'Let me out here,' demanded Róisín in an urgent whisper. 'I can't take the risk of being caught in the minibus.'

'I can't let you out now,' said David.

But Róisín had already slid back the side door and was stepping out of the van.

'Pick me up on the other side of the security gate, or we'll reunite on board the ship. Either that or I'll see you on the inside of a Russian prison.'

David was about to say something, but was cut off by the slamming of the door.

With the brim of her straw hat pulled firmly down to shield her face from high-level CCTV cameras, Róisín walked purposefully towards the security gate. She took care to stay out of sight of the returning minibus driver, and on reaching the gate looked for the most senior of the uniformed immigration officials. Spotting a captain, she delved into her pocket and pulled out the wallet Nicolai had given to her. She flashed it at the official, who stiffened at an identity of such high rank.

In a quick stream of heavily Moscow-accented Russian, Róisín explained she was there to keep her eye on a vehicle. But the captain and his subordinates should ignore her. She was undercover and would be gone soon enough.

Róisín shrank into the shadows of the security building and avoided the gaze of more cameras. There she waited until the migration police had let half a dozen vehicles through the gate. The minibus was five vehicles away from the barrier when Róisín went back to the captain. She told him that she had seen what she needed to and asked if one of his men could take her towards one of the docked cruise ships. The captain offered to take Róisín himself, but she said his duty was leading his men in the critical job they were doing. The officer nodded and barked an order. A subordinate jumped into a hard-top GAMI jeep, saluted Róisín as she climbed on board, and gunned the vehicle down the port towards the docked cruise ship.

A little way before the ship, and affecting Nicolai's most official manner, Róisín brusquely told the young officer to stop. She told him she needed to speak to some other officials and ordered him to return to his duties.

She sauntered to the cruise ship, timing her arrival at the gangplank with that of some returning passengers. She presented her identity card to the dock police and security people. More saluting followed. Once the officials had turned their attention back to checking credentials, Róisín slipped behind them, removing her hat and donning dark glasses as she did so. She presented her boarding pass to a crew member and stepped onto the gangplank amidst a gaggle of returning passengers, who swept her onto the ship.

Removing her jacket and keeping well out of sight a step or two back from the ship's rail, she saw the white minibus draw up, and David take her suitcase out and give it to a deckhand, all the while looking around surreptitiously for his ward.

She watched her minder slowly climb the gangplank. Once he had reached the main deck, she tapped him on the shoulder and said, 'It's good to see you made it.'

David turned around. 'How on earth did you get on this ship?' he asked. 'Please don't do that to me again.'

'In case you don't know, this isn't about you, David. This is about me: my escape, my life, my choice. I have no intention of getting caught at this stage, and keeping me in that minibus was asking for trouble.'

'And jumping out of the bus wasn't?'

'I'm here, aren't I?'

David exhaled. 'Look, we have got off to a bad start.'

'No, you've got off to a bad start. I'm on board a British ship heading for Greece. I would class that as a good start.'

'I meant us.'

'Us? I take it you are an interrogator – the first of several, I imagine. There is no us. So, when do the questions start?'

'Tomorrow morning, after breakfast.'

'Sleep deprivation, white noise or waterboarding?'

For the first time, Róisín noticed David smile. She thought it made him look rather attractive.

'I think we can be more civilised than that. Look, I'm just tasked with finding out who you are and getting you to Piraeus. Although I would love to know how you got to the ship. I saw the officer at the security gate jump to attention when you spoke to him. How did you do that?'

'Tradecraft,' said Róisín with a smile. She thought about how easily everything could backfire if David saw her fake identity card. New suspicions would be raised, and further questions asked. She would have to destroy the card once the ship was in international waters. 'Plus, I've had a lot of practice,' she added. 'Now, I could do with some rest.'

David saw Róisín to her cabin.

'One more thing,' she said, as he turned to go.

'Yes?'

'Good luck.'

'Good luck with what?'

'You said you wanted to find out who I am. After all these years, I should love to know the answer to that myself.'

CHAPTER
TWENTY-EIGHT

'Mara's on board and they are out of Russian waters,' Sir Bidian said to Eliza, during one of their increasingly regular telephone calls.

'That's good. How did it go?'

'Our man said it was touch and go getting onto the ship. There was an unexpected security crackdown by the local migration police – nothing to do with Mara, just one of their irregular and irritating spot checks. But Mara seems to have taken control. She managed to get onto the ship without a passport or any bother. Our man says he doesn't know how she did it, but it was very impressive.'

'That suggests a cool mind and some good training.'

'If that's so, then I would like to know who trained her.'

'You have a good point. How's the debrief going?'

'Our man says he thinks Mara is getting more from him than he is from her.'

'You didn't send a proper interrogation team?'

'She will be back here soon enough. Then she'll get the crack team.'

'When will that be?' Eliza asked.

'She should arrive here in about eight days. We will have a passport under an assumed name for her by the time she reaches Piraeus. Then we will put her on a British Airways flight from Athens to Heathrow. Our man will stay with her all the way. We have two others shadowing them just in case there's any trouble. Mara will be in a safe house within hours of her landing. Then the real debrief can begin.'

'Where will you put her?'

'The Pheasant's Tail in Hampshire. You won't be familiar with it, as it's after your time, but it's one we reserve for high-value, low-risk assets that we need to lose for a while in a comfortable environment. A couple of weeks should give us enough time to get all the information we need. I'm having it made ready as we speak. Mara has said two interesting things to her handler.'

'Which are?'

'She told us to look into Moscow House in London.'

'Moscow House? That rings a bell.'

'It did with me too – a loud bell, as it was the second time in four weeks that I had heard the name.'

'Wasn't it some sort of Russian club?'

'It was, and it still is. We've known about it forever, but it's always been as clean as a whistle. It's an independently funded, non-state-run UK charity. Originally, its raison d'être was supporting Russian culture. It was started in 1952 by some Russian émigrés, together with British enthusiasts and sympathisers to the Russian cause.'

'I remember,' Eliza said. 'It started out as a non-political organisation – as far as any Russian organisation can be non-political. In its early days, it supported the Russian way of life and language. So, what has happened to it?'

THE ART DEPARTMENT

'We were pleased to get the intel. The membership has changed. Many of the old guard have either died off or resigned their memberships. The club, society or whatever you choose to call it, relies on donations. But according to the records at the Charity Commission, there doesn't seem to be any lack of money. In fact, it is very well funded.'

'Wasn't it based in Fitzrovia or Bloomsbury?'

'It still is – in a beautiful house in Fitzroy Square, a few doors from where Virginia Woolf lived. The freehold was bought in the early sixties after the group benefited from a large bequest. It must be worth a fortune now.

'They have some function rooms for events – a music room, a gallery, a lecture and meeting room, and a library with a good collection of Russian literature, including some important first editions and rare novels, apparently. They hire out some of the rooms for extra income. The Inland Revenue tells me they appear to do very well. Outwardly, it seems all above board.'

'So why is this Russian group suddenly of interest?'

'Two reasons. Besides the tip-off, we managed to get hold of the current list of members. It makes for interesting reading. Volkov is there with all his friends, including Mrs Mirova. There are also dozens of other wealthy Russians from the post-Yeltsin era. It's like a who's who of ex-pat oligarchs.

'However, we now think this organisation has been taken over by another, altogether more sinister group of Russia supporters – a secret society. As you will know, the Russians have a history of secret societies, such as the Decembrists, Black Repartition and Union of Prosperity.'

'What do you think this group is for?' Eliza asked.

'We think it might act as part of the Russian military or security apparatus, like the FSB.'

'What, some sort of Russian undercover unit made up of oligarchs true to the cause?'

'That sort of thing, perhaps, but I did wonder if it could play a part as Putin's instrument of retribution beyond Russian borders.'

'Bidian!' Eliza exclaimed. 'You are treading close to the absurd. You are making it sound like James Bond and SMERSH.'

'I don't need to remind you that SMERSH *was* real. It was not a figment of Ian Fleming's imagination.'

'I know, I know, Smert Shpionam – Death to Spies. A counterintelligence agency under Stalin.'

'So, why not again under Putin? We believe that Nemizida could be an elite unit of the GRU, specialising in subversion and assassination.'

'It all sounds very far-fetched,' said Eliza. 'But if you are right, you might have found the meaning and function of the group.'

'We need to know more – and soon.'

'How will you do that?'

'Well, I think we have someone who can help us.'

'Who's that?'

'Roger Strand.'

'Roger?' said Eliza in amazement. 'He's a florist. How on earth does Roger fit in?'

'It seems that Roger and Volkov have a thing.'

'A thing?'

'I think in modern parlance, they have made a connection.'

'Volkov's gay?'

'So Roger tells me from direct experience. We have had to re-evaluate Volkov. It may be that he is not our focus now so much as another.'

'And who might that be?'

'Maria Mirova. She seems to run a committee within Moscow House.'

'This thing gets more extraordinary by the day,' Eliza said.

'Well, we are working up a plan to keep a closer eye on Mirova. She might be putting the thumbscrews on Volkov to do something he's not happy about. Or that is what Roger thinks.'

'Do you think this has anything to do with Bezrodny?'

'Possibly.'

'You said there was something else Mara told her handler.'

'I did. She revealed that her name was Róisín Kelly.'

CHAPTER
TWENTY-NINE

Ten days after Róisín had left the ship in Piraeus and shortly before nine o'clock in the morning, Felix arrived at Somerset House for the fortnightly internal meeting of The Art Department.

All team members were in the studio when Sir Bidian walked in. 'I have to say, I've been extremely impressed with the work you have all done so far,' he said. 'You have already proved the value of this new department. Each of you has played an essential part in this operation. Your joint efforts have enabled us to get closer to a person of interest and find out more about him than I would ever have thought possible.

'But the job is not yet over. As sometimes happens with operations, our focus can change in the light of events.'

'What do you mean?' asked Rani.

'We thought that Yuri Volkov posed a major threat, but now we think he may not be all we originally thought or, to a certain extent, feared.'

'How is that?' asked Ellie.

'We wanted to investigate Volkov's private life. As we

suspected, it seems that he does lead two lives, but it turns out that his secret one might be more personal than political in nature. As far as we can determine, Volkov has not done anything illegal up to now. Indeed, he has done a great deal of good for the arts during his time in the UK. He's also paid a substantial amount in tax. The Treasury has run a forensic check on his finances, and he is a model citizen in that respect. Oh, I'm sure he's not squeaky clean. There must have been some shortcuts made, and blind eyes turned. Few billionaires get to where they are without a few shady dealings.

'But we should not be blinkered; Volkov has flirted and continues to flirt with danger through his Russian connections in London. He is still in our sights, as we think he could be being persuaded or forced into doing something he may not want to do – something that could be terrorist related. We must prevent this at all costs. But at the same time, we must find out more about the person we now believe is forcing Volkov's hand. If we can eliminate Volkov as the threat, we can narrow down any second party's options. We can then gain control and eliminate the threat altogether.'

'Who is this second party?' asked Ellie.

'Her name is Maria Mirova. She is the wife of a deceased oligarch and lives in Kensington.'

'So, why is she so dangerous?' asked Rani.

'We think Mirova has something to do with a cell working closely with the Russian Government, but possibly autonomous from the Russian Embassy. I'm not going to go into any more detail. The less you know, the better. But we think that up to now, this cell has operated only in an eyes-and-ears capacity, perhaps with some logistical and financial assistance thrown in. However, that might now have changed, and the group could have gone operational. Our job is to find out what is going on and, if it's bad, prevent whatever it is from happening – with a particular emphasis on protecting the public. The last time the Russians did something like this, they didn't achieve their objective, but a British citizen was killed. It was a blunder that had tragic consequences.

'So, I am here today to see if we can prevent another tragedy.'

Sir Bidian studied the members of his team. Each looked downcast and as though they had lost their enthusiasm.

'Look, let me tell you that in this business, no plan survives first contact with the enemy. We plan as best we can, with the knowledge that things could change at any moment. It is the law of unexpected consequences. How good we are isn't just down to how well we plan, but how well we deal with the unexpected when it happens – for it will always happen.'

'But does this mean we won't continue with Volkov and the Saltanov miniature?' Ellie asked. 'If so, it seems more than a pity after all the work we have done, especially Tiya and Petro. And what about Volkov? Won't he be suspicious if we just disappear?'

'I agree, Ellie, it would look suspicious. But let me assure you all that none of your time and hard work has been wasted. Far from it, in fact. I think we can use it to our better advantage.'

'How?' Rani asked, brightening a little.

'Mirova shares with Volkov an interest in collecting Russian art. But we understand that her interest is more of a fixation. She possesses an extremely obsessive personality. We've discovered she competes with Volkov and appears jealous of what he acquires yet crows when she adds something new and important to her own collection.'

'So, do you think we could turn our attention to this Mrs Mirova with the Saltanov miniature?' Ellie asked.

'I do,' replied Sir Bidian. 'There are three excellent advantages as far as I can see. First, we can use the miniature to get close to Mirova and try to gain some trust, just as we have done with Volkov. Second, if we manage to sell the miniature to Mrs Mirova rather than to Volkov, it will drive more of a wedge between them. We know that Volkov dislikes Mirova. That could be the final straw. At that point, although he won't know it, Volkov will already be on our side.'

'Our enemy's enemy is friend,' Petro suggested.

'Precisely,' Sir Bidian replied with a smile.

'What's the third advantage?' Ellie asked.

Sir Bidian laughed. 'The third advantage is that Her Majesty's Government won't be guilty of selling fake art to an innocent collector.'

'But it would be guilty of selling fake art to a guilty collector,' Rani said.

'That is another matter entirely, Rani. You of all people should agree with me when I say that sometimes the end justifies the means.'

Rani laughed. 'With our record, it would be difficult for me to deny it.'

'So, you see,' Sir Bidian continued, 'we might get even more from your hard work than any of us originally thought.'

'What are you going to do with any money we do make?' Felix asked, knowing it was a question the team had been discussing among themselves.

'We will invest it back into the department. Our friends at the Treasury will be pleased about that – and you will all be happy too, no doubt, as it will keep you in a job. And if it all goes well, we may add a little bonus.'

'So, how are we going to reach Mrs Mirova?' Petro asked.

'That is a good question, Petro. I think we shall ask you to go into the field if you feel OK with that?'

Petro looked alarmed. 'I didn't think you were going to use me like that.'

'Nor did I. It would be your decision, of course. But I think this role is ideal for you.

'I think you might be a dealer who was also contacted by Chorney's brother. You will be anxious to find a buyer, having discovered that Volkov is interested in the miniature through another dealer. Ellie, you will be ignorant of this. Mrs Mirova's greed and motivation to get the better of Volkov should drive up the price significantly. If we can get her to pay well over the amount of Volkov's offer, he should be even more infuriated.'

'Divide and rule,' Felix said.

'The time-honoured principle, precisely.

'Petro, you would be a Ukrainian art expert and dealer, often working in stolen or black market items of immense value.'

'I suppose that should not be too difficult for me,' Petro said, but he still looked concerned.

'Yes, you will be on familiar ground. We will work up a backstory for you and give you the credentials you will need. This would be a simple business transaction, Petro. You shouldn't have to meet Mirova more than twice, and then you can disappear into the ether, never to be seen or heard of again by her. Anyway, we intend her to have far more important things to deal with than wondering where you have disappeared to.'

'What will I do?' Rani asked.

'Up to the critical point, you just continue with the Volkov deal. He can't know that it has turned sour until it is too late. That should annoy him even more.'

'When do we start?' Felix asked.

'We will start as soon as we have worked out Petro's cover story. That should only take a few days. Then he can make contact.'

'How are you going to do that?' Rani asked.

'I think through a Russian so-called cultural group in London called Moscow House. Both Mirova and Volkov are members. Mirova stealing the deal from right under Volkov's nose at an event they are both attending should add further insult to injury. Petro will be visiting London on art-dealing business. He will have been recommended to visit the Moscow House group for one of their social evenings.'

'I don't feel confident,' Petro said suddenly.

Sir Bidian thought for a moment and then said soothingly, 'I understand. Let me think about it for a while. Perhaps I can come up with a solution that will make you feel easier. Is that okay, Petro?'

Petro nodded.

'Good,' Sir Bidian said. 'Now, I had better get on with this plan. Felix, could we have a word in my office? There are several things about Volkov I need to go over with you.'

* * *

Felix surveyed Sir Bidian's office, which was now decorated with twentieth-century paintings. On the wall behind him was a nude by Modigliani. Other walls sported pictures by Matisse and Dufy.

'So, you want us to change our focus to Mrs Mirova,' Felix said.

THE ART DEPARTMENT

'Yes. I understand why that didn't go down too well with the team at first. But they must learn that we are not the only people who determine how things work out. There are so many moving parts and unknowns. But from what we have learned, principally from Roger Strand, it seems the antagonist in this story could well be Mirova. We've discovered from the French police that she is probably guilty of bumping off her husband – either on her own account or on the orders of her masters in Moscow. But the French can't prove any of it.'

'So, what's our next move, do you think?' asked Felix.

'I still want us to get close to Mirova, and I think using the miniature is the best way to do it. I'm going to have to find a way of making Petro comfortable. I still think using him is a good idea. He is completely believable. His language is authentic, and he knows as much about Russian art as just about anyone.'

'But for all his expertise, if he's not comfortable, then he might not be able to pull it off.'

'Of that, Felix, I am painfully aware.'

'What if you had a babysitter with him, someone who puts him at his ease, feeds him his lines and covers any nervousness?'

'Mmm, that is a possibility. But we can't use Ellie or Rani, as Volkov knows them. And Tiya is not made to do that sort of thing,'

'So, there's no one left,' said Felix.

'I wonder,' Sir Bidian replied.

CHAPTER
THIRTY

For Róisín, the past weeks had been a whirlwind. She had enjoyed her days of comfort and relaxation on board the cruise ship. For the first time in as long as she could remember, she could, up to a point, relax and not worry about the disastrous consequences of being discovered as an imposter. If her fellow passengers' questions strayed from art and life in Russia and became a little too personal, she gently deflected them. But she loved the conversations about culture, current affairs and simple everyday domestic matters with the sort of friendly, informed, unthreatening people she understood and recognised from long ago in her past. Overall, these people were non-judgemental and keen for fresh experiences and to learn about new cultures.

The small cruise ship was spacious enough for its hundred passengers. The ship's team gave briefings each day, and evening talks from the guest speakers took place in the comfortable main lounge. Róisín had been given a promenade deck suite with a private balcony. Already, she felt a million miles away from Moscow. Yet the experience also made her reflective about a life she could have had.

She stayed on board when the ship docked in Odessa, Constanta, Nessebar and Istanbul. She had been nervous while they were in a port and relieved once they had put to sea again.

While most passengers disembarked to enjoy days of exploration in new places, Róisín spent the time talking to David, although their conversations did not reach the level of a debrief. Róisín knew that would come later. They spoke instead about life, love and loss – the sort of conversations she had enjoyed with Nicolai. Róisín came to discover that while David worked for MI6, he was not a spy or even an analyst but a psychological profiler. He wasn't there for information so much as emotional truth: his aim was not to demolish but to build – to help Róisín decompress from years of double-life pressure and glean any useful information that cropped up along the way.

Whoever had chosen David to accompany her knew what they were doing. The sessions were another way of helping her to get back to a new normality.

In the evenings, the passengers returned to the ship with newfound experiences and knowledge to share. These were served up as fresh conversation over dinner, and afterwards over coffee and drinks. When asked by passengers why she didn't disembark, Róisín reminded them she had work to do.

Finally, the cruise ship had docked in Piraeus. Fond goodbyes were said among the passengers. Contact details were swapped, and promises to keep in touch were made. Róisín was sorry to see her fellow passengers go. Mostly because it meant that her life was to move from fantasy to reality. She had told David her name was Róisín Kelly, but soon someone was going to find out who she really was.

* * *

Now she sat in her bedroom at Pheasant's Tail, the house to which she had been taken after landing at Heathrow from Athens. It was a mid-Victorian building commissioned, she learnt, by an industrialist who enjoyed fishing. From the large bay window that looked down the wide sweep of lawn, she could see the River Test. The chalk stream slid by, waving long strands of trout-concealing weed within its shallow water.

When Róisín had arrived at the house, she saw several fishing rods propped up in the spacious hall. She had learned how to cast a fly as a child. Later, in Northern Ireland, she had sometimes fished for brown trout on the Lower Bann, west of Belfast. It was a beautiful spot where she found sanctuary.

The staff at the house had encouraged Róisín to use the fishing tackle, so she often fished the river after dinner and before dusk, when the trout were rising. She never saw her watchers, but she knew they were there.

She had expected high walls or fences and lots of security around the house, but there was none apart from a gatehouse and CCTV cameras here and there. She didn't overtly feel like a prisoner, but she knew if she simply walked, she wouldn't get far. Besides, where would she go? There was one place, but she hadn't dared even think about that. She was too afraid of what she might, or might not, find.

In some ways, Róisín couldn't remember a more contented time in her adult years. The Black Sea cruise, followed by a stay at this beautiful house and grounds, gave her time to reassess her life and try to work out how to make the best use of her future.

She quickly fell in with the daily routine. A buffet breakfast was available between eight and nine. The morning's work began at ten. A light lunch was served at noon, after which there were further sessions with the debriefing team. There was a mid-afternoon cup of tea, and drinks at six-thirty in the library, followed by dinner at seven in the dining room.

The debrief team consisted of two analysts from the Russia department, a psychoanalyst and a senior interrogator acting as an observer. David provided continuity between the cruise ship and the house.

Some of the sessions were exhausting. They required Róisín to recall minute details of whom she had met and what had been said to her over many years in Moscow. Day by day, the team skilfully extracted more memories and opinions. They learned about Róisín's affair with Nicolai Rykov, and they found out about the cast of military and security personnel that she had come to know, in addition to information on their partners, wives and girlfriends. The team drilled down to the smallest detail of her relationship with the FSB, and then her activities in discovering useful intelligence and passing it on through the dead drop.

Most days, Róisín walked in the garden with David. After a rocky start, she had come to quite like him – at least within the bounds of their circumstances.

Róisín had been trained in debriefing techniques: hers unfolded in a slow and anticipated way. David had already worked through the first stage of the programme on the cruise ship, where he had kept the topics of discussion to innocuous cultural, social and mildly personal issues. His aim was to gain Róisín's confidence, and she let him do so.

Then the process shifted to more focused topics: this was all part of well-planned information gathering, always with a specific goal in mind.

The job of the two Russia department specialists was to identify with Róisín on the basis that the more knowledgeable they were, the better the result was likely to be. The debriefing was non-aggressive and designed, through a relaxed, collaborative approach, to trigger a substantial flow of useful information.

Meetings with the psychoanalyst separated the sessions with the two intelligence analysts. These were aimed at gaining specific and more complex information from Róisín. The psychoanalyst wasn't just looking for answers but seeking opinions and evaluations.

Róisín answered the relentless questions about her past as fully and as honestly as she could.

One day, she told David, 'I can see that psychoanalyst coming a mile off, you know. It's all textbook stuff to make me more cooperative. How can I be more cooperative, for goodness' sake? As for finding a comfortable interview environment that reflects my usual surroundings, he's going to struggle to turn a riverside fishing lodge in Hampshire into a cramped Moscow apartment. Tell him I am comfortable here and he needn't bother.'

David laughed and said, 'I'll let him know.'

'Actually, David, there is something that would make me more comfortable.'

'If I can help, I will.'

'I need some clothes.'

'Ah, I hadn't thought about that.'

'I can't continue with three sets of Russian clothes and what I wore in Sochi – not to mention underwear.'

David smiled. 'I'll get one of the staff here to help. You could pick out some things online.'

Up until then, Róisín had been denied access to the internet, using the telephone or spending money. 'That would be nice, thank you,' she said.

'I'm sorry you had to ask. But in return for this favour, I should like to know something.'

'That sounds very transactional.'

'Sorry.'

'Go on.'

'Your names. Which is the real you?'

Róisín laughed. 'You are wondering which name to use?'

'Exactly. To the service, you were always Mara. Then you became Róisín Kelly. We can't find any reference to a Róisín Kelly anywhere.'

'And you won't.'

'Why not?'

'David, this is after hours, not the debrief.'

'Actually, it is all part of the debrief.'

'Let's continue with Róisín for now. I think I have been Róisín for longer than I have been anyone else.'

'So, I can at least presume you were someone else before that?'

'For that information, David, you will have to interrogate me – not debrief me over a post-dinner drink,' Róisín smiled, and added, 'Anyway, as I don't think your real name is David, and you probably won't tell me what it really is, I don't think that is very fair, do you?'

David smiled.

'Do I still get my new clothes?'

'Yes, Róisín, you still get your new clothes.'

In the advanced stages of the debriefing, Róisín was

increasingly asked for clarification. Her interrogators became more robust, and her statements were challenged. Róisín took this in her stride and at the end of each tough day went fishing.

Finally, the day came when the questions on Russia stopped. Two new Irish analysts replaced the Russian ones, and the whole process started over again. Róisín felt wrung out by the first round and began to lose patience at the thought of having to go through it all again. But David persuaded her that it was something that had to be done.

* * *

'There won't be any debrief today,' David told Róisín over breakfast one morning. It was a week after the Irish questions began.

'Oh, why not? Are you running out of things to ask me?'

'Not quite. It's just that the head of the service is coming down later and would like to meet you. Would you be OK with that?'

'Why not? It's not as if I am going anywhere. But what's this all about?'

'I can't say, I'm afraid.'

'Can't say or don't know?'

Róisín was sitting reading the newspaper in the drawing room after breakfast when she heard the scrunch of car wheels on gravel. A black Range Rover drew up, and a tall, athletic-looking man in a well-cut, dark blue suit, white shirt and striped tie got out from the back seat. Róisín heard the front door open and the sound of David's voice greeting the visitor.

Moments later, the drawing room door opened, and David came in with the newcomer.

'Róisín, I would like to introduce Sir Bidian de Butts,' said David. 'Sir Bidian, this is Róisín Kelly.'

Róisín stood up and walked towards the two men. The new man briefly raised his eyebrows and then held out his hand. Strange, Róisín thought, that he seemed suddenly off guard. It wasn't at all what she had expected from the head of a security service. But by the time she had shaken his hand, he seemed to have collected himself.

'It's good to meet you, Sir Bidian,' said Róisín.

'And you, Ms Kelly. I've been looking forward to it.'

Turning to Sir Bidian, David asked, 'Do you want me here for this?'

'I don't see why not. But before we start, is there any coffee, David?'

'I'll go and rustle up some.'

'Well, let's both sit down, shall we?' Sir Bidian said to Róisín.

Róisín sat down on one side of the fireplace and Sir Bidian on the other.

'Are you comfortable here, Ms Kelly? Is everyone looking after you well?'

'I'm very comfortable, thank you, and yes, everybody is very kind. But please call me Róisín; everyone else does around here.'

Sir Bidian smiled. 'Then Róisín it is, and please call me Bidian.'

David came into the room with a tray of coffee.

'I have been kept abreast of your time here, Róisín,' said Sir Bidian. 'David tells me you have been most cooperative.'

'I have no reason not to be.'

'Apparently so.'

'Then you believe me?'

Sir Bidian smiled. 'I have no reason not to, either. Why I came down here today, as well as to meet you in person, was to ask you to do something for us.'

'What's this, the final test?'

'Do we need a final test?'

'Not in my opinion.'

'Nor mine.'

'Then you trust me?'

'Strange as it might sound, Róisín, I do.'

Róisín frowned. 'Then what is this something you would like me to do?'

Sir Bidian explained about Volkov and Mirova and how he thought Nemezida and Bezrodny, names Róisín was familiar with, were connected to a possible Russian black operation.

'I should say your presumption is a good one from what one of my girlfriends said in Moscow,' said Róisín.

Sir Bidian nodded and said, 'I'm glad you agree.'

'So, what part do you want me to play? Do you want me as an analyst?'

'I was thinking something a bit more hands-on.'

'Fieldwork? Don't you think I'm too long in the tooth, and isn't it too big a risk? You are going to put me in touch with the enemy when I've been sleeping with them all these years.'

'I have some good reasons, and from what you tell us, you've not been idle in the field for the past thirty years, so one last outing shouldn't be too hard. Besides, this task fits your particular skillset to a tee.'

'How?'

'I want you to help persuade Maria Mirova to snatch an important piece of art from under the nose of Yuri Volkov – to unsettle their relationship further. Volkov has already negotiated a deal with a seller, but it hasn't yet been concluded. You will be another dealer working with a representative of the seller.'

'What's the piece of art?'

'A miniature by the Russian artist, Bogdan Saltanov.'

'Saltanov? For an obscure artist, he seems popular at the moment. That's the second time I've heard his name in a few months, and as far as I know, he didn't paint miniatures.'

'Well, whether he did or not, he certainly didn't paint the one we want to sell to Mirova.'

'How's that?'

'Because we painted it.'

Róisín laughed. 'You are selling a fake?'

'Yes.'

'And who is the seller's representative?'

'Actually, he's one of ours. He's the artist who painted the miniature.' Sir Bidian took out a photograph from his inside pocket and passed it to Róisín.

She inspected it and said, 'I should like to meet this artist. This painting is exquisite.'

'We certainly hope it is good enough to convince Mirova to outbid Volkov. But that's your job, if you are prepared to do it. We will put you up in a good hotel – suitable for a successful international art dealer.'

'What about clothes?'

Sir Bidian smiled and said, 'David mentioned that to me. I think we can run to an appropriate wardrobe – especially as this is now operational. I will speak to the quartermaster about it.'

'With the greatest respect, I don't want your quartermaster choosing my clothes, thank you.'

Sir Bidian laughed. 'I didn't mean he would pick them out,

just that he would arrange the funds. Perhaps we could do that through David.'

'Will David accompany me to London – as my minder?'

Sir Bidian looked at David. 'The thought did cross my mind if that's OK with you?'

'I'd be only too happy to tag along.'

Sir Bidian stood up to go and looked out of the window. 'My cast isn't so good with my left hand, but I'm sorry I can't stay for a spot of fishing.' He turned to look at Róisín and added, 'Talking of fishing, once this operation is over, will you help us to discover your life before Moscow?'

Róisín met the security chief's eye. 'Once this operation is over, Bidian, will you help *me* discover my life before Moscow?'

Sir Bidian bowed. 'Róisín, I can assure you it will be my pleasure.'

Sir Bidian bade Róisín and David goodbye and told them he would see them during the following week, before she met Maria Mirova.

'So, you're stuck with me for a little longer,' Róisín said to David, once Sir Bidian had gone.

'Seems like I am,' he replied.

Róisín thought he didn't look unhappy at the idea.

CHAPTER
THIRTY-ONE

Róisín ended her debrief at Pheasant's Tail in some confusion: she had imagined the time would be cathartic, and while it had been, it was only up to a point. It had been a phoney fortnight, she thought: two weeks spent in a heavenly never-never land, where the issues of everyday life – from the mundane to the challenging – were removed. She had spent most of the time reliving her past. The days had been long, and by the time she had told her questioners everything she could, she was exhausted. The debrief team had unpeeled as much as possible, but she had left herself one final layer.

At Pheasant's Tail, her relationship with David had moved on. He had lost much of his early professional distance and become companionable. That was why Róisín felt relaxed with him as he drove them past Salisbury and onward towards Blandford Forum. Her bags containing new clothes, gleefully purchased from various online sites, were stowed in the back.

It was a beautiful day, with the trees in full leaf.

'This is lovely,' Róisín murmured, almost to herself. 'It's been a long time since I've seen Salisbury Cathedral. I love this time of year in England. But you haven't told me what today is all about.'

'Sir Bidian suggested it might help if you got out and about before London.'

'That was thoughtful of him, though I'm not sure I buy it.'

David smiled. 'You're right, of course. But I have to say I'm a little confused. Something happened when Sir Bidian came to Pheasant's Tail. His attitude towards you changed. I asked him about it, but he only said something about a gut feeling. He didn't elaborate further. Anyway, he thought you might like to have a glimpse of the man who seems to have got himself caught up with Nemizeda and Maria Mirova, especially as we aren't too far away. He is going to an auction preview today. I thought we could have a pub lunch somewhere on the way.'

'That sounds nice. Some more gentle acclimatisation?'

'Something like that, but we won't be able to leave the car once we're at the event. We don't want to come face-to-face with Volkov. But we can spy from afar.'

'A stakeout, how very cloak and dagger.'

* * *

Felix and Ellie joined dozens of others, all clutching sale catalogues, as they walked from the parking field through faded formal gardens to the front of Binfield House, where they had arranged to meet Volkov. Binfield House was an Elizabethan manor that had, as Felix could see only too clearly, fallen into a sad state of disrepair. The house was perched on a wooded hillside with unbroken views across the pretty Elder Valley. It was a classic timber-framed building with three gables, leaded windows and tall brick chimneys.

Volkov arrived half an hour late. He was unapologetic, ungracious and seemed in a foul mood.

'This is not the sort of house that is good for what we are looking for,' he said. 'It is a waste of my time.'

'What's up with him, and why doesn't he like this? It's beautiful,' Ellie whispered to Felix, as Volkov stomped off through the front door.

'I don't think he's having a good day. We'll just have to humour him,' Felix said.

The pair caught up with Volkov in the entrance hall, the surroundings of which did nothing to improve his humour. Like the exterior, the internal decoration was tired. Felix's heart sank. Most of the furniture looked as if it belonged on a bonfire rather than at an auction sale.

'This house is a dump,' said Volkov with contempt, and in a voice loud enough to make people around them stare. 'There will be nothing here for me.'

'I thought the dining room might have something,' said Felix. 'I think it will be through here.'

Once inside, Felix pointed to a table and two chairs. 'What do you think about those?' he asked.

Volkov gave a small shrug.

'Yuri, the catalogue says these are genuine Hepplewhite and have good provenance. They have the original bills of sale from 1768.'

'Is Hepplewhite good?' asked Volkov.

'Excellent, Yuri. Along with Chippendale and Sheraton George, Hepplewhite is one of the big three English furniture makers.'

'These would suit Courtlands?'

'As if made for it,' Felix assured Volkov, who was by then showing a little more interest.

* * *

David parked the car in the corner of the designated field. It gave him a good view of all the comings and goings at Binfield House.

'Volkov should have arrived by now,' he said. 'He should be here with a couple of his people.'

'And who are they?'

'He didn't tell me that.'

* * *

As they passed through the rooms, Felix sensed Volkov's mood lift. He was paying more attention and asking questions.

As they toured the house, Felix, Ellie and Volkov wrote comments in the margins of their catalogues, drew large asterisks beside selected items and referenced the separate price guide sheet.

By the time they had seen everything, Volkov's mood had improved further, and he even looked as though he was enjoying himself.

The three of them sat down at a plastic table in the garden. They had just visited a tea and coffee stall, and they drank stewed tea from Styrofoam cups.

'This reminds me of the catering van at Courtlands,' Volkov said with a laugh. He looked directly at Felix and Ellie. 'I must apologise for my behaviour earlier. I have been under considerable strain. It is a problem that is proving difficult for me to resolve. I have not been sleeping well. But I am enjoying this event. It is far more crowded than I imagined. It is a nice feeling; it is like a festival. It helps my mood.'

'I'm sorry to hear that, Yuri. Is there anything we can do?' Felix asked.

'No. I must find my own way out of the problem. It is something I have to do alone. But thank you for asking. Now, tell me, are all these people art dealers, do you think?'

'Oh no, Yuri,' said Felix. 'While there will be a large number of dealers here, others are private collectors, local souvenir hunters or sightseers out for the day. But it's easy to spot the dealers.'

'How?'

'They're the ones trying hard not to look too interested in any particular lots – just in case another dealer sees them and gets curious. Each is secretly hoping to find a hidden gem among all the other items in the sale that no one else has noticed – including the auctioneers. They call them dark lots.'

* * *

'There's one thing I haven't found out about you,' said Róisín to David as they sat in the car.

'Only one? And what is that?'

'You've never told me your real name.'

'That question again. But you've never told me yours.'

'So that's how it's going to be?'

'Seems only fair.'

'I can't tell you, David – see how easy I use your alias? It was well chosen as it suits you. It'll be difficult to get used to a different name in the future. And the longer you don't tell me, the more difficult it will be.'

'You mentioned the future?'

'Don't change the subject. For too many reasons at the moment, I just can't tell you.'

'You can't or you won't?
'Both. I have to be sure.'
'Sure of whom? Me?'
'Not of you. It's a long and complicated story, and not without risks.'
'On a personal or professional level?'
'Both, in a way. Besides, knowing your real name would at least stop me speculating.'
'And where has that got you?'
Róisín smiled. 'Not very far. First, I thought Sigmund, then Carl.'
'Flattering.'
'I can't see why you won't tell me. Your boss told me *his* name.'
David sighed. 'And there, in a simple statement, you have the winning argument.'
'So, you will tell me. Go on, then.'
'I hope you can handle the truth.'
'Try me.'
'It's David.'
'David. You've been David all along?'
'For as long as I've been alive. If you remember, it was you who jumped to the conclusion that David was an alias.'
'In the café?'
'Yes.'
'Why didn't you correct me?'
'It was more fun not to.'
'Callous beast. But even if your name had been different, I should always have thought of you as David.'
'Always? Now, we had better concentrate on what we came for.'
Róisín laughed. 'Oh, I've already got what I came for.'

***

'Dark lots, you say. This is exciting to me,' Volkov said. 'I am glad now I came. It is a very British day out, I think.'

Felix looked at Volkov and wondered if he was seeing more of what Roger saw in him. Here was a man enjoying a simple pleasure. Volkov had immense wealth and could afford whatever he wanted. He could buy all his furniture from the very best antique dealers in London and around the world if he so desired. But where was the fun in that? Half the pleasure was in discovery. Volkov didn't want to order his contents, he wanted to collect these things himself and be part of the process of putting his home together. He wanted to become part of each object's story.

'I'm afraid these estate sales are becoming rare events,' Felix told him. 'Most of the big house collections will have been sold by now – unless they are owned by very wealthy families who can afford to keep and display them. But this decline has taken place over the past hundred years.'

'This is part of what you were telling us over dinner,' Volkov said.

'Why yes, it was. The significant era for these sales was the 1930s. Sotheby's had a small group called The Flying Squad, who tore around England with the contents of country houses.

'Sotheby's ran over twenty of these auctions at various country piles during that time. I like to think they were a bit like a pop-up shop today, and I imagine these sales must have created the template for the larger events that followed.'

'There were much larger sales?' Volkov asked, clearly interested in learning more.

'The greatest was probably at Mentmore Towers in 1977. Then in 2010, there was a sale of items from the attics and various properties and outhouses of the Chatsworth Estate. Those I have spoken to who went say they will never forget that day. Those enormous house sales helped to establish the Sotheby's of today.'

'I am learning a great deal here,' said Volkov.

'So, what items that we've seen today do you think you might bid for, Yuri?'

Volkov consulted his catalogue. 'I have marked down the George III mahogany musical bracket clock and the 1802 John Broadwood grand piano.'

'The piano has a beautiful mahogany case,' agreed Felix, nodding his approval.

'Then I have the George III mahogany armchair, made by France & Bradburne in about 1765. It says here there is a pair of similar chairs at the Metropolitan Museum in New York.

'I also liked the mahogany and upholstered sofa and two armchairs by Gillows of Lancaster.'

'I think they are all lovely choices,' said Felix, 'but don't forget the Hepplewhite table and chairs. I think those are the best lots in the sale. Ellie, what have you earmarked?'

'The oil on panel of Sir Nicholas Stockton painted in 1564, when Stockton was aged 49. He was the son of the original owner of this house. He has a magnificent long red beard. The painting has an inscription in gold. There is no note of the artist, the catalogue just says English School.'

'Is that the chap who looks like those two in ZZ Top?' Felix asked.

'Trust you to lower the tone,' Ellie said. Volkov looked slightly bemused but didn't say anything.

'Talking of English School, I think this picture is interesting,' Ellie said, pointing to an illustration in the catalogue. 'Look at it. Really look at it,' she demanded.

Felix and Volkov looked. Staring back at them was a seated young woman turned slightly to the right.

'What about it?' Felix asked.

'This is exactly the sort of thing I was talking about a few weeks ago. It's an oil on canvas, three-quarter length portrait of a twenty-one-year-old young woman called Lady Henrietta Downes. The catalogue marks it as English School, which means the artist is unknown.'

'Is this an important picture?' Volkov asked.

'It depends which way you look at it, Mr Volkov. As it stands, it isn't very valuable,' she said, lowering her voice. 'But as you can see, it is a beautiful portrait. Look at her. She rests her right hand elegantly in her lap. Her hair is dressed high on the head with a blue ribbon, and she wears a white dress with gold braiding. There is a gold embroidered Turkish scarf at her waist and a white gauze shawl with more gold braiding wrapped over both her shoulders and arms. Look how expertly the clothes have been rendered. This was a very skilled artist. Whoever it was, he or she was extremely accomplished. Look behind the sitter in the centre of the picture. There are some trees, and on the right is a distant landscape view with more trees and a cloudy sky. It is a very familiar Arcadian scene of the eighteenth century, and it is beautifully executed.'

'Yes, I can see all that,' Felix said.

Volkov added, 'I too can see. But what can you see, Ellie?'

Ellie smiled at Volkov. 'I see a young woman painted in 1771. Her hair and clothes are perfect for the period. But the composition is perfect too. The background is what we would expect for the era – so far, so authentic. We are very familiar with this look through principal artists of that era. I have to say, this picture would be perfect for Courtlands, Mr Volkov.'

'I can see that,' said Yuri. 'It would be excellent. But I sense you are thinking something more.'

Ellie lowered her voice even further. 'When Henrietta sat for this portrait, Joshua Reynolds was forty-eight. Three years earlier, he had become the first president of the Royal Academy, and a year after that, in 1769, he was knighted – only the second artist to be given that honour. Reynolds was at the height of his career.'

'So?' Felix said.

'It makes me think of Mr Volkov and his daughter.'

'My daughter and me. Why, how? Volkov asked.

'I imagine a very wealthy man with vast estates and great influence. His darling and beautiful daughter, the apple of his eye, has reached the age of twenty-one. The father commissions a portrait of his beloved daughter to celebrate her coming of age. If I were this man, which artist, I wonder, should I have commissioned to paint this important picture?'

'I would have commissioned Sir Joshua Reynolds,' said Volkov without hesitation. 'Nothing is too good for my daughter.'

'You don't think—' Felix started.

Ellie held up her hand. 'I don't think anything. I just ask the question and suggest that as it stands, this would be a wonderful picture for Courtlands. But after Mr Volkov has bought it, we should look into the history and painting technique of this picture forensically.' Turning to Yuri, Ellie said, 'That, Mr Volkov, is how you build an art collection in the twenty-first century.'

Volkov bowed his head. 'Chapeau, Ellie! That is what you call a dark lot?'

Felix laughed. 'By the sounds of it, an extremely dark lot! You catch on quickly, Yuri.'

'So I've been told,' Yuri said, with the air of someone always one step ahead.

But Volkov wasn't one step ahead with everything in his life right now. Felix thought how difficult things must be for him.

After tea, Felix and Ellie saw Volkov to his car.

* * *

Róisín and David sat in silence watching the people return to their cars from the house. Suddenly, David pointed and said, 'There he is.'

Róisín followed the line of David's finger and saw two men and a woman talking by a black Mercedes limousine.

One of the men had his back to Róisín. 'Which is Volkov?' Róisín asked.

'The one facing you,' David replied.

* * *

'Thank you very much,' said Volkov. 'We have a good list of furniture, and Ellie, I think the pictures you pointed out will work very well in Courtlands. I wasn't expecting today to work out so well.

'In a funny way, it has helped me. I think I know now what I must do – if not yet how. I can't explain it; it is a business matter.'

Ellie replied, 'Then, Mr Volkov, by the end of the day tomorrow, I will let you know what I think you should bid on each of the pictures.'

'And I think we should play it by ear on the furniture,' said

Felix. 'Let's see what happens on the day. You are coming to the sale, aren't you, Yuri?'

'I certainly intend to be here; it will be fascinating,' Volkov replied. 'There are several pieces I shouldn't miss.'

'Well, if you don't mind my saying, Yuri, you will have a big advantage over all the other bidders.'

'Because I have such good advisers?'

'No, Yuri, because you can outbid everyone else.'

Volkov laughed. 'You make an interesting point, I think. But there is one thing you must learn about great wealth, Felix.'

'How to get it?'

'Besides that.'

'What else?'

'No matter how much money or power you have, there is always someone with more. You have to hope that one of those wealthier people doesn't want what you want on the day you want it.'

Yuri climbed into his car and Felix and Ellie waved him off.

* * *

'OK, we've seen him,' said Róisín. 'What next?'

'Now we go to London.'

'That's it?'

'Yes, that's it.'

'So really just a nice day out.'

'I hope you think so.'

'I do, David. It's been a very nice day out indeed, and I feel much more acclimatised. Now, as Volkov has gone, I think I will stretch my legs for a moment and then we can be on our way.'

'May I stretch my legs with you?'

'Afraid I'll make a run for it?'

'It's certainly not a good career move to lose a prime asset.'

'So, I'm a prime asset, am I?'

* * *

'Well, that went well – after a rocky start,' Felix said to Ellie as they made their way to the car.

'I thought so,' Ellie agreed, 'but I wonder what Yuri meant when he said, "I think I know now what I must do – if not yet how".'

'I wondered that too,' said Felix.

'I'm beginning to see what Sir Bidian means about Yuri,' Ellie said. 'He seems quite ordinary really, once you get to know him.'

'But we shouldn't let what we think about him now blind us to the threat Bidian was telling us about.'

'I suppose not, but I'm glad we're not going to sell him a fake. I'd have felt bad about that.'

Felix suddenly stopped. 'See that woman over there, getting into the black Range Rover? She reminds me of someone, but for the life of me I just can't think who it is. That will irritate me now.'

'These things often come back to you when you least expect them.'

Felix and Ellie were halfway back to London when Felix exclaimed, 'I've got it!'

'Got what?'

'The woman in the car park, the one who reminded me of someone.'

'I told you that you would remember when you least expected it,' Ellie said. 'As a matter of interest, who is it?'

'She looked just like that guide I spoke to at the gallery in Moscow.'

'The one you gave your drawing to?'

'Yes, she could have been her twin.'

'Don't they say one's double is walking around the globe somewhere?'

'No, that was more than seeing double. It was like a kick in the heart. I can't explain it. I wonder if the woman in Moscow kept my drawing.'

* * *

'It's going to be hard coming back down to earth after the cruise, Pheasant's Tail and now this five-star hotel,' said Róisín to David as they waited for the lift to take them to their floors after checking in. 'The trouble is, I'm not at all sure what comes next.'

'I think Sir Bidian has a few thoughts on that. But he didn't mention what they are.'

'Well, I think I'm going to order a sandwich from room service, have a long, hot bath and then an early night,' said Róisín. 'It sounds like tomorrow will be a long day. Perhaps we could meet for breakfast. Around eight?'

David agreed and they went their separate ways.

After breakfast the next day, the pair took a stroll along Piccadilly and then across Green Park to Buckingham Palace. On the way back to the hotel, they had a light snack at Fortnum & Mason. Later in the afternoon, they took a taxi to Somerset House, where Sir Bidian was set to brief Róisín.

She enjoyed more London sights on the way, and once

THE ART DEPARTMENT

inside Sir Bidian's office, gazed admiringly around the walls. She counted two Pissarros, two Gauguins, a Matisse and a Van Gogh.

'You have a nice spot here, Bidian,' she said, eyeing the pictures.

'They're on loan.'

'I should imagine they are. Now, what is it you would like me to do?'

'In a moment, I am going to introduce you to the artist who painted the Saltanov miniature. He will be with you tonight. The two of you are going to a lecture on the Mongol invasion of Russia in the thirteenth century. There you will see Yuri Volkov and Maria Mirova.'

Sir Bidian passed a photograph of Mirova across the desk. 'I want you to find a way to speak to Mirova alone and introduce yourself.'

'Introduce myself as whom?'

'Well, you can't be Róisín Kelly. It would be far too easy for Mirova to check up on you. Using a cover of anyone from Russia or the old Soviet states would also be dangerous. How's your German?'

'Good.'

'Can you speak Russian with a German accent?'

'Yes, especially with a few hours' practice.'

'Then how about you are a German dealer specialising in Russian works of art? I will leave you to work up a cover from there.'

'You seem very confident in me.'

'From what I've seen and heard, I have every reason to be.'

'Any doubts at all?'

'Should I have?'

'No.'

'That is as I thought.'

'You are very trusting.'

'I have my reasons.'

Seeing this line of questioning wasn't going further, Róisín said, 'And what about my companion this evening?'

'His real name is Petro. His cover is that he is working directly for the seller of the miniature.'

'Who is the seller?'

'The brother of an assassinated Ukrainian crime boss.'

'Who assassinated him?'

'Actually, it was Petro. But don't let that influence you; he had good cause, and he is a master artist.'

Róisín raised an eyebrow but said only, 'So what's our objective?'

'I want you to convince Mirova that you've heard that Volkov, whom you saw yesterday in Dorset, is keen to buy the miniature. But the seller wants much more money than he has offered. You will have a photograph of the miniature and can tell Mirova the piece is now in London. If she agrees to your price, she can have it.'

'What is the price?'

'Volkov thinks he is the only one interested and has offered a black market £10,000. I think you should ask for £75,000. It is nothing to Mirova, and most of the value to her will be pipping Volkov to the post.'

* * *

Róisín and Petro settled into a taxi. 'Fitzroy Square, please,' Róisín told the driver.

'So, how did you get roped into all this, Petro?' Róisín

asked in English. She had been intrigued by what little Bidian had told her about the Ukrainian.

'I had nowhere to go. Sir Bidian gave me a home.'

'Bidian told me you had a tragic experience with this gangster, Vasyl Chorney.'

'It is a long story.'

'The traffic is slow,' said Róisín.

'I am a monk artist. My abbot made me paint an icon for Vasyl.'

'Did you know him?'

'We were altar boys together. But he grew up bad. He played at devotion but was an evil man – drugs, prostitution, people smuggling. He murdered my family when he was a young man and later lived like a royal in a grand dacha.'

'So, what did you do?' Róisín asked, appalled.

'I mix paint with arsenic. I hear he kiss an icon every night and morning. He thought he kiss hand of God. But he kiss devil's hand. Over few years, with damp climate, he got stomach cancer and died.'

'So, you poisoned him slowly?' Róisín said. Then she laughed and added, 'Sorry, I know it's not funny, but an artistic assassin, how creative.'

'Yes. Others try kill him with guns and bombs; I use colour green.'

'Remind me not to kiss any of your artwork, Petro.'

'It is better not to,' Petro replied with a straight face.

The taxi arrived at Fitzroy Square and stopped outside Moscow House. Róisín paid the driver from the cash she had been given for the evening, and with a new respect for her companion, she and Petro made their way into the building. An attendant directed them to the lecture room, where a woman sat at a table selling tickets for the evening's talk. Róisín handed over twenty pounds and was given two tickets. She and Petro then walked over to a table to collect their complimentary glass of wine.

'I don't think I have seen you here before,' a man by the table said to Róisín and Petro in Russian.

'No, we are in London on business,' said Róisín. 'We heard about Moscow House from a friend, so we thought we would come. My colleague here tells me he is homesick.'

'Then you have come to the right place. This is a little corner of Russia in another country. Come, let me introduce you to some friends.'

While Róisín made polite conversation, she kept one eye on the door. The room was filling up quickly now. Eventually, she caught sight of her target who, with a small group of men, including Volkov, had entered the room from another direction. Somehow, she was going to have to separate Mirova from the group. Fortunately, she didn't have to consider this manoeuvre for long, as she saw Mirova say something and leave the room. Guessing she was probably heading for the cloakroom, Róisín excused herself and followed. Once inside, she positioned herself in front of a mirror and attended to her make-up so that she would be standing next to Mirova when she came to wash her hands.

Mirova appeared from a cubicle and stood at a basin. She glanced at Róisín's reflection in the mirror. 'I don't think I know you, do I?' she said without warmth.

Róisín smiled. 'No, this is the first time I have been here. I am with a colleague.'

'Your Russian is good, but I detect a slight accent. I am Maria Mirova by the way.'

'Most of my business is transacted in Russia. But I am German. My name is Ute Lange,' Róisín said.

'And what business brings you to London, Ute?'

'You do, Maria.'

Mirova looked surprised and alert. 'Me? Why?'

'I am a dealer in Russian art. I think that is a passion of yours.'

'It is. But what makes you think I will be interested in meeting you?' Mirova said bluntly.

Róisín took from her bag a photo of the miniature and put it on the vanity top.

'What is this?' Mirova asked.

'This is a miniature of Tsar Alexis I, by the artist Bogdan Saltanov. It is quietly on the market.'

'So?'

'If you don't buy it, Yuri Volkov will.'

'Ah, now it makes sense.'

'What makes sense?'

'Just a conversation on miniatures I came in on recently. How far has Volkov got with this?'

'He has already made an offer.'

A cruel smile crept across Mirova's face. 'I need to know more. Who is selling this piece?'

'I am with the representative of the seller tonight.'

Mirova thought for a moment. 'There is a library down the corridor. We won't be disturbed. Meet me there with your representative in ten minutes.'

Mirova dried her hands and left the cloakroom without another word.

Róisín found Petro deep in conversation with two men. Interrupting them, she extracted him and explained what had happened as they walked.

Mirova was already in the library. Forgoing any preamble

and not waiting to be introduced to Petro, she said, 'What's this all about and who is selling this miniature?'

'The seller is the brother of the man, Vasyl Chorney,' Petro said.

'Vasyl Chorney, the dead Ukrainian mobster?' Mirova asked in surprise.

'The same,' said Petro.

Mirova grilled Petro on Chorney. Róisín was pleased that he could answer all the questions. She then questioned Petro and Róisín on the miniature's history, its provenance and, finally, its price. Eventually, she seemed satisfied and asked, 'Is the piece here in London?'

Petro told her it was.

'Then bring it to me. Tomorrow evening is convenient.' Mirova didn't wait for agreement and took a card from her handbag. 'This is my address. Be there at seven o'clock. Don't be late. I will have an expert there to look at the miniature. Do not try to cheat me and do not sell it in the meantime. It will go badly for you if you do.' With that, she left the room.

'That easy part over,' said Petro to Róisín. 'Tomorrow different.'

The following evening, Petro and Róisín arrived by taxi at Mirova's house in Kensington Palace Gardens. The sizeable Italianate building over three floors stood behind high iron railings with plenty of security cameras on show. A butler ushered Petro and Róisín into a large drawing room: it was a room in Imperial Russian style, substantial and decorated in white and gilt. Róisín could see that Petro was fascinated by the artwork.

THE ART DEPARTMENT

After several minutes' wait, Maria entered the room. She was accompanied by an effete man with a goatee beard trimmed to a point and a waxed moustache. He was flamboyantly dressed in a black frock coat over a patterned waistcoat. Around his neck was a cravat kept in place with a pearl-topped pin.

Petro unwrapped the miniature and laid it out on a card table. The man studied the painting in great detail using a powerful magnifying glass and torch. Eventually, he finished his inspection and proceeded to question Petro and Róisín. Some of the questions about provenance were the same as Maria had asked the evening before.

When the enquiries came to an end, Maria asked Petro and Róisín to step outside into the hall. Ten minutes later, she appeared at the door and invited them back into the drawing room.

She went straight to the point. 'You asked for £75,000?'

'Correct,' Petro said.

'I will give you £65,000. Take it or leave it.'

Róisín felt a surge of pleasure. But the feeling was short-lived, as she heard Petro say, 'Then we will leave. The owner will not take less than £75,000. If you pay by bank transfer now, I will leave the masterpiece with you.'

Róisín held her breath as Mirova looked sternly at Petro and considered the counteroffer. Finally, she nodded. 'It is too much, I think, but it will be worth it.'

Róisín noticed the cruel smile had returned to Mirova's face.

* * *

'You did amazingly well, Petro,' Róisín said as they walked towards Bayswater Road to find a taxi. 'I thought you had asked too much.'

'My work is worth every rouble,' said Petro with a smile.

When Róisín arrived back at her hotel, David was waiting for her in the bar. 'By the look on your face, mission accomplished,' he said.

Róisín sat down and replied, 'I think a glass of fizz is in order. Mirova bought the story and the painting hook, line and sinker.'

'Sir Bidian will be delighted. It means he can press on with the next part of the operation.'

'But our part in the operation has come to an end, David.'

'I have been thinking the same. I must say, Róisín, it has been an unexpected time for me.'

'Unexpected in what way?'

'In a nice way.'

'For me also.'

'From my point of view, it would be a shame not to stay in touch.'

'From mine too.'

'If you would like me to, I could help you with the next stage of your readjustment. I promise Sir Bidian isn't behind this.'

'He'd better not be. But are you sure? My life holds much sadness. It starts well, with love and security, but then it becomes full of risk, dreadful loss and more danger. Revisiting my past will bring to the surface things I have pushed to the back of my mind.'

'What sort of things?'

'Oh, upbringing, sacrifices, partings, those sorts of things.'

'Are you sure it's somewhere you want to travel?'
'Is that the psychologist asking?'
'The psychologist, but also now a friend, I hope.'

CHAPTER
THIRTY-TWO

Eliza picked up her phone.

'Is that you, Eliza?'

'Who else would it be?'

'It's Bidian.'

'I would never have guessed, especially as your name comes up on this new phone Felix has given me. It's the latest iPhone, apparently. So, what's your news? I think that is the only thing this phone can't tell me. Or perhaps it can, and I haven't worked out how to find a mind-reading app yet.'

Sir Bidian laughed. 'Well, the news is that Róisín and Petro have sold the miniature to Maria. I wasn't sure if it would happen at first. Petro wasn't happy about playing his part in the operation.'

'I'm not surprised, are you? It was a huge responsibility. None of the team is trained for this work. They are creatives with difficult and repressive backgrounds. They are a bunch of talented mavericks, not a group of highly trained and disciplined field agents.'

'You're right, of course,' Sir Bidian said with a note of resignation.

'You know I am,' said Eliza firmly. 'I should very much like to visit Somerset House some time and meet the group; they sound fascinating. But I suppose that's out of the question on security grounds.

'Anyway, how much did Mirova pay for the miniature?'

'Seventy thousand.'

'That was well done. And Róisín has come up trumps, too. I thought there was something about that woman. How is she, by the way? You haven't told me about her debrief. I appreciate that you can't say much.'

'Well, I shouldn't. But I can say it has been like unpeeling an onion, as David put it. There is layer after layer. We took it slowly whilst aware we might have been dealing with a Russian double.'

'But are you satisfied that Mara – or Róisín – is *our* double?'

'I can say with almost total confidence that she is.'

'You've reached that level of unpeeling?'

'Yes, we have, although there are quite a few years yet to cover. But those years don't involve Russia.'

'Can you say what they do involve?'

'No, I can't for certain yet. I may be able to tell you a bit more in a few weeks. In the meantime, Róisín seems very well and settled back at Pheasant's Tail.'

'You've let her stay on?'

'For the time being.'

'She shouldn't get too comfortable; she will have to move on before long, won't she?'

'She will. It's something I am working on, though I'm not quite sure what to do.'

'MI,' said Eliza.

'MI?'

'Masterly inactivity.'

'Oh, I see. Well, you could be right. Things just might work out without my involvement.'

'It is often the way. What does your psychologist think about it?'

'That is a very good question. He and Róisín seem to be getting along very well – professionally and personally. It was the last thing I anticipated.'

'What do you mean by getting on personally?'

'David spoke to me the other day about seeing Róisín as a friend once this is all over. He also mentioned he'd like to help her pick up what pieces she can from her previous life. He is a great stickler for protocol.'

'What did you tell him?'

'I told him I was OK with it. But I advised him to take it slow until we have completed our evaluation. You never know, he may yet help in getting to the bottom of this.'

'Róisín is still being taciturn over some areas?'

'Extremely.'

'Oh, well, no doubt all will be revealed in the fullness of time. Meanwhile, what is happening to Volkov?' asked Eliza.

'Ah, Roger Strand called me. He says Volkov is beside himself about losing the miniature. Strand thinks he is at breaking point. And Felix also called to say that he was not at all himself at the sale preview.'

'So, what are you going to do to tip Volkov over the edge?'

'It is going to have to be a direct approach.'

'And how do you propose doing that, Bidian?'

'Well, it can't be Strand, Felix or anyone Volkov knows.'

'And in case you were thinking of Róisín, Bidian, I do not think that would be a good idea.'

'I agree, but why do you say so?'

'If you have Volkov wrong, it could backfire, and if he makes enquiries back in Russia, you could put Róisín in harm's way – again.'

'I take your point, but I had been thinking about a gentle strong-arm tactic with Volkov.'

'That would be better. Will you get someone from the roughhouse department to have a quiet word? Or, I am sure West would be pleased to oblige. He seems at his happiest when he is threatening one or more with violence, although I fear he is rather out of practice. There is not much need for that at Witch's.'

'I am sure West would be ideal, but I thought I would have a word with Volkov myself – with perhaps a little tactical support for window dressing.'

'Ah, that sort of direct approach,' said Eliza. 'I think that should do nicely.'

They were interrupted by the sound of running outside. West rushed into the room.

'Hang on the line, Bidian, will you, please,' said Eliza. 'West seems a bit concerned about something.'

'About what?'

'Well, hang on a moment, and I'll tell you.'

'We seem to have some activity in the grounds,' West said. 'Something or someone has set off one of the motion sensors.'

'Not again. It's probably one of the muntjacs like last time.'

'Maybe so, but we can't be too careful, especially after what Sir Bidian told us about Mrs Mirova poking her nose into things. I'm going to have a look. I'll send Cairo and Frankie in here just in case.'

'What on earth is going on?' Sir Bidian's voice came down the phone.

'It's probably nothing, but one of the sensors in the woods has been activated. No doubt it's only wildlife.'

'Yes, but what sort of wildlife?'

'West is going to have a look now.'

'Do you want me to stay on the line?'

'No, don't worry.'

'Well, keep me updated. I do worry about you.'

'I know, and I appreciate it, Bidian.'

* * *

Cairo and Frankie arrived to sit with the lady of the house.

'I am sure this is a lot of fuss about nothing,' said Eliza.

'Well, we can't be too sure,' Cairo replied. She held a Glock handgun.

'As you're both here, one of you might as well pour us all a stiff gin and tonic,' said Eliza.

'I'll just have the tonic,' Cairo said.

The three women sat down, sipped their drinks and chatted whilst they waited.

'Do you think West is OK?' Eliza asked after about twenty minutes.

'I don't think it is West you should worry about,' said Cairo. 'He will be the most dangerous thing out there. If there were anything more dangerous, it would have been here by now.'

'Well, thanks for that comforting thought,' said Frankie.

A little while later, there was the sound of a crash from the kitchen, followed by West shouting.

'Stay here with Frankie, Eliza, I'll go and see what's happening,' said Cairo.

'Do take care, my dear.'

'That is why I'm here.'

Cairo returned a few minutes later. 'You'd better come and see,' she said. 'It's quite safe.'

The three women went into the kitchen, where West was standing over a man secured hand and foot with heavy-duty cable ties. His clothes were muddy, and blood seeped from his nose.

'Did you rough him up, West?' Eliza said with an accusing voice.

'More like I tripped over him. He'll live. I found him on the other side of the lake, in the tower. He had made himself quite at home. And I found these bins.'

West pointed to a high-powered pair of binoculars and a night sight on the kitchen table. 'I'm not sure if he speaks English; he's not yet responded to anything I've said to him.'

Without blinking an eye, Eliza started speaking to the man in Russian. He looked startled.

'Well, that answers that,' West said. 'What did you say to him, Eliza?'

'I asked him what he was doing here and why he was spying on an old woman and her carers.'

West slapped the man around the head. 'Answer the lady,' he shouted.

Eliza translated.

West slapped him again.

Slowly, the man began talking.

Eliza listened, and now and then asked more questions.

Finally, she said, 'He says he doesn't know why he is here. His orders were to observe and report back.'

'Report back to whom?'

Eliza again spoke in Russian.

'He says he can't say.'

'Or perhaps won't say,' said West. 'Do you want me to be a little more persuasive?'

'Let's leave that to Bidian. I don't want any unpleasantness here in the house if I can avoid it. Was he armed?'

'No.'

'So, just here for a look-see I should think. I'll call Bidian, and he can send a team.'

'What do you think will happen to him?' asked Frankie.

'He will disappear,' said West.

'Permanently?' Frankie asked with alarm.

'Depends on what he knows and what he tells,' said West. 'But I don't think he'll taste freedom for a while. Serves him right; he wasn't much good. I caught him cold. He's not the brains of the outfit, that's for sure. Anyway, I wouldn't feel sorry for him. He deserves what he gets.'

'Well, we don't want him dripping blood on the floor,' said Eliza. 'Frankie, why don't you clean the man up a bit while I make a call?'

* * *

Eliza picked up the house phone and dialled.

'What on earth's going on? Are you OK?' Bidian's voice was full of concern.

'It's all over, Bidian, we had a small rodent problem – a Russian rodent.'

'But are you all right?

'Yes, yes, yes. Thanks to West, we are. Can you send in pest control?'

'I'll arrange a team now. Are you sure there are no more rodents?'

'West thinks not. But it might be best to have a look

around. If this one was on his own, I think it is only a cursory look. If they suspected anything serious, I'm sure they would have sent in a team that was far better prepared and trained. But one thing is certain, we are poking the bear.'

'That is exactly what we are doing, Eliza, and it's a big Russian bear.'

'Mirova?

'I have no doubt about that at all, but I think at this stage she is only being cautious.'

'Well, you be cautious too, Bidian.'

'I shall. I'm sending a couple more caretakers up to you until this is over.'

CHAPTER
THIRTY-THREE

It was a beautiful Sunday morning, and Yuri Volkov took what on any other day would have been an enjoyable walk from his house to Sloane Square. The bells from St. Margaret's rang out as he walked, which made him think of Dimity. He bought *The Sunday Times* and that week's issue of *Country Life* magazine at the newsstand in the square. In Piette, he was shown to his favourite corner table by the window.

He should have been in good humour, but he wasn't. He felt he had a precipice in front of him and wolves behind him. For some reason, he had been placed in an impossible situation. If he did what had been asked of him, he would become Maria Mirova's next husband. That was bad enough, but he would also be a murderer and a permanent puppet of his old friend at the Kremlin. Who knew what requests might follow? In some ways, there was no question about what he should do. The consequences of disobeying his masters would be devastating and undoubtedly involve his daughter. But rather than jump into the precipice, something in Volkov made him want to turn and face the wolves. It was an illogical feeling that went against all the odds.

All this, Volkov was certain, was about Moscow getting full control of his company – one way or another. Maria Mirova was just a convenient way of achieving that. He didn't know what was worse, the thought of losing his business or having Mirova as his wife.

Fortunately, he had taken precautions in case he lost his company and, over the years, had diverted hundreds of millions to various banks, properties and institutions. But now Mirova had taken the Saltanov miniature from him, and something in him knew this was just the beginning.

Volkov felt frozen out. He had seen it happen to dozens of other Russian oligarchs. Now it was his turn.

He had been thrilled to become a member of Nemezida, as he wanted to proclaim his fealty to Russia. But he hadn't been told how the real cost of membership would be the loss of everything he had gained in life. Volkov's only conclusion was that Russia, or the man who ran it, had forsaken him and therefore no longer deserved his devotion.

Over the past few weeks, his well-ordered life had spiralled out of control and gone through a significant change. While all the business with Mirova, the miniature and Nemezida was going on, he had met someone. Roger Strand had burst into his world. Volkov had hardly dared to think that his life could change in such a way. For the first time, he was thinking about the possibility of a meaningful relationship with another man rather than superficial one-night stands. He wondered how it would be not chasing younger, beautiful men for ephemeral pleasure. The florist had changed everything. But now, just as this unexpected event was nudging his life into a new and exciting direction, something else threatened to snatch the chance away. Volkov suddenly thought of the danger he could be putting Roger in. He would have to take that into account.

A waiter came to take his order.

'I'll have a double espresso and a plain croissant, thank you,' Volkov said, craving the stimulus of caffeine and the comfort of pastry. He idly turned the pages of his magazine, studying the houses for sale and comparing them with Courtlands. Moments later, he sensed someone standing over him. Thinking it was the waiter, he told him to put his order down without looking up.

'Actually, I'm serving up something else for you today, Mr Volkov,' said a polished English voice he didn't recognise.

Volkov looked up with a start to see a smartly dressed man looking down at him. 'Who are you and how do you know who I am?' he demanded.

Sir Bidian de Butts smiled. 'May I sit with you for a moment? My friend here will occupy the next table.'

Volkov looked around to see a second man watching him closely. He noticed he had a coiled wire that ran from an earpiece and disappeared under his jacket collar. He immediately understood his position. He shrugged and waved towards the chair opposite.

'Most kind of you,' said Sir Bidian. 'For the time being, I won't introduce myself, if you don't mind. But I can't help but think that you are sitting in this delightful café and wondering if it is for the last time.'

'What are you talking about? I don't follow you.'

'Oh, I think you do. I work for the longest-established and most effective secret service organisation in the world. We have had our eyes on you. You are an intelligent man, Mr Volkov. You must know that we would take a keen interest in a gentleman of your power, influence and wealth living in our country – a gentleman with close links to a government with which, how shall I put it, we don't exactly see eye to eye these days – if we have ever done.'

The waiter arrived with Volkov's order, put it on the table and looked at the new arrival expectantly. 'Nothing for me, thank you,' said Sir Bidian, 'but I'm sure my friend at the next table will have something.'

The waiter departed.

Turning back, Sir Bidian said in a soft voice, 'To be honest, we like you, Mr Volkov. You have been discreet and have most generously supported our arts and institutions. You pay your taxes, and you seem to be a good and loving father. I'm sorry if all this sounds patronising, but you contribute to our society and seem to be making your home here – several homes, in fact. Who knows, you might wish to have British citizenship one day. We would like to help you.

'But I sense you are at a crossroads. I have certain information that suggests all you have built here is now in jeopardy. It would be such a pity if everything you have worked for comes to nothing: worse still, if it ends with you in a British jail for the rest of your life. We could invite you to explain to us where all your money comes from under an Unexplained Wealth Order. However, Mr Volkov, I hope you believe me when I say I would take no pleasure in your imprisonment, nor in expelling you from the UK, seizing all your possessions in this country and freezing your international bank accounts indefinitely. We can do that, you know. It would also be hard for your daughter, I think, to leave her school friends and go back to an unwelcoming Russia with a disgraced father.'

Sir Bidian brightened. 'So, I'm here to extend my country's hand of friendship. But I will extend it only once. If you help us, I think there is a great deal we can do to help you.'

Volkov sat listening to the stranger, seething with conflicting emotions. On the one hand, he was appalled that he had been under surveillance. How did this man know these things? It felt like being back in Russia. But then he had a point; he could hardly imagine that he wouldn't come under some form of scrutiny from the UK's security services.

Slowly, Volkov came to realise this might just be the help he needed to avoid jumping into the precipice or facing the wolves. It might get him out of this nightmare and rid him of Maria Mirova.

'Mr whatever your name,' he said eventually. 'Can you even begin to understand the danger I and those close to me would be in if it were found out that I had betrayed my country?'

'As it happens, I have a vivid picture, Mr Volkov. It would undoubtedly be an unpleasant end for you, but it would be even worse for your innocent daughter if she were taken from you and put to work as a heroin addicted sex worker in Norilsk. Yes, I have a very clear idea of the danger you would both be in. But the alternative is to court a protracted financial, social, personal and reputational decline. It would cost you your fortune and your freedom. Some might argue that is better than the first option. But think what it would do to your daughter.'

'I could go back to Russia.'

'To be under the Kremlin's control or buried in a gulag somewhere? I think you know neither makes an attractive proposition. If you have come to the end of your usefulness and Oliniya continues to provide great wealth, there must be those who would like to see the back of you – some ambitious apparatchik or even your leader. No, I don't think returning to Russia would be my first choice. But then I'm not you.'

'I would be a traitor.'

'But ask yourself what sort of country and leadership you would be a traitor to.'

Volkov weighed up these words. He could imagine Maria Mirova being at the top of the list of those wanting to get rid of him. He looked the stranger in the eye and said, 'What do you have in mind?'

Sir Bidian flashed a smile. 'Finding a way to get you out of any current predicament you are in, without plunging you into another one. Getting rid of your enemies without creating more. It won't be easy. But first, I want to know everything you know – with no omissions. Please finish your coffee. Then why don't we take a leisurely walk back towards your house? My friend here and my driver will follow.'

* * *

It was the day of the sale at Binfield House. Volkov had received detailed instructions from Maria Mirova. She had handed him one of two identical, small, rigid boxes and told him to treat it with the utmost care. Volkov would go to the house contents sale and then drive on to Bridport. Mirova wouldn't be far behind to ensure everything went as planned.

As Volkov drove his Audi down the M3, he went over the next hour and the varied ramifications following success or failure. Never in his life had the saying 'failure is not an option' been more apt.

He called Mirova's mobile number when he passed a sign saying Fleet Services was eight miles away, just as instructed by a small detail of hard-looking men. Volkov took them to be

SAS – they had the confidence, humour and quiet menace of elite forces while remaining unfailingly polite.

'I thought I told you not to call me unless it is an emergency,' Mirova spat.

'It is an emergency,' said Volkov testily. 'I need to use the lavatory.'

Over the airwaves, he heard an impatient sigh.

'Then I will stop too. I will be at the back of the car park, watching.'

Volkov parked amongst other cars close to the facilities and, leaving the vehicle unlocked as instructed, went into the service station.

When he returned, a man he hadn't met before was bent low and out of sight in the passenger seat. He was wearing the same colour and style of clothing as Volkov.

'OK, Mr Volkov,' the passenger said. 'Just as you practised, please let down your seat as far as it will go and climb into the back, staying low. There's a crash helmet on the seat. Put it on. Then put both seatbelts around you and clip them in place. Whatever you do, stay down and out of sight.'

Volkov complied. 'Where's the box that was on the passenger seat?' he said in sudden panic.

'Please take it easy, Mr Volkov. It's been taken away by someone from Porton Down, our chemical and biological warfare research laboratory.'

The passenger slid nimbly across and into the driving position, raised the seat again and said, 'I know this will be hard, but first I want you to try to relax. It will be better for you in the long run. In about four or five minutes, I'll tell you to brace for impact. There is going to be a loud crash, and we are going to swerve violently. It will be very uncomfortable for a while, I'm afraid.'

'I take it you have done this before?' Volkov asked nervously.

'You could say that. Now, please try to relax.'

'Where's Mirova?' Volkov said as the car was driven out of the service station.

'She's behind. We have her in a box. Our cars, vans and lorries are surrounding her vehicle, preventing her from getting too close and seeing that it isn't you doing the driving. Now, please get ready. Hold very tightly on to those seatbelts.'

Looking up and out of the car's offside window from his position low on the back seat, Volkov saw a giant lorry passing the Audi. Suddenly, the truck swerved to the left and struck the car with a sickening sound of metal on metal. Volkov felt the car go out of control. It lurched to the left and then swerved right, only to clash with the lorry once again. This time, the car was pushed over the hard shoulder and onto a low, grassy embankment. It hurtled along the bank. Volkov was thrown about despite the seatbelts. Then came a violent judder and the alarming crack of splitting timber.

The next thing Volkov saw was a bright light above him and a woman dressed in green scrubs bending over him.

'Welcome back, Mr Volkov. You've been involved in a motor accident. Do you remember?'

Slowly, Volkov recalled the lorry and then the car bouncing around with him in it. 'I remember,' he said. 'Who are you?'

'My name is Frankie. I'm a nurse. You're in an ambulance on the way to the hospital. We just want to make sure nothing's broken. Your head has been immobilised by a neck brace. You've been shaken about and will have some large bruises and feel stiff for a week or two, I'm afraid. Otherwise, I'm sure you'll live.'

'That is most gratifying to know.'

Volkov recognised the man sitting next to the nurse. 'You risked my life,' Volkov said accusingly.

'That's not entirely correct, Mr Volkov,' Sir Bidian de Butts replied. 'Your life is far more valuable to you than it is to us, so the way I see it, you risked it yourself. You will have to tell me if it was worth that risk to get a new life. You've been reborn, Yuri. Not many people get to do that. But now you're in very good hands. Frankie is used to this sort of thing. She worked for us in Afghanistan. We are going to take you to a military hospital in Frimley, where they will give you a proper once over.'

'How is the driver?'

'It's very good of you to ask,' said Sir Bidian. 'He's fine, just a few bumps. But he practised that manoeuvre in Hereford many times over to ensure you would both be OK. He wrecked several cars in the process. We even consulted film stunt specialists for safety advice and maximum visual effect.'

'What happened?' asked Volkov.

'From what I have been told, it was a spectacular crash, especially when the car broke through a fence. Few who saw the accident would have expected anyone inside to survive. And your car is a complete write-off, I'm afraid.'

'It's insured,' Volkov said dryly.

Sir Bidian laughed and replied, 'I'm delighted to hear it.'

'Where's Mirova?'

'The last time I heard, she was heading to Bridport – to finish your mission by the looks of it. She had a front row seat at the accident. She couldn't have thought it was anything other than a fatal crash caused by the lorry blowing a tyre. However, boxed in as she was, she couldn't stop and had to drive by. But she would have seen enough. Now Mirova – although she doesn't know it yet – is up a creek without a paddle, while you, Yuri, can start your new life without her. Tomorrow, we will announce that you survived the crash following a life-saving procedure in the hospital. That should satisfy your old masters.'

'And what do we do now?' asked Volkov.

'I thought we might discuss your future.'

'And your role in my future, I take it?' Volkov said wearily.

'I am so pleased that we understand each other, Yuri. Oh, may I call you Yuri?' Sir Bidian asked cheerfully.

* * *

A week later, at the Sloane Square café, Volkov, who was still wearing a neck brace, met the security man again.

'I think I can now tell you that my name is Sir Bidian de Butts.'

Volkov nodded. 'Thank you, Sir Bidian, I have had time to appreciate what you have done. May I ask what happened after the accident? There has been nothing in the media.'

'I don't see why I shouldn't tell you. We followed Mirova to Bridport as per the plan you outlined. She was under tight surveillance, both on the ground and from a drone overhead. But she suspected nothing – our people are experts, as was your driver, who is back at work by the way.

'Mirova was apprehended the moment she walked into the hall where the chess club were meeting. Bezrodny was there. As you told us, the plan was to contaminate a chess piece with the fatal nerve agent Novichok.

'We arrested Mirova under our anti-terrorism laws – well before she could administer the poison. It was the same toxin you were carrying on your passenger seat, Yuri. The members of the chess club were understandably alarmed, but we told them it was a drugs arrest.

'Mirova was fast-tracked in secret through the courts and convicted of terrorism and intent to murder.'

'What will happen to her?'

'It has already happened. She is in a deep black hole, where she will stay for the rest of her life. There will be no parole. There will be no spy swap: she wasn't a spy. She was an assassin, and we don't swap assassins. The court has confiscated all her UK assets, including her house, her belongings and her money: her worldwide bank accounts are also frozen. Mirova's son is already back in Russia, where they might not be so forgiving about his heroin addiction. It's hard on the son, but we had to make Mirova an example in case any other Nemezida members, now or in the future, become tempted to carry out orders from the Kremlin on UK soil.'

'That would all have happened to me?'

'It certainly would, Yuri, had you not invited us along for the ride.'

'I wouldn't have carried out the murder, you know. I had decided that,' said Volkov wearily.

'I believe you, which is why I was happy to give you a way out – as long as you helped us to deal with the real terrorist.

'Our foreign secretary spoke to the Russian ambassador yesterday and made a formal complaint. I don't think it was a comfortable interview for the ambassador, especially as I'm certain he had no knowledge of the operation. Of course, the Kremlin is denying everything. They say it must have been a rogue operator. We have asked them what a rogue operator was doing with a military-grade biological weapon.

'So, all's well that ends well, but I'm sorry that you were unable to get to your sale in Dorset.'

'Even that worked out well in the end,' said Volkov. 'My advisors were able to make bids on my behalf and secure the items I wanted.'

Sir Bidian already knew this. 'But that is splendid news,' he said.

Volkov's attention was suddenly drawn to the entrance door. 'Actually, I am meeting someone else here, and he has just arrived.'

'Oh, well, I had better leave you. I think we have covered everything.'

'No, please don't go, Sir Bidian. I would like you to meet my friend.'

'Hello, flower,' said the new arrival, kissing Volkov on each cheek.

Volkov said, 'Sir Bidian, I should like to introduce Mr Roger Strand. Roger, this is the gentleman who has been helping me out with an immigration issue. These things can be complicated.'

'I'm delighted to meet you, Mr Strand,' said Sir Bidian. 'Are you by any chance the florist Roger Strand?'

'The very same,' said Roger, giving Sir Bidian the very slightest of knowing smiles. 'Here, let me give you a business card. You never know when you might want someone expert in the secrets of floristry.'

'Thank you very much. You are right; the services of a helpful florist are often invaluable.'

'Always at your service,' said Roger with a beaming smile.

'Roger and I are going to make a garden together at my house in the Cotswolds,' said Volkov proudly.

'That sounds like a fine plan; I should very much like to see it one day,' Sir Bidian said.

'You would be very welcome. I'm also going to invite the

THE ART DEPARTMENT

Prince of Wales when it is finished – Roger knows him, you know,' Volkov added with equal pride.

'Knowing how much the prince enjoys gardens, I'm sure he will love it. Now, I must be on my way, but before I go, I have something for you, Yuri. It is a small token of thanks for your assistance in this matter.'

Sir Bidian took a small package out of his leather case. Volkov undid the wrapping and stared at the Saltanov miniature in his hand.

'How did you get this?' he asked in astonishment.

'You mentioned that Mirova had snatched it away from you. We had a few minutes to make an inventory of the contents of Mirova's house before anyone else arrived, so we removed it. Just one word of advice, Yuri, please don't ever try to sell it.'

'Because it might come up on a police list as missing?' Volkov asked.

'Something like that,' replied Sir Bidian with a smile.

CHAPTER
THIRTY-FOUR

Following the successful conclusion of the Bezrodny Affair, as Sir Bidian had come to call the operation, Róisín and he had a further discussion. Sir Bidian wanted to talk about her future, a topic she was also most interested in exploring.

But there was one issue that interfered with Sir Bidian's plans. Róisín remained tight-lipped about her life before she went to Moscow. He had asked the debrief team to press her further, but she remained resolutely mute on the subject. Even a thorough search of top-secret documents in the security archives had brought up no mention of her. It was as though she had never existed before becoming Róisín Kelly.

In the end, Sir Bidian had concentrated on more pressing practical matters. He had asked Róisín where and how she thought she would live. She had no money of her own, so he made a decision that would help in the short term. With Treasury approval, he agreed on an ex gratia payment in recognition of Róisín's service. Until the funds came through, he let her remain at Pheasant's Tail. There she could explore her options with the continued support and careful encouragement of the agency's psychological and planning teams.

David became a regular visitor to the house on the Test. He and Róisín walked, talked, fished and further strengthened their relationship until, as Sir Bidian gently suggested to her on one occasion, the question over what she would do next seemed well on the way to taking care of itself. Róisín had been equally tight-lipped on the subject.

* * *

The Moscow agent's past was also a regular topic of conversation between Sir Bidian and Eliza, and it surfaced again now.

'Still no luck with Róisín?' Eliza asked her former trainee.

'No breakthrough yet, I'm afraid. That subject is a closed book with her. I scoured all the records from the Troubles, but it's as if she never existed. Either she didn't exist, in which case, who on earth is she? Or she did exist, and all records have been expunged. In which case, who deleted them, and why? Then the question still remains: who is Róisín? All roads lead to the same quandary.'

'Do you think she has something dark to hide?'

'If she does, then it must be pretty major, like an IRA bombing or a revenge killing.'

'Perhaps so, Bidian, but then why is there no record of her? And why did she return here and risk exposure? She has me baffled. It may be something that we will never fathom. Perhaps it is not even something you want or need to know. Some stones are better left unturned. But do you think her past is impacting her future?'

'That is a question I can't answer, I'm afraid. But whatever

Róisín's past involves, she has created for herself the very best get-out-of-jail-free card: she has become the handler of our most important mole in the Russian Government. It's already bearing fruit. We are receiving vital information concerning Russian intentions in Ukraine. But our new mole will only make contact through her.'

'Do Róisín and the mole have a history – a personal history?'

'She told us there was a brief affair, but she said when it ended, it left them with an unexpected but strong friendship.'

'That's unusual but not unheard of. It's certainly good for you. I must say, on Róisín's part, it seems a very well organised defection – or re-defection,' said Eliza. 'I have never heard of a re-defection before.'

'Nor I,' said Sir Bidian.

'The whole plan seems to have been cleverly worked out and executed,' said Eliza. 'Our mole, Róisín, comes in from the cold, but before she does, she turns her most valuable informant into a full-blown asset. It provides the asset with a secure and trusted conduit, and it makes Róisín immensely valuable to us – thereby securing her a perfect insurance policy. You have to admit, Bidian, as espionage plans go, it's touched with genius.'

'Worthy of one of your own, I think, Eliza. It makes me even more curious about her.'

'Do you wonder, as this is such a clever plan, if she is a triple agent working for the FSB or GRU?'

'That's crossed my mind on many occasions. But it makes no sense when you take into consideration the value of the information the asset has been providing. As well as useful intel on Ukraine, there's also a lot on the Russian cyber warfare and cyber espionage unit known as Fancy Bear.'

'Fancy Bear, that's an odd name.'

'It comes from a coding system used to identify hackers. We think Fancy Bear was active in secretly backing a positive Brexit vote. And, in the US, for hacking Democratic National Committee emails to try and influence the outcome of the 2016 presidential elections.'

Eliza shook her head and said, 'It sounds like science fiction to me. I don't pretend to understand anything about the cyber world. I knew where I was in the Cold War when it was analogue. But I realise that cyber is a big threat, and I want to try to understand.'

'It is a considerable threat, Eliza. Róisín's asset also told us about a Russian tech whizz who is working undercover for Fancy Bear at a social media company based in East London. If we don't tip our hand, it means we might be able to reverse hack into the heart of the Russian cyber-espionage machine. Or that's what the boffins at GCHQ think. I hardly understand a word they say either. But the director of GCHQ seems pretty excited about it.'

'Making the new asset priceless, and therefore Róisín equally priceless. She's a clever one.'

'So it seems.'

'I know what you mean, Bidian; her background is very intriguing.'

'Perhaps one day we will find out. In the meantime, I have an invitation for you.'

'An invitation to what?'

'To a party.'

'Oh, I believe my party days are long over, Bidian.'

'You might change your mind about this one. You asked about visiting The Art Department a while ago.'

'Yes, I did. But I didn't for a minute think it would be possible.'

'Would you still like to go?'

'If it wouldn't be too much trouble, yes, I most certainly would.'

'It wouldn't be too tiring for you?'

'Well, it may be tiring, but West could drive me door to door, and I could have Frankie manage the contraption. And Cairo will have to come too, of course.'

'Contraption?'

'Wheelchair.'

Sir Bidian laughed. 'Oh, I see. Look, I know how much you hate being pushed about, Eliza, but wheelchairs do have their uses – especially at Somerset House, where this party is being held. I often think I could do with one myself in those long corridors.'

Eliza laughed. 'I suppose you're right. So, why the party?'

'I'm having a little get-together for the troops to celebrate a good and successful operation. They will all be there. I wondered if you would like to come and join us?'

'Will it involve champagne?'

'It wouldn't be much of a party without it.'

'Then count me in,' Eliza said. She laughed before adding, 'But how will you explain me away to everyone else at the party, especially when, at the very least, West, Cairo and Frankie will be with me? And what about Witch's while we're away?'

'I've thought about that, Eliza. I can send some caretakers to look after the house. Also, I don't mind telling our little art group that you are the inspiration for their department – without going into too much detail. No one needs to know anything more.'

'In that case, I gratefully accept your invitation, Bidian, even if I may not be able to stay too long. Will there be dancing?'

'No, Eliza, I can't think for a moment that there will be dancing.' Sir Bidian laughed.

'Thank goodness for that. These days, I don't seem to have the stamina I once had. But Felix and Dimity will be there, won't they?'

'Yes, and I think even Roger might show up.'

'Now, that does sound like a good celebration. I think it will be just up my street.'

* * *

On the day of the party, West drove Eliza to London, accompanied by Cairo and Eliza's nurse, Frankie. West did as Eliza asked and took the busier route through the centre of the West End. Eliza loved seeing the bustle on the streets, the shops, and the familiar landmarks and theatres along Shaftesbury Avenue. She enjoyed seeing Piccadilly Circus, where, in her much younger days, she had often dined at the Criterion Restaurant and at the nearby Café Royal. Finally, West drove by Trafalgar Square, along the Strand and around Aldwych, before arriving at Somerset House.

'It has been a long time since I was here,' said Eliza, as West and Frankie helped her into the wheelchair. 'It's good to be back.'

'How are you feeling?' Frankie asked her.

'Ready for a party. Now, don't fuss, Frankie. West, do you know where you are going? I think you should be going this way.'

THE ART DEPARTMENT

Eliza waved imperiously in the direction she thought they should be heading.

'Yes, thank you, Eliza, I know where I'm going,' replied West, ignoring her directions.

A young man, who introduced himself as Gregory, met Eliza, West and Frankie at the reception and, using the lift, guided them upstairs to Sir Bidian's office.

'How lovely to see you here,' Sir Bidian said as he greeted them with a beaming smile. 'And particularly on a special day like this.'

'I see you don't bother much with decorating your office, Bidian,' Eliza said, eyeing Édouard Manet's *A Bar at the Folies-Bergère*, which was hanging behind Sir Bidian's head.

'I'm beginning to wish I'd never started having these pictures hung here. All I seem to get from Felix are sarcastic comments when he's here. Even Róisín did the same. Now you.'

'I'm pleased to hear it,' said Eliza with a smile. 'It will keep you grounded.'

Gazing around further, she noticed Vincent van Gogh's *Self-Portrait with Bandaged Ear* practically looking at her.

'We should go through to the studio,' Sir Bidian said. 'Felix called to say he and Dimity are running a little late. Dimity has had a committee meeting of some sort. But they shouldn't be too long.'

'I'm very much looking forward to meeting the others,' said Eliza. 'I've heard so much about them that I feel I know them already.'

Sir Bidian ushered the group along the corridor and into the studio. In one corner, chatting around a table with some bottles, glasses and plates of food were five people. 'Eliza, let me introduce Ellie, Rani, Tiya and Petro – and I think you know this other gentleman.'

'How could I ever forget Roger?' Eliza said. She laughed and accepted a stooped kiss from the florist. She shook the hands of Ellie, Rani and Tiya, then, turning to Petro, said in Russian how pleased she was to meet him. Petro beamed and replied in kind.

'Roger, will you do the honours with the champagne?' Sir Bidian asked.

'Your servant, flower,' replied Roger.

Once Roger had poured the drinks and handed out the glasses, Sir Bidian said, 'I will leave proposing a formal toast until Felix and Dimity are here. But until then, cheers everybody.'

'Cheers!' they all cried in return.

Eliza talked to Petro about his work, and he showed her a painting he was working on for the Institute. Turning to the others, she chatted with Rani and Tiya about Calcutta and then spoke to Ellie. 'I think you and I have a dangerous escape in common,' she said.

'Really?' Ellie said. 'Which escape was that?'

'I understand that one of your family, another Louise-Emmanuelle, escaped France during the French Revolution, under the protection of a certain Englishman.'

'Why yes, the man was called Robert Arrow.'

'Robert Arrow was my many times great-grandfather.'

So engrossed was Eliza in telling the story that at first, she didn't notice the studio door open. Then, from the corner of her eye, she saw Gregory enter with a man and woman, although she couldn't guess who they were. She could see a tall, elegant man, but the woman was partially obscured from her view by Gregory, and her eyes weren't as good as they once were. She saw Bidian stride over to meet the pair. He exchanged pleasantries and then steered the couple towards her.

'I have a surprise for you, Eliza,' said Sir Bidian. 'I'm very pleased to introduce you to Róisín.'

Then, looking directly at the woman, Eliza suddenly felt the hairs on the back of her neck stand up. Spilling some of her drink, she murmured, 'Oh, oh.'

'Are you all right, Eliza?' Frankie said, applying a paper napkin to Eliza's damp skirt.

'Oh my,' whispered Eliza, almost to herself. 'Oh my.'

'Oh my what?' said Frankie, becoming concerned at Eliza's sudden agitation.

Eliza looked into Róisín's eyes, gasped and said, 'This is not Róisín.'

Róisín stared at Eliza for a moment and then, dropping to her knees, threw out her arms, buried her head in the old lady's lap and began to sob.

The rest of the party looked on in amazement as Eliza cradled Róisín's cheeks, kissed the top of her head and said, 'Athene.'

'I... I never thought I would see you again, Mama.'

'Any more than I thought I would see you, my darling girl. But now I understand everything.'

'Witch's?' Athene asked.

Eliza smiled. 'Witch's is just as it was the day you left it. Nothing has been changed. I wanted it to remain as it always was – just in case.'

The two women were in tears, as was everyone else by then, although no one quite understood what they were crying about. Everyone, that was, except Sir Bidian.

Eliza turned and asked him, 'Did you know about this?'

'I didn't know for certain, Eliza. But when I first met Róisín at Pheasant's Tail, the facial resemblance took me aback. Róisín – Athene – wouldn't tell us enough about her past, which made me suspicious on several fronts – not all good, I might add. But the whole Ireland connection and Russian mole thing made so much more sense when I put Athene in Róisín's shoes. I didn't tell you any of my suspicions, Eliza. It was the longest of shots – far too long to get your hopes up. It seemed the only way I could find out for certain was for the two of you to meet. I just had to hope that you wouldn't have a heart attack if my suspicions proved correct – I'm glad to see you haven't had one.'

Sir Bidian turned to Athene and said, 'Why wouldn't you tell us – tell me?'

Athene didn't reply, but Eliza did. 'Athene didn't say anything because she was keeping the family secret, however much she might have wanted to tell you. That was the reason.'

Athene wiped her eyes and, without letting go of Eliza, said, 'Of course it was, Mama. I couldn't expose the family and Witch's. Once in Ireland and then in Russia, I could never put the family in jeopardy. I couldn't even risk making any enquiries. So, I put myself into exile and isolation.

'Once I was back in England, I wasn't quite sure whom I could tell or ask. I thought enough time had elapsed to separate my past from my present. How wrong could I have been? I was going to look into things quietly, once the dust settled and I found the opportunity. But I never expected this.'

Athene shook her head in astonishment. 'But you are surely not still involved in all these affairs, are you, Mama?'

Eliza smiled and replied, 'In an advisory capacity. Bidian indulges me a little – a lot, in fact. After all, I am an Arrow.

THE ART DEPARTMENT

Once a spy, always a spy, but it's a very long story, best told around the fire at Witch's.'

'You can't know how long I have dreamed of the fire at Witch's,' said Athene. 'But where are my manners, Mama? This is my friend, David.'

'Ah, so this is Róisín's David, is it?' Eliza released her right hand from Athene's tight grasp to greet David.

'How do you do? Thank you so much for taking such good care of Athene over the past few months.'

Athene looked confused and asked, 'You know about David?'

'I know about a lot of things, darling.'

'Of course you do, Mama,' said Athene.

'I am delighted to meet you, Mrs Arrow,' said David. 'The pieces are beginning to slot into place. But I must say, it would be good to understand the Arrow family history.'

'That would take about five hundred years,' said Sir Bidian dryly.

A chair was found for Athene and placed beside her mother. Holding Eliza's hand, she said, 'I conditioned myself to never see you again, Mama. I tortured myself that the Arrow line ended with me.'

Eliza suddenly gasped and threw her hands to her face.

'What on earth is it, Mama?' asked Athene. 'What have I said?'

'Oh, good heavens,' Sir Bidian exclaimed. 'In all the drama, I had completely forgotten.'

'What have you forgotten?' Athene asked.

Eliza had turned ashen and said, 'Athene, there is some—'

But she was interrupted by the arrival of two more guests.

Roger hurried over to Felix and Dimity. 'Darlings, it is gorgeous to see you.'

'And it's good to see you,' said Felix, slightly surprised by his appearance.

'Roger, have you been crying?' Dimity asked.

'It's an emotional party,' replied Roger, wiping his face with a large handkerchief of a colourful, botanical design. 'So far it's been full of surprises.'

'What do you mean?' Dimity asked.

'Take a look at Eliza,' Roger said.

Felix and Dimity turned to look. 'She looks upset, Roger,' said Felix. 'Has she been crying too? What on earth has happened? Has someone died?'

'It's more the opposite,' Roger said.

It was then that Felix noticed the woman sitting next to his grandmother: she was staring back at him.

'You were at the gallery in Moscow,' Felix said. 'I don't understand. What are you doing here?'

Athene looked as confused. 'Felix?'

'What are you doing here?' Felix repeated. He might also have asked why the woman was sitting so close to his grandmother.

Eliza held out a hand to Felix. 'Darling, I know this will be hard for you to take in, but this is Athene, my daughter.'

'Your daughter? But how? But your daughter is... and you're my grandmother... that means—'

'It means Athene is your natural mother, Felix.'

'This is *my* Felix?' said Athene. 'But that's impossible.'

'Unlikely, yes, but impossible, no,' said Eliza. 'Can't you see the family resemblance?'

'But, Mama, how did you know that I had a baby all those years ago? I never told you.'

'I didn't know until Bidian here worked it out quite recently.

'But it was a closely guarded military secret – to keep the family safe.'

'It was top secret,' said Sir Bidian, 'almost *too* top secret. We may never have known, Athene. With the records deleted and you having disappeared – like so many others during the Troubles – we assumed you had been killed by the IRA, along with your husband, Phillip.'

'You know about Phillip?'

'Yes, we do.'

'Phillip saved my life: he drew any suspicion the IRA had about me onto him. He paid with his life. But *this* Felix is our son?'

'Yes, your own flesh and blood – our flesh and blood – Arrow flesh and blood,' said Eliza.

Felix was numb and said nothing. Dimity looked just as shocked.

Athene continued to stare at Felix. 'It's very strange, but I felt there was something about you that day in the gallery. It was why I turned back to look at you again – after you gave me your drawing. I still have it by the way; it's one of the few things I brought with me from Moscow. Right now, it's on the mantelpiece in my room. In many ways, it was that drawing that brought me back here. But that's another story.'

Felix looked at his natural mother and finally uttered, 'I felt something strange that day too. Although I couldn't explain it, it felt almost like looking at myself. That was why I gave you the drawing. I was sure I saw you again at Binfield House, but then I thought it was my mind playing tricks on me.'

Still feeling stunned, Felix added, 'Oh, I'm sorry, I must introduce you to Mitten – Dimity – my wife.'

'Your wife? How lovely to meet you,' said Athene. Then she smiled and added, 'I'm sorry I missed your wedding.'

Everyone laughed.

Felix said to Athene, 'I'm afraid I don't know what to call you – Róisín, Athene?'

'Well, call me old fashioned, but I don't think either is very appropriate, Felix,' said Eliza sternly. 'What about Mum, Mother or Mama?'

'But I am not the mum who raised Felix,' protested Athene.

'I suppose I'm lucky to have two mothers,' Felix said, 'but now that my adoptive mum has gone, I'm sure she wouldn't mind if my natural one took over that name. After all, I have had to get used to calling Eliza Grandma. So, Mum it shall be.'

'I should be honoured to take up the name, Felix. Now, please may I hug my son? The last time I did so was many lifetimes ago.'

Eliza said to Sir Bidian with a big smile, 'A third Arrow is back in the quiver.'

'God help our enemies,' Sir Bidian said, as Roger handed Athene, David, Dimity and Felix glasses of champagne.

'Thank you, Bidian,' said Eliza.

'What on earth for?'

'For two things. One, you brought Athene home to Felix and me.'

'And the other?'

'You have just thrown the most memorable party of my long life.' Eliza raised her glass and added, 'Peace and lesser sorrow.'

'Peace and lesser sorrow,' replied Athene, Felix and Dimity in unison, while raising their glasses.

Sir Bidian frowned and said, 'I think I'm missing the point.'

Eliza, Athene, Felix and Dimity all laughed.

'Don't worry, Bidian,' Eliza said. 'It is the point – the Arrow point.'

ACKNOWLEDGMENTS

Once the characters in my debut novel *Witch's Lawn* introduced themselves to me, they refused to go away. The result is *The Art Department*. But there were also some non-fictional characters who were essential in bringing this story to the page. My thanks go to Colin, Nettie and Martin for beta reading and, of course, to Susan for her endless support and assiduous correcting. I should also like to express my deep gratitude to Danielle Wrate for once again copy editing, proofreading and publishing this novel.

ABOUT THE AUTHOR

Having spent a long and successful business career in property marketing, Nick followed a long-held desire to write. His debut novel, *Witch's Lawn*, and his collection of children's stories, *Sheep Bleating*, have been followed by *The Art Department*, the second of the planned Arrow series.

Nick lives in Hertfordshire, England, and has two children and three grandchildren. After many years of travelling the world for his work, he now spends much of his time between his homes in England and the beautiful Mediterranean island of Menorca.

ALSO BY NICK CHURTON

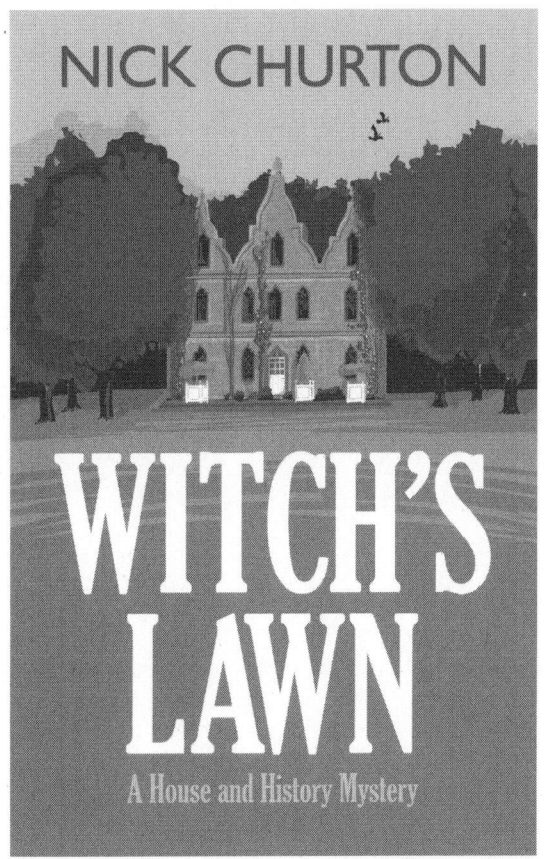